"WHERE DO WE GO FROM HERE?" JO ASKED

The worry left Brad's eyes, replaced by a loving warmth. "I don't know about you, but I've always wanted to visit an art museum," he said, purposely ignoring the true meaning of her question. "Do you know if Denver happens to have one?" He stood and held out his hand.

There were moments in Jo's life when having the feel of someone's arms around her became almost as necessary as breathing. Right then was one of them.

Almost as if he could read her mind, he gathered her into his arms. "I wish I knew a way to tell you how much you mean to me," he said, looking deeply into her eyes.

"I think you just did," she said. Her arms came around his waist, and she lightly touched her lips to his before asking, "Are you really interested in art?"

ABOUT THE AUTHOR

Georgia Bockoven, a talented California author, has been a steady contributor to the Superromance line. But one of her more recent contributions made Harlequin especially proud: at the 1986 Romance Writers of America Conference, Georgia was awarded a Golden Medallion for *Today, Tomorrow, Always*, her fourth Superromance. Always innovative, Georgia plans to continue the story of some of the characters introduced in *Love Songs* in an upcoming Harlequin Temptation.

Books by Georgia Bockoven

HARLEQUIN SUPERROMANCE

82–RESTLESS TIDE
102–AFTER THE LIGHTNING
138–LITTLE BY LITTLE
179–TODAY, TOMORROW, ALWAYS
222–THE LONG ROAD HOME

HARLEQUIN TEMPTATION

14–TRACINGS ON A WINDOW
57–A GIFT OF WILD FLOWERS
94–A WEEK FROM FRIDAY

Don't miss any of our special offers. Write to us at the following address for information on our newest releases.

Harlequin Reader Service
901 Fuhrmann Blvd., P.O. Box 1397, Buffalo, NY 14240
Canadian address: P.O. Box 603,
Fort Erie, Ont. L2A 5X3

Georgia Bockoven

LOVE SONGS

Harlequin Books

TORONTO • NEW YORK • LONDON
AMSTERDAM • PARIS • SYDNEY • HAMBURG
STOCKHOLM • ATHENS • TOKYO • MILAN

Published February 1987

First printing December 1986

ISBN 0-373-70246-9

CHAPTER ONE

JOSEPHINE WILLIAMS chewed on her bottom lip as she looked around the small utilitarian office. With its gray metal desk, vinyl-covered sofa and neutral-colored walls, the room had all the charm and personality of the interior of a battleship. Still, the place managed to intimidate her. What was it about a police station, especially one as large and impersonal as Denver, Colorado's, that could make even the most innocent search their souls for guilt?

She crossed, then recrossed her legs trying to get comfortable in the straight-backed wooden chair. Perhaps if she were more confident in her quest she wouldn't feel so hesitant about stretching the truth. No, that wasn't it. She was absolutely sure that what she was doing was right— even if it wasn't straight-arrow honest.

She looked down at the gleaming two-carat diamond ring she wore on her third finger, left hand—the only finger it would fit—and thought of the bitter old woman who had given it to her shortly before she died. Mabel Tyler had lived the last eight years of her life in a lonely hell of her own making, distraught over the alienation of her only child and too stubborn to seek a reconciliation.

Unable to sit still any longer, Josephine wandered over to the bulletin board and absently perused the notices stuck to the cork with brightly colored pushpins. She was in the middle of a memo recruiting players for the police athletic club's softball team when she heard someone enter behind her. She turned, prepared to launch into the speech she had spent the past week polishing. "Alex..." she gasped, her heart sinking.

Alexander Reid had changed in the eleven years since she had last seen him; he had filled out some and his hair was about seven inches shorter. But he hadn't changed so much that she didn't instantly recognize him. He'd been as much a fixture in her house when she was growing up as her mother's macrame wall hangings. And about as useful, as far as Jo had been concerned. He and her brother, Mike, had been inseparable from the moment they'd met as toddlers and swapped baby bottles while being strolled through Southside Park in Colorado Springs—or so the family legend went.

She noted that it took him a fraction of a second longer to recognize her. She wasn't surprised. The changes she'd gone through between fifteen and twenty-six were far more dramatic. The last time he'd seen her she'd worn nearly waist-length braids. Now her hair was much darker blond and cut short and sleek in an easy-to-care-for, wash-and-wear style. But that wasn't all that had changed. After years of despair spent thinking she would be forever flat-chested and hipless, she had finally rounded out in most of the right places. She was definitely not the tomboy Alex had once bossed around with the same proprietary ease as her own brother had.

Big talk. If she was really so grown-up, why did she instantly feel like Alex's kid sister again, despite the eleven years that had passed since they'd last seen each other? Why was she overcome with guilt about what she was planning to do? And why did she fervently wish she could slink out the back door before he started asking her questions?

"As I live and breathe," Alex said, "if it isn't Josie Williams."

Josie…how she hated that nickname. "The name's Jo now," she said emphatically. "In a pinch I'll answer to Josephine." She softened her tone, realizing not only was she coming on like a punch-drunk fighter, she was being rude. "I left 'Josie' behind when I graduated from high school."

He studied her, a smile touching his eyes. "Still haven't forgiven me, I see."

"Forgiven you?" She was instantly on guard. "What for?"

"For telling Tony Erickson you had a crush on him."

It took a moment for the memory to click. When it did, a fury of emotion gripped her. "*You* were the one. That slimy excuse for a male pursued me my entire freshman year because he was convinced I was playing hard to get." She should have suspected Alex would be behind something that rotten.

Alex laughed and crossed the room, catching her to him in a bear hug. "So, other than fighting off the attentions of lustful young men, what else have you been doing these last eleven years?"

Eleven years *was* a long time; there was no point in holding a grudge. And, she had to admit, it felt fantastic to see him again—like finding a long-lost brother. She returned his hug. "Not much."

"Not much? That's it?"

She extracted herself from his arms and walked back to the chair she had been sitting in earlier. Frowning, she sat down with a dejected plop. Over four thousand days had passed between the last time she had seen Alex Reid and now. She would have been ecstatic had she met him on any one of those days and in any other place. Why

today? And, for God's sake, why in the inner sanctum of
the Denver Police Department? She would never be able
to pull off what she had come here to do if Alex was to be
her inquisitor. He'd see through her ploy in a second.
"What would you like to know?" she said, finally answering his question.

"You could probably satisfy me with a few of the high
points."

High points? There hadn't been any. Not even a grand
passion to leave her scarred and wistful and mysterious.
"Just remember, you asked for it." She let out a resigned sigh. "I finished high school in Bakersfield." The
oil company her father worked for had transferred him
to California at the end of her freshman year. The move
had been traumatic for the entire family but especially
hard on Mike, who had desperately wanted to finish his
senior year of high school in Colorado Springs. "I was a
junior at UCLA when my grandmother fell and broke her
hip, and I came back to Colorado to take care of her for
the summer." She shrugged. "That was five years ago."

"I thought Mike told me your grandmother died."

Although Mike and Alex had not seen each other since
high school, she knew they still occasionally corre-
sponded. "She did. But by then I had taken over a fro-
zen-yogurt shop and was pretty much entrenched in
Boulder, so I stayed on." She crossed her legs and nervously began tapping the toe of her shoe against the file
cabinet. "And you?"

Alex went around the desk and sat down, facing her.
"I'm doing all right. Barbara and I had a rough couple
of years, but I think they're behind us now. We're em-
barrassingly normal: 2.5 kids, one dog, two cats and a
mortgage." He leaned back in his chair and put his feet
up. For long seconds he studied her. "Enough of this

sparkling wit and brilliant conversation. As much as my ego would like me to believe you came all the way into Denver just to see me, that stunned look on your face when I walked into the room tells me different.''

''I came here to find someone who could help me locate a missing person.''

Alex settled deeper into his chair and supported the back of his head with intertwined hands. ''Well, it seems I'm your man. Who is it you're looking for?''

''A guy named Brad Tyler.''

He reached into the desk to take out a tablet of forms and then into his pocket to remove a pair of horn-rimmed reading glasses. ''How long as this Brad Tyler been missing?''

She flinched, knowing what was coming next. ''Eight years.''

Alex lowered his chin and looked at her over the top of his glasses. ''Why such a long delay in filing a report?''

She had already traveled this road with the police department in Boulder and wound up with nothing but detours and dead ends. ''Because there was never any pressing reason to find him before.''

''And now?''

''There's a large sum of money coming to him and I'd like to see he gets it.''

Alex laid the pencil down on the tablet and leaned forward. ''Enough of this beating around the bush, Josie. Just who is this Brad Tyler...and what is he to you?''

Several possible answers sprang to mind and she wished she knew which one would induce him to help her. Realizing that she'd probably be stretching the truth enough as she got further into the story, she decided to play it straight for now. ''Actually, I've never met the man. He's the son of a friend who died a couple of months ago."

"And this friend left him her estate?"

"Not exactly."

"Then what exactly?"

"She left her estate to the Gray Panthers. What I'm holding for Brad was given to me for safe keeping about a year ago."

"Done all nice and legally, I assume."

She swallowed. Lie number one. "Oh, yes. Mabel's lawyer handled the whole thing."

He picked up the pencil again and rotated it slowly between his fingers. "What have you done to find this Tyler up until now?"

"I've gone to the Boulder police, but they told me I'd have to be a relative before they would even consider talking to me."

"They were right, you know. The privacy act protects people who want to disappear." He looked at her through narrowed eyes. "What gave you the idea that coming here would make any difference?"

She adjusted her position in the chair, glancing up at the ceiling, over at the bulletin board and then at the pencil Alex was methodically tapping against the green desk blotter—anywhere but at him. She cleared her throat. "I was planning to claim I was Brad's sister. But then, I didn't know I'd be running into you."

Alex tossed the pencil down and groaned. "It's a damn good thing you did. You could have gotten yourself into one hell of a lot of trouble if a file had been opened and then someone found out you were lying."

"Does that mean you're not going to help me?"

"On top of losing my job if I got caught, it happens to be against the law for me to help you, Josie."

"Jo."

"Have you considered a private detective?" he asked, ignoring her correction.

"I don't have the money for anything like that."

"Well, then, have you considered using some of the money his mother left? I can't see that he'd have grounds to object if it was a matter of either not getting his inheritance at all or spending a little of it to find him."

Again she positioned herself in the chair, then recrossed her legs, squirming under his questioning but trying to hide her discomfort with natural-looking movements. "Actually, I misled you a little. It's not money I'm holding for him; it's jewelry. And if I sold the jewelry to get money, there wouldn't be any reason to search for him because there wouldn't be anything to give him when I did find him."

Alex's chair gave a loud protesting squeak as he leaned back again. "Even if you were his sister, you must realize that after being gone eight years, there's not much any police department could or would do to help you find him. Unless, of course, you could prove he disappeared under suspicious circumstances."

She thought a minute. "How suspicious would these circumstances have to be?"

His face twisted into a scowl.

"Oh, all right. Why don't you just tell me how you'd go about finding him if he *had* disappeared under suspicious circumstances and I'll do the work myself?"

"You couldn't because you wouldn't have access to the files."

"What files?"

"Files that would tell us whether or not Brad Tyler had come in contact with the law in any way."

"You mean if he had robbed a bank or something like that?"

"Or was in an accident, received a ticket or applied to operate certain businesses."

"Oh . . . I see." She looked at him thoughtfully. "And there's *no way* I could gain access to these files?"

Slowly, purposefully, he shook his head. "Besides, they would only be useful to you if you knew for sure that he'd settled in this area."

"I don't have the slightest idea where he might have settled," she reluctantly admitted.

"What have you done besides come here and contact the Boulder police?"

"Nothing. I didn't know what else to do."

He pushed his glasses back up to the bridge of his nose with his index finger. "Is there any reason Tyler would have changed his name?"

"Not that I know of."

"Do you happen to know why he disappeared in the first place? That would make a difference to whether or not he'd feel a need to hide his identity."

"He and his mother had a fight over the woman he wanted to marry—her name was Karen Patterson. Mabel—his mother—told him that if he went ahead with the marriage, as far as she was concerned, she would no longer have a son."

"And he did and his mother changed her mind about her daughter-in-law—this Karen—too late to get in touch with him herself?"

Jo nodded.

"Do you think he would have stayed in the west?"

"Since he was born and reared in Colorado, that seems likely. Why?"

"Well, it's a long shot, but you might try the library. I know the main branch has the phone book for just about every major city and quite a few of the smaller ones. Even if you stick to neighboring states you'll probably wind up with more Brad Tylers than you know what to do with. But at least it's someplace to start."

She had never thought of looking in a phone book—probably because it was such an obvious solution. Anyone who was purposely trying to disappear would never be found that way. But Brad had no reason to hide. "Thanks, Alex," she said, heading for the door, eager to get started.

"Wait a minute. You're not going to take off before we've had a chance to talk, are you?"

"Next time I'm in Denver, you can take me to lunch. It's the least you can do after telling Tony Erickson I liked him." She started to leave, then added, "Come to think of it, you'd better make that dinner. Someplace fancy."

He laughed. "Sounds good to me. Barbara's a fantastic cook—and there's no place like home."

THREE HUNDRED MILES northwest of Denver, Brad Tyler flipped the left-turn signal in his pickup truck. He waited impatiently for the traffic to pass, then pulled into the third construction site he had visited that day. As he stopped in the skeletal shadow of the new hotel he was building, he quickly assessed the progress of the project. Satisfied that everything was as it should be, he reached for a dog-eared set of plans, climbed out of the truck and hailed Jack Hargrove, the site foreman. A middle-aged man with forearms and face tanned a deep cinnamon hurried over to him.

He stood beside Brad and tipped back his hard hat to wipe the sweat from his face. "I told Shirley not to bother you with this," he grumbled. "You've got enough to do downtown without running all the way out here just because some inspector isn't up on his codes."

Brad gave him a puzzled frown as he combed his fingers through his thick black hair, then put on his own hard hat. "I haven't talked to Shirley since yesterday. I came out here to go over the clearances on those air-conditioning shafts you said didn't fit. Now, what's this about an inspection?"

"Nothing—it's all been taken care of."

Because he had supreme trust in Jack's judgment, he let the matter drop. "Then let's get to work on this other thing. I've got to be back in town for that damned awards banquet by eight, and I've still got the meeting with Van Alsteen this afternoon." Brad's voice was decidedly reluctant. For a man who was to be the recipient of the major award given at the banquet, he was showing a surprising lack of enthusiasm.

That morning the paper had carried a full-page article, complete with pictures, extolling the remarkable young man who, at thirty-three, owned the construction company that was almost single-handedly changing the skyline of Casper, Wyoming. The anonymity he had enjoyed during the past six years as he gradually developed his construction company into the largest in the state had abruptly ceased with the publication of his photograph. It amazed him how many people had seen the photograph in the morning paper. Everywhere he had gone that day there had been comments—from the electrical contractor he'd met for breakfast to the girl behind the counter at McDonald's, where he'd stopped for a cup of coffee.

It wasn't that he harbored any false modesty about his accomplishments. He'd worked damned hard to get where he was and felt he owed no one any apologies for the success that had come his way as a result of that work. However, being honored for what he'd accomplished for purely selfish motivations was not only a nuisance, it was embarrassing. Afterward, people would have all kinds of expectations about how he should handle himself, expectations that might interfere with his freedom to do his work the way he chose. And like it or not, his work was all he had—it was his lifeblood.

Years earlier it had become the only drug that could effectively numb the pain and dull the edge of loneliness. For a long time after losing Karen, he had been one of those men described by Thoreau; he, too, had led a life of quiet desperation. Then he'd found a new mistress—Tyler Construction Company. It had been a steadfast and demanding mistress, and it never failed to get him through the days. The nights he had learned to cope with in other ways.

Brad followed his foreman into the core of the building, moving with a long, self-confident stride that had become second nature to him after the years he had spent as a champion pole-vaulter in high school. In addition to the stride, he had the vaulter's build, with arm and leg muscles that were lean, and a flexible body. At times, the graceful way he carried himself seemed almost choreographed. He traversed narrow steel girders a hundred feet in the air with the same surefooted steps he took on the ground.

Brad spent the next two hours going over the specs for the duct clearances with Jack. They compared the actual construction with the specifications called for in the plans. In the end, they determined that the sheet-metal contractor had made the mistake. Whatever ductwork couldn't be used elsewhere on the project would have to be returned to the shop and refitted.

By the time Brad had finished at the hotel site, met with a group of subcontractors about the hospital they would be starting in a month and then gone back to the office to review a bid on a new industrial complex, it was almost six-thirty. A quick shower and shave at his nearby house put him at Donna Jackson's condominium only fifteen minutes later than he had told her he would pick her up.

"How handsome you look this evening," she said, opening the door and stepping aside to let him enter.

"You don't look so bad yourself," he answered, giving her a quick perfunctory kiss. Actually, she looked stunning. She'd pulled her shoulder-length platinum hair up on one side and attached a white moth orchid. Her moss-green silk dress was cut enticingly low, accentuating full breasts and creamy skin. A cloud of tantalizing scent surrounded her, and her eyes flashed a promise as she offered to fix him a drink.

Brad felt a familiar nagging sense of guilt. He had never meant to let things go as far as they had with Donna. Almost overnight he and Donna had drifted into what was for him an impossible situation. But every time he attempted to break things off between them, he ended up postponing the moment of truth, unwilling to hurt her while realizing that eventually his hesitancy would make things harder for both of them.

Even though they would be late for the dinner, he followed her inside. She moved with a natural gracefulness, an erotic sensuality as she went over to the bar and poured him a shot of bourbon over ice. "How's the hotel coming?" she asked, handing him the drink.

"We're still a week off schedule, but I think we'll manage to bring it in on time."

She stepped closer to put her arms around his neck and provocatively snuggle her hips into his. Her fingertips played with the thick waving hair at his nape, still damp from his shower. "Does that mean you can stay with me this weekend?" she asked, dropping her voice to a husky whisper.

Donna was the kind of woman who could set men's hearts racing with only a glance. Yet no matter how hard he wished it would happen, for him there had never been any magic between them. "Donna...we have to talk about us." He gently removed her arms from around his neck.

As if sensing what he wanted to say, she put him off as she had been doing for the past month whenever he tried to talk to her. "Not now, Brad." She took his glass. "If you recall, we have a party to go to."

Because he was basically a kind man and had no more desire to hurt her than he could avoid, he went along with her delaying tactics. But he promised himself that he would make the break and make it clean and quick when he brought her home at the end of the evening. That way, they could both get on with their lives. For an instant he caught a blinding glimpse of what that life would be like for him, and the overwhelming loneliness almost made him change his mind.

Forcefully he repeated the phrases he had etched into his consciousness over the past eight years. He would live his life the only way he could without Karen—one day at a time, never looking too far into the future, never allowing himself to dream of what might have been.

CHAPTER TWO

JO WALKED to the front door of Yogurt, Etc. and turned the Open sign over. As usual, there were no lines of people pushing and shoving to get inside. She glanced up and down the walkway that ran in front of the small shopping plaza. Now that summer had officially arrived, marked by the exodus of university students, a cannon could have gone off and not hit anyone. She knew it was silly to open at ten when it was rare for anyone to come in before noon and things never really picked up until about two. But her hand-painted sign said she opened at ten, so that's what she did.

Since she always cleaned up and filled the bins for the dozen yogurt toppings before she left at night, there was never anything to do in the morning. This particular day, however, was an exception. She had seven hundred and eighty-two addresses and telephone numbers for B. Tylers, plain Brad Tylers and Brad Tylers with a variety of middle initials, all of whom she had to contact.

Alex's suggestion had been a good one—almost too good. The result of her day at the library had been overwhelming. She had started with Colorado and then moved on to its seven bordering states, refusing to consider how easily she could miss Mabel's son if he decided to move from one state to another while she was using her clumsy but methodical methods to chase him down. For the listings that had given telephone numbers

but no addresses, she'd copied down the numbers anyway, with the thought that if no one responded to her
letter, she could always try giving these Tylers a call later
on.

Before she'd even had a chance to spread out her pa-
perwork on one of the round ice-cream parlor tables that
were used by her customers, the bell over the front door
sounded, making her jump. She looked up and saw
Howard Wakelin, one of her favorite people from the
senior-citizen complex across the street. Howard was accompanied by a leggy girl in white shorts and a pink T-
shirt. Jo guessed the girl to be around ten or eleven.

"Oh, I'm sorry, Jo," Howard said. "We didn't mean
to frighten you."

Jo took her hand from her heart. "I was off in another world. Hardly anyone ever comes in this early."
The young girl shoved her hands in her back pockets and
critically surveyed the shop. "This wouldn't be the
granddaughter we've all been hearing so much about,
would it?" she asked. Not expecting a reply to her rhetorical question, she smiled brightly and went on, "What
can I do for the two of you today?" It was no secret
Howard Wakelin hated frozen yogurt and only came to
the shop for company.

"Seems frozen yogurt is Sandy's favorite treat. So I
thought we'd stop by before we headed for the park."

Jo got up to walk over to the twosome. Howard feed-
ing his granddaughter the health-food version of ice
cream at ten o'clock in the morning had to mean the visit
was not going as well as he had hoped. Jo put her hand
out to the girl. "Hi, I'm Jo Williams."

A startled look crossed the girl's face before she
reached up to take Jo's hand. "Sandy Channing."

"I'm pleased to meet you, Sandy. I understand you're from California. What part of the state do you live in?"

"Modesto."

Jo smiled. "I used to live in Bakersfield. The central valley can sure get hot in July. I'll bet you were glad to get away for a while to visit your grandfather."

A sullen pout marred the girl's pretty features. "Yeah, I guess so," she replied.

Jo felt like kicking herself when she saw the disappointment in Howard's eyes. She'd put Sandy on the spot with her question and had received a typical ten-year-old's answer. More than likely, Sandy had been shipped to Colorado so her parents could have some time to themselves—not by her own choice. "I'll bet by the end of the week your grandfather's going to have to drag you to the airport, you'll be so sorry to leave here." Both of them gave Jo a skeptical look. It was time to change the subject. "Now, then, what can I get for you?" she asked, stepping behind the counter.

"A medium strawberry with chocolate bits and toasted almonds in the middle and peanuts and coconut on top," Sandy commanded.

Jo made the concoction with extra everything and handed it to Sandy with a flourish. When Howard started to dig in his pocket for the money to pay her, Jo waved him away. "Not this time. It's my treat."

Howard shook his head in reproof. "How many times do I have to tell you that you can't keep giving away your product and still stay in business?" He pressed a five-dollar bill in her hand. While he waited for his change, he looked around. "What's this you're doing?" he asked, noticing the stack of papers on what was normally a spotlessly clean table.

Jo hesitated before answering. She wasn't sure how much she should tell Howard about her latest project. The gossip network at the complex was incredible, and she was afraid that if the people who had known Mabel found out she was looking for Mabel's son, the chances of getting away with the story she planned to tell Brad would be virtually nonexistent. But then...there was always the possibility someone might be able to help, too. "I've decided to try to find Brad Tyler."

"Mabel's son? What in heaven's name for?"

"I just figured he might want to know his mother had passed away."

"So he could come back here to dance on her grave?"

Mabel and Howard had not been the best of friends, which, as far as Jo was concerned, was in his favor. "Actually, I thought it might put his mind at ease to know the feud was finally over."

"There are times you're too tenderhearted for your own good, Josephine. If Brad Tyler is anything like his mother, you'll not get thanked for your efforts."

"It's not thanks I'm looking for, so I don't think I'll be disappointed." She had learned to accept that as long as she operated her business in this location, the majority of her customers were going to treat her as a youngster who was in need of parental advice. She didn't mind. Especially with Howard. He was special—a gentleman in a world that was no longer gentle or had much use for the manly courtliness he had been taught as a child. He had become a widower ten years earlier and, to the keen disappointment of half the women in his apartment building, had remained single ever since.

Before coming to Boulder, Jo would never have believed she'd find such pleasure in becoming friends with people three times her own age. Occasionally, there seemed to be a disproportionate number of cantankerous souls in the lot, but they were more than balanced out by the ones who willingly, even eagerly, shared the richness of their lives with her. The friends she had made comprised the sole reason she had not moved her shop to a more lucrative location near the college or left the business altogether and gone back to school full-time to finish her degree.

"Well, I guess we should be on our way." Howard motioned for Sandy to follow. "Don't want to take up any more of your time when you've got that stack of work ahead of you."

Jo walked them to the door. "Be sure you get your grandfather to bring you back to see me before you leave, Sandy."

Sandy mumbled an affirmative answer through a mouthful of yogurt.

As soon as they were gone, Jo went back to her papers, sorting through the stack to find her writing tablet so she could begin the letter she'd be sending out. She'd never been much good at putting thought to paper; the mere prospect of composing a compelling yet properly businesslike message was almost enough to make her abandon the whole project.

An hour later, when she heard her second customer of the day enter the shop, she still hadn't got past the salutation. She looked up to see Florence Pickford, the woman Mable Tyler had considered her best friend. Jo laid the pencil aside. "If you'd been here a little earlier, you could have met Howard's granddaughter. She's going to be a real beauty when she grows up—if she ever gets that scowl off her face, that is."

"I met her last night, when I went to Denver with Howard to pick her up at the airport. She was scowling then, too. Something tells me she's going to be a real handful this next week. I offered to act as a buffer, but Howard said he thought he could handle everything all right.''

There were times when Jo was convinced Howard and Florence had something going between them, but then at other times, they would act so cool toward each other she would wonder if they were even friends.

Florence came across the room and sat down at Jo's table before Jo had a chance to get up. With her slim, erect figure and deep-blue eyes that snapped intelligence and wit, Florence made being seventy-three years old look enviable. ''I'm not going to beat around the bush about this, Josephine. Louise told me what you're up to, and I want you to know I think you're asking for trouble if you keep up this search for Mabel's son.''

Jo shook her head in wonder. It had only been a little over an hour since Howard had left and already the news about her search for Brad had made it through the apartment building. Surely the relay team had set some kind of record. ''Tell me why you feel that way and I promise I'll give it some thought.''

Florence sat back in the wrought-iron chair. ''Finding that young man is going to bring him nothing but grief when he learns Mable didn't leave him so much as a fare-thee-well. And then, what if the hurt makes him angry and he decides to contest the will just for spite? Think of the scandal and the heartache something like that is sure to bring. Remember, for all its size, Boulder is still a small town and the Tylers were one of its founding families. Brad would be better off not knowing.''

''Do you really think he would contest the will?''

It was as if Jo's question had stuck a pin in Florence's agitation, deflating it. She let out a sigh. ''No . . . I don't think Brad's the type who would ever fight for money. It wouldn't be at all like the young man I remember to do something so crass.''

"Florence, you're the only one I know who knew both Mabel and Brad. Won't you please tell me about him? What was he really like?" Up until then, all of Jo's information about Brad had come from Mabel. Everything she'd been told was so negative and one-sided, Jo had necessarily found herself leaning in the opposite direction until she'd begun to think of Brad as practically approaching sainthood. She knew she needed another person's viewpoint to find some balance.

Florence thought for a moment. Finally she blinked and started to speak, her indecision over. "I know it's difficult to understand the loyalty I feel toward Mabel, especially the Mabel that you knew. But there was a time when she was a much different person, someone you would have been proud to call a friend. I've never been able to forget that Mabel, and I can't quite shake the feeling that I'm being disloyal by talking about her now that she's gone.''

"If you'd rather not, I'd understand.''

"No...it's all right. It's time you heard the story, especially if you're intent on going ahead with this thing." She hesitated, took a deep breath and began. "Brad was born long after Mabel and James had given up hope of ever having any children. As you might expect, Brad wanted for nothing when he was growing up. The only surprising thing is that all the attention they lavished on him didn't ruin him. But it didn't. He was the most levelheaded kid I ever knew. And that's including my own. I don't mean to say that Brad didn't sow a few wild oats or to imply that he didn't get into his share of trouble, because he did. But, all in all, he was everything parents could hope for in a son."

Without knowing any of the facts, Jo had suspected as much. Often Mabel's bitterness had seemed to spring from a feeling of betrayal. If Brad had always been a thoughtless, uncaring son, his final action would not have been so devastating.

"Everything went along fine until James died when Brad was in high school," Florence continued. "After that, Mabel lost control. She became possessive and demanding. No matter how well Brad did, it wasn't good enough for her. Now that I have the advantage of hindsight, I think she was terrified at the prospect of being near sixty and suddenly having a teenage boy to raise all by herself and she simply overreacted."

"With all that was happening with teenagers back then, I can't say that I blame her for being concerned, not to mention a little scared."

Florence lightly shrugged. "Every generation rebels; some more dangerously than others. It's a test all parents must take, and how they conduct themselves determines their score. I'm afraid Mabel failed her test... worse than most of us."

Jo couldn't help but compare the way her own parents had guided her through her teens with the way Mabel had handled Brad. A long overdue thank-you was in order—one she would give that night when she called them in California.

"By the time Brad was ready for college, Mabel had clutched him so tight she was unable to let go. Naturally, he could hardly wait to get away. When he insisted on going to an out-of-state school instead of staying in Boulder and going to the University of Colorado, she told him she wouldn't pay his tuition. That didn't stop him—

he applied for scholarships and took on a second job. In the end, when she saw that he meant to go to the University of Iowa even if he had to support himself, she changed her mind.''

Jo let out a low whistle. ''Now I understand how Karen's appearance could cause so much trouble. Mabel was nowhere near ready to let go of her son.''

''Brad tried for over two years to get Mabel to change her mind about Karen.''

''What was it Mabel hated so much about her?''

Florence couldn't restrain. ''It would take the rest of the day and I'd only be halfway through the telling. Mostly she didn't think Karen was good enough for Brad. He made the crucial error of telling his mother that he had met Karen in a bar where she was a cocktail waitress. The kids he ran around with used to go there regularly for the happy hour. They would order a beer and fill up on the free food so they didn't have to fix themselves dinner.''

Jo smiled. When she was in college, she and her friends had done the same thing more times than she cared to remember. The meal they got was never well balanced, but dinner for the price of a beer helped stretch a meager budget.

''Working in a bar wasn't the worst of it,'' Florence went on. ''Although they were both sophomores, Karen was older than Brad by three years...and she had a child but she'd never had a husband.''

It wasn't necessary for Jo to hear more. She had come to know Mabel well enough in the last two years of her life to realize how her friend had probably reacted to this news. In Mabel's eyes, having a child out of wedlock would have branded Karen a scarlet woman with no possible hope of redemption. Straightlaced was a kind description of Mabel; narrow-minded was more accurate.

"Brad tried every way he could think of to bring Mabel around, but she wouldn't budge. Their arguments became more and more bitter until finally Brad was forced to accept his mother for what she was and to understand he was never going to get her to change. They had a terrible fight before he left that last time and he never came back. He's probably got a passel of kids of his own by now and made a real success of himself as an architect."

"Architect?"

"That's what he was studying. He wanted to open his own firm here in Boulder. Said he wanted to have a voice in the new direction he saw the town heading."

Jo filed the information away for future use. Surely architects had organizations they belonged to. If the letter she was getting ready to send out didn't work, at least she had her next step planned. She felt a shiver of excitement. Looking for Brad had begun to develop an unexpected fascination. "Did you like Brad, Florence?"

A slow, warm smile appeared. "I liked him a lot," she said softly. "He was the kind of young man who could make old women like me remember what it was like to stroll through a flower-filled meadow on a sunny summer afternoon. There was a touch of the rogue in him that showed through when he smiled. And those blue eyes of his were real heartbreakers. Mabel near drove me crazy complaining over the number of girls who used to call him when he was in high school. She'd tell them it was unseemly for girls to be calling boys. But it never stopped them for long."

"You realize, don't you, that you're making him sound like a combination of Richard Gere and Robert Redford?"

She gave Jo a sage smile. "When you find him you'll see for yourself. *Then* you can tell me if you think I've exaggerated."

"Does this mean you've changed your mind about whether or not I should keep looking for him?"

Florence hesitated before answering. "I guess he does have a right to know Mabel's gone. Maybe it'll bring him some peace. If anyone ever deserved it, he does." She stood up and turned to leave.

Jo walked her to the door. "Thanks for telling me about Brad," she said. "I really needed another perspective. It's made me more convinced than ever that I'm doing the right thing in looking for him."

"Let's just hope you'll still be thanking me after you've found him."

Before Jo could get back to her letter, the usual assortment of noontime customers began straggling in, providing a welcome distraction from the blank paper she still had to face. It was almost four before she had any real chance to return to her task. The "Dear Mr. Tyler" looked forlorn, perched at the top of the page all by itself. To give it company, she added the date.

By the time she was ready to close up shop for the day, she had what she considered a fairly decent first draft. It was straightforward and succinct, giving just enough information without encouraging anyone but the real Brad Tyler to step forward and claim his inheritance...or so she hoped. She'd let it sit a day or two, make corrections and then borrow her friend Amy's typewriter for the final copy. Since all the letters were addressed to the same generic Mr. Tyler, she could run off the almost eight-hundred copies she needed and save considerable work. Only the envelopes would have to be individually typed. She quickly figured out the cost involved in photocopying and mailing and gave a soft groan. The promise she'd made to herself three months before not to dig into her meager savings anymore was going to have to be broken—again.

BRAD PULLED HIS CAR into the driveway of his single-story tract house, waited for the garage door to open and parked inside. Even though it was mid-July, with daylight lasting until almost nine, he had arrived home from work under a sky full of stars. Weary from a day of meetings with subcontractors and the planning commission in Cheyenne—all of which had entailed an almost four-hundred-mile round trip from Casper—the only things on his mind were food, a quick shower and bed.

Walking through the cavernous house, still bare of all but the most basic furniture after four years of occupancy, he passed the day's mail, sitting on the coffee table where his once-a-week housekeeper had left it. He glanced down at the small stack while untucking his shirt from his pants. The buttons slipped through the buttonholes, revealing a deeply tanned chest covered by a light wedge of curling black hair. His back and shoulders felt stiff from hours of driving and he tiredly rubbed the tight muscles in his neck. Exhausted, he considered letting the mail wait until morning. And then the return address of the top letter caught his attention. Boulder, Colorado. Slowly he bent and picked up the envelope, his fatigue, his hunger, instantly forgotten.

With unsteady hands he held the innocuous rectangle of white paper in front of him. J. Williams. He searched his memory for a Williams—nothing. He headed for the kitchen, tapping the envelope thoughtfully against his thigh as he walked down the hall. Tossing the letter on the counter, he went to the refrigerator for a glass of milk before returning to stare at the typewritten return address as he drank. Mechanically he rinsed the glass and left it in the sink. Still unable to bring himself to look inside the envelope, he carried it with him into the bedroom.

After all this time, was it possible Mabel had broken down and was trying to make contact with him? It didn't surprise him that the contact would be through someone else; he knew his mother too well to think she would be direct in her dealings with him. This way, if he still refused to see her, she wouldn't have to endure the humiliation of hearing it from him.

A sudden, self-deprecating laugh escaped him when the realization finally struck that there was every possibility the letter had nothing at all to do with his mother. He no longer hesitated tearing the envelope open and extracting the single sheet of white paper.

Dear Mr. Tyler:
I'm writing in an attempt to locate the Brad Tyler who is the son of Mabel and James Tyler of Boulder, Colorado. I am holding a message and a small inheritance for him which was entrusted to me by his mother before she died last spring.

Please, if you are the man I'm looking for, or if you have any information that might lead me to him, I urge you to contact me as soon as possible.

Regards,
Josephine Williams

P.S. When you do write back, if you would add a

line or two about Uncle Henry, it would expedite matters considerably.

His mother was dead. The news left him numb. How was it possible she had died and he hadn't felt anything? Shouldn't there have been a sense of loss? Shouldn't there be one now?

Instead of a feeling of loss, a profound sadness swept over him as he stared blindly out the bedroom window and mourned not so much for the death of a woman who had lived a long full life, but for all the years that had been wasted.

After several minutes had passed, he turned from the window, unshed tears glistening in his eyes. *Damn it,* he silently swore, throwing the crumpled letter across the room. What perverse game had he played in his mind to make him think he and his mother had forever?

CHAPTER THREE

STANDING NEAR the front entrance to the three-story Victorian apartment building she called home, Jo bent to peer into the mailbox marked #3, trying to see if she had anything worth the effort of digging her keys out of the bottom of her purse. The corner of an envelope stuck out an eighth of an inch past a slick advertisement for Hanley's Department Store. Her heart skipped a beat in anticipation. The envelope had to mean a letter; it was either too early or too late in the month for the usual bills. She started digging for the key ring that held the mailbox key—one of three sets of keys she carried around with her.

"How many times do I have to tell you, if you'd get rid of that damn suitcase you call a purse, you wouldn't have to spend half of your life locked out of places? Purses were never meant to carry a sample of everything you own, Jo. Just a few of the essentials."

Jo looked up and smiled at Amy Feinstein, who was walking up the sidewalk toward her. Scarcely a year older, a scant two inches taller and a curvaceous five pounds heavier, Amy's coloring so closely resembled Jo's that they could be, and frequently were, mistaken for sisters. Not only had Amy become Jo's best friend during the three years they had occupied the apartments directly across the hall from each other, she had been privy to countless dumpings of the entire contents of Jo's purse while Jo struggled to find her elusive keys.

"I cleaned it out last week," Jo said, grabbing the sides of the floppy cloth bag and giving it a vigorous shake. "But then I discovered I was so used to carrying the extra weight I couldn't maneuver without it, so I put everything back." Again she shook the bag. "I can hear them," she groaned. "Why can't I see them?"

"Watch this," Amy commanded as she reached into her own purse and effortlessly withdrew a small chrome ring with five keys attached. "See how easy life can be?"

"Show-off." Jo thrust her hand deep into her bag for yet another try.

Amy took out her mail and leaned against the wall as she sorted through the collection. "Catch anyone slinking around the shop today? Better yet—did you see any strange men hiding in the bushes as you walked home?"

Jo gave a disparaging snort. She had invited Amy over for cake and coffee two nights before, and somewhere between telling her about seeing Alex again and relaying the tale of the mass confusion she'd had at the yogurt shop when thirty-five preteens had stopped by on their way home from a scouting trip, she had let it slip that she'd used her home address on the eight hundred letters she'd sent out. Amy—always practical and with few illusions about her fellow man—had ranted and raved for half an hour. Jo was sure to be the victim of some deranged B. Tyler, she insisted, some lunatic who was convinced that she either was carrying a fortune around with her or had one hidden in her apartment.

"If you don't develop a little trust in humanity, Amy, you're going to wind up just like Mabel Tyler."

"At least I'll reach old age. Which is more than I can say for you if you keep advertising for someone to hit you over the head."

"Ah ha!" Jo said triumphantly, producing her keys and ignoring Amy's crack.

"Did you tell the police about that weird phone call you got last night?"

"At one time or another in their life, everyone gets weird phone calls, Amy."

"In other words, you didn't."

"If he calls again, I'll report him—Scout's honor."

"That's going to look terrific written on your tombstone."

Jo jiggled the temperamental lock on her mailbox in an attempt to get it open. Finally it yielded and she extracted her mail then turned to Amy. "If I invite you over for dinner, will you promise not to talk about this anymore tonight?"

"You can't buy my silence that easily."

Jo laughed. "Since when?" Of all her friends, Amy was by far the most inept in the kitchen and the most grateful for a free meal.

"Since I happen to already have an invitation to dinner. Steve and I are going out for Chinese and then to a movie."

Suddenly Jo realized how much she had counted on Amy being home that evening—just in case. *You're behaving like an idiot,* she railed, squaring her shoulders as she sought to regain her earlier bravado. There had been no one lurking in the bushes, and there was no one waiting to pounce on her in her apartment. She was letting Amy's overactive imagination find fertile ground. "Does this mean things are heating up between you and Steve?"

she asked, valiantly trying to hide her unease about spending the evening alone.

"Not a chance. Steve is too in love with himself to ever find room in his heart for anyone else."

"Then why do you bother going out with him? I would think that even reruns on television would be more stimulating than an evening with someone who was the president of his own fan club." Jo sorted through her mail as she walked toward the front door. The letter she had spotted through the slot was from a Brad Tyler in Provo, Utah. Unable to wait until she was inside, she slipped her finger under the flap and tore open the envelope.

"Actually, once we get past how dashing he looks in his new 'whatever,' he can be a lot of fun—just not the type you'd want to spend a lifetime with." Amy nearly bumped into Jo, who had stopped to read her letter. "What's so interesting?" she prodded, her curiosity instantly piqued.

Instead of answering, Jo held the single sheet of paper up so Amy could read over her shoulder.

Dear Ms Williams,
I was terribly distressed to learn my dear mother had passed away. To know that she thought of me to the last, however, was heartening—even if the inheritance was a small one.

Since you didn't mention what type of proof you required in order to release what my mother so kindly left to me, I have taken the liberty of enclosing my birth certificate.

I would sincerely appreciate any expediency you might use in getting the funds to me as my youngest child—a beautiful, fragile little girl who looks remarkably like my dear mother, Mabel—cannot be admitted to the hospital for heart surgery until I can supply a rather large deposit.

As for Uncle Henry, I'm not surprised Mother mentioned him to you. Not only was he her favorite brother, I was his favorite nephew.

Impatiently yours,
Brad Tyler

Jo carefully refolded the single sheet of paper and tucked it back into the envelope. She glanced over at Amy and wasn't surprised to see an "I-told-you-so" look on her face. "All right. So maybe there are one or two people in this world who might try to get something that didn't rightfully belong to them."

Amy put her arm around Jo's shoulders and gave her a commiserating hug. "Just be glad this particular person is in another state, far far away."

"You must admit, he was pretty clever to say he was enclosing his birth certificate and then 'accidentally' forgetting to put it inside. Surely if he were crazy, he wouldn't think up something like that?" She strived to sound confident but failed miserably.

Amy took pity on her. "I'm sure he's nothing but an opportunist. When you don't answer, he'll let the whole thing drop."

Jo shoved the letter in her purse. "It's at times like this that I know why I like you so much."

"Come on. I have a few minutes before I have to get ready. We'll go upstairs and grab a quick glass of wine. I think we could both use one." She held the door for Jo to enter first.

As always, the windowless lower hallway in the three-story Victorian was dark and sinister looking. Jo hesitated a second to let her eyes adjust before crossing to the stairs. "I hope there aren't too many more letters like this one," she grumbled. "I might be forced to reassess my feelings about man's basic nature."

Amy snorted. "If I thought there was much chance of that, I'd sneak off and send a few myself. Maybe it's a good thing this is happening. You needed something to shake you up. Everyone should have a little healthy fear in them."

"You must think I'm a complete wimp if you really believe one little letter is going to shake me up."

"Not even when you add weird phone calls to it?"

"Phone *call*, Amy—in the singular." Jo reached the second-story landing and, as usual, was instantly blinded by the light streaming in through the hall window. On familiar ground, she didn't wait for her eyes to adjust before taking the four familiar strides over to her front door. She was sorting through her keys when she heard a sharp gasp of surprise from Amy. Jo felt a tightness in her throat and a tingling along the base of her scalp. *Amy never lost her composure.* Slowly she turned to look at her friend, who was staring at the opposite end of the hallway. Jo followed her gaze.

Amy's warnings about midnight phone calls and men lurking in the bushes came crashing down around Jo as she detected the barely discernible shape of a man standing in the shadows. She felt a cry of alarm tear at her throat, but no sound broke the ominous silence. The man stepped forward, moving out of the darkness into the dusty streaks of sunshine. Jo tensed, preparing to flee.

BRAD FELT LIKE kicking himself for not making his presence known the minute the two women had reached the top of the stairs. "I'm sorry...I didn't mean to frighten you." He held out his hand in what he hoped would look like a friendly gesture. "My name is Brad Tyler. I'm here to see—"

Jo let out a groan and took a step backward. "How did you get here?" she managed to say past the lump in her throat.

"I drove," he answered, puzzled by her question but willing to play along.

"Why?"

"Because someone who lives here and goes by the name of Josephine Williams wrote to me, and I have a few questions I'd like to ask her about her letter."

"What kind of questions?" Amy asked.

Brad stopped his forward motion, folded his arms and leaned one shoulder against the faded tea-rose wallpaper. "I've never been wild about repeating myself, so if you don't mind, I think I'll save them for Ms Williams."

"She doesn't live here anymore," Amy answered before Jo had a chance to say anything. "She moved to Denver last week."

"Kind of sudden, wasn't it?" Brad glanced from one woman to the other, assuming they were roommates and trying to decide which one of them had written the letter. He shrugged, affecting nonchalance. "And here I thought she was dying to find out what happened to Uncle Henry."

Jo dropped her keys. They made a discordant jangling sound as they bounced off the hall runner and hit the oak floor. "Why don't you tell us?" she suggested, ignoring the keys. "We'd be happy to pass the information along when we see her."

"How do I know I can trust you?" He could feel a smile tugging at the corners of his mouth and reached up to wipe it away. He wasn't sure whether it was because of his lack of sleep over the last three days or because of his sometimes perverse sense of humor, but he had the feeling that he'd somehow stepped into the middle of an Abbott and Costello comedy routine.

"It's us or nothing," Amy replied.

"I see." He hesitated before saying more, as if considering her offer. "Since you don't leave me much choice, I guess I'll have to tell you." He settled more comfortably against the wall, pausing for dramatic effect. "Uncle Henry and I go back quite a few years. We met in a junkyard when I was eight years old and we became instant, inseparable friends. I invited him home for dinner—he stayed ten years. Then one morning he just disappeared." Again Brad paused. "Without a doubt he was the ugliest dog God ever put on this earth, but what he lacked in looks, he made up for in personality." His voice dropped. Intuitively deciding which of the two women was Josephine Williams, he intently met her gaze. "My mother hated Uncle Henry, and since she became the kind of person who'd talk about something she hated long before she'd talk about something she loved, I'm not surprised she told you about him."

Jo felt the weight lift from her shoulders. *So this was Mabel Tyler's son.* Responding to the directness of his last statement, she said, "How did you know I was Josephine Williams?"

He grinned. "You mean other than having the keys to her apartment in your hand?"

"Uh-huh."

"Your friend's rush to protect you was a dead giveaway."

As if reinforcing her position, Amy came up to stand beside Jo. "Are you absolutely sure this guy is who he

says he is?'' she said to her friend, not taking her eyes off
Brad.

Jo nodded. "I'll be all right. You go ahead and get
ready for your date."

Amy cast a final warning glance in Brad's direction. To
Jo she said, "Just remember, I'm right across the hall if
you need me. All you have to do is yell."

After Amy had disappeared into her own apartment,
Brad stepped forward to pick up Jo's keys. He handed
them to her. "I take it you've had some problems with
replies to your letter?"

Jo opened the door. "It hasn't been as bad as our behavior would make you think. You just caught us at the
wrong time." She stepped inside and motioned for him
to follow. After she'd closed the door again and tossed
her purse in a chair, she put her hand out. "As you already know, Mr. Tyler, I'm Jo Williams."

He took her hand, pleased by the firmness of her
handshake. "Brad," he corrected.

"I'm sorry we had to meet under such unfortunate
circumstances, Brad—both the news about your mother
and what happened out there in the hallway."

"Don't worry about it." He liked this Jo Williams. "I
believe you said in the letter that my mother died last
spring?"

"Suddenly and quickly. She was watching television in
Florence Pickford's apartment. Florence said Mabel
complained about a heavy feeling in her chest and then
closed her eyes. She was gone before the fire department
arrived."

"I'm glad Florence was with her." It made him feel
better that she hadn't died alone.

"They were inseparable these last few years. Your
mother didn't have too many..." Would her mouth for-

ever be disconnected from her brain? "Uh, what I meant to say was that your mother didn't have a very active social life toward the end. But those who were close to her—"

"I know how abrasive my mother's personality could be," he said, trying to spare her further embarrassment.

Jo smiled her appreciation. "Why don't you have a seat while I fix us some iced tea? Then we can talk about why I wrote to you."

"Thanks, I'd like that." But after she'd gone, instead of sitting down, he shoved his hands into the back pockets of his jeans and wandered over to the window. It felt strange to be back in Boulder. But nothing like he had anticipated. He'd expected to feel overwhelmed by memories of his last visit and its devastating aftermath. But he felt only a profound sense of sorrow for the wasted years. He had thought he could never return. Yet here he was, reliving the happy memories instead of the bad ones. Being able to do so brought him a sense of peace, as if something long unfinished had at last been completed and he could get on with his life.

Jo came back into the living room carrying a tray with glasses of tea and a plate of cookies. She was surprised to find Brad so deep in thought that he didn't even notice her return. Wondering whether she should clear her throat or bump noisily against the table to announce her presence, she wound up doing neither. Instead she took the opportunity to study Mabel's son.

It was difficult to discern any family resemblance. The years had not been kind to Mabel's craggy face; Brad had yet to reach his prime. Mabel had been crippled and hunched over by arthritis; Brad was tall and straight. Her hair had been a shimmering gray; his was midnight black. But the most obvious difference between them was the lack of bitterness in Brad's intense blue eyes and the lack of compassion that had been in Mabel's. He wasn't unusually tall or massively built, but he dominated the small room, somehow looking out of place as he stood next to the garden of chintz flowers on her sofa and the mauve paint on the walls. And Florence had been right—he radiated a masculine sensuality that connected directly to a woman's secret fantasies.

"Do you think we looked alike?" he asked, turning from the window.

"No." She understood he hadn't asked the question to embarrass her; he was simply curious. "You're nothing like I expected."

His face twisted in a half grin. "Is that good or bad?"

"Good. I was afraid..." Damn, she'd done it again. "Uh...I thought you might—"

"You don't have to explain. Better than anyone, I know what my mother was like."

Jo swallowed. This was as good an opening as she was going to get. "That's one of the reasons I was so anxious to find you, Brad." She handed him a glass of tea. "Mabel changed a lot the year before she died. I don't know why. Maybe she was aware of her heart trouble and it made her realize her remaining time was limited, or perhaps she simply began to mellow. Whatever it was that caused the change really doesn't matter, does it? Only that the change took place." Jo knew she was talking too fast but she couldn't slow down. Lies had never come easily and this was the granddaddy of them all.

"She desperately wanted to find you and Karen," Jo went on, "and to tell the two of you how sorry she was for the trouble she'd caused. Toward the end, all she could talk about was the possibility that she had grandchildren she might never see and that the two of you might never have the chance to make up.''

''What you're telling me would represent an amazing turnaround from the last time my mother and I saw each other,'' Brad said. The years hadn't softened the ugliness nor lessened the impact of that final confrontation between him and Mabel.

Jo couldn't tell by his reaction whether she was pulling off the fabrication or not. ''As I mentioned in the letter, Mabel left a small inheritance with me—actually, it's some jewelry—to give to you if you ever returned to Boulder. She said they were all pieces that either had been passed down to her through the family or that your father had given her. She couldn't bear to see them sold to strangers as part of the estate.'' Now came the tricky part. ''I'm afraid the inheritance is just the jewelry. There isn't any money. Mabel said she never doubted you would be successful and in no need of financial help from her. So she felt you wouldn't mind if she gave what money was left to her favorite charity.''

''Which was?''

Jo swallowed. Her credibility was on the line, but she knew better than to fudge this one. It would be too easy to check out. ''The Gray Panthers.''

Brad considered her answer and then laughed aloud. ''How perfect. I'm sure she never belonged but she'd have loved the idea of old people sticking it to the government.''

Because many of her friends from the senior-citizen complex were active members of the Gray Panthers, Jo's immediate impulse was to tell him he had a slightly lopsided view of the organization. But she decided it wasn't important enough to pursue when she still wasn't sure she'd managed to convince him about Mabel. ''The only

piece of jewelry I have with me at the moment is this.''
She took the diamond ring from her finger and handed
it to Brad. ''The rest is in a safe-deposit box at my
bank.''

Brad looked at the ring resting on his palm. The diamond had belonged to his grandmother. She had given
it to him in her will, along with instructions that he was
to save the ring for his bride. Mabel had kept it for him
with her other jewelry. Bittersweet memories touched
him, momentarily transporting him to another time and
place. So much pain...so many lives twisted and
warped...for what? Purposefully he shoved the memories aside. ''Thank you,'' he told Jo.

She had been right. A rush of vindication swept
through her that made her feel marvelous. Her plan had
worked; she couldn't resist pressing it a little farther.
''I'm only sorry I didn't think to contact you before she
died.'' The wry, knowing smile he turned on her in reply
forced a tentacle of doubt to creep into her newfound
confidence. ''I hope you don't mind that I've been
wearing the ring,'' she said in her haste to change the
subject. ''Your mother insisted that it shouldn't be locked
away, but worn and enjoyed. She put particular empha-
sis on letting you know she wanted the ring given to
Karen. And then if you had children, she requested that
it eventually be passed on to one of them.'' Jo cringed a
little at that bending of the truth. When Mabel had given
her the ring, it had been with the particular admonition
that the ''trollop'' Brad had married never get her hands
on it.

Brad stared at the brilliant pear-shaped diamond,
turning it over in his hand before dropping it into his

pocket. "There are no grandchildren," he said softly. "There is no Karen."

Jo's eyes opened wide. "What do you mean, there's no Karen?" she demanded.

CHAPTER FOUR

BRAD STARED at Jo, taken aback by her passionate outburst. What possible difference could Karen's disappearance make to her? "I haven't seen Karen in over eight years."

"Eight years? You mean to tell me that you and Mabel maintained a feud all that time over something that never happened?" Jo threw her hands up in the air in frustration. All the days, the *weeks* she had spent stewing over Mabel's jewelry, the guilt she had felt over keeping something that she felt rightfully belonged to someone else, the plans she had devised to find Karen and Brad—all for nothing. "I don't believe it. I thought Mabel was stubborn, but you . . . you take the cake."

Brad's reaction was immediate, his tone subdued but angry. "I don't know how you managed it or why you'd even bother, but it's obvious you know quite a bit about me. But there's no way you could know it all."

"What's to know?" Jo nearly shouted. "Bone-deep dumb stubbornness is undoubtedly an inherited trait. Like mother, like son."

Brad put his tea on the table beside him, folded his arms across his chest and stared at Jo. This was insanity. A woman he had met barely ten minutes before was reading him the riot act about something that was none of her business. *And he was standing there listening to her.* "Would you mind telling me what in the hell this is all about? In case it's slipped your mind, Ms Williams, I didn't go looking for you.''

Jo's anger disappeared as quickly as it had come. Wearily, she let out a deep sigh. ''I'm sorry,'' she said. ''I had no right to yell at you like that.''

Despite his better judgment, Brad responded to the conciliatory tone in her voice. ''Why don't we start this conversation over again?''

Jo looked at him over the rim of her glass. The air filled with tension as an unnatural silence grew between them. Finally, in an attempt to bridge the gap her outburst had caused, she asked the first question that came to her mind. ''So... which one of my Brad Tylers are you?''

Despite the lingering traces of anger, he smiled. ''How many do you have?''

''Almost eight hundred. And that only covers Colorado and its bordering states.''

''I'm the one from Casper, Wyoming. Or was there more than one of us there?''

''No, as I recall, there was just one.'' She took another sip of tea, staring at him the whole time. Florence had been right. Brad's eyes were an incredible color—not quite like any she had ever seen before. The band of light blue that surrounded the black center was itself encircled by a band of dark blue. ''It surprises me that there's enough work to keep an architect busy in a place the size of Casper,'' she said conversationally. ''But then, I guess the beautiful country must make up for the lack of work.''

''What makes you think I'm an architect?''

''You mean you're not?''

''Is that what you are?'' he asked with deceptive calm. ''An architect?''

"Me? Goodness, no. Whatever made you think that?"

"What made you think I was one?"

"Since you studied architecture in college, I just assumed—" Too late she saw the trap he had laid.

"Do you have any idea how disconcerting it is to have a complete stranger tell you about yourself?"

Jo shrugged. "I can't help it. I feel as though I already know you. Or at least I felt that way before we actually met."

Realizing his anger and resentment were wildly out of proportion to the situation, Brad groped for a way to stabilize his feelings. Perhaps, he reasoned, it would help if he turned the conversation away from himself. "Why don't we even things up a little?"

"What do you mean?" She knew very well what he meant but hoped to sidetrack him.

"Tell me about yourself."

Jo hated talking about herself. She didn't like admitting that for someone who had been alive twenty-six years, there was a remarkable lack of anything interesting to tell. But giving Brad some of her own background was probably the only way she would get him to tell her about Karen, so she unenthusiastically began reciting the details that had led to the crossing of their paths. "I moved to Boulder five years ago to take care of my grandmother when she fell and broke her hip. That's how I met Mabel. Your mother's apartment was across the hall from my grandmother's, so whenever I went to the grocery store I'd check with Mabel to see if there was anything I could get for her. After a while we became friends."

"I take it you don't live with your grandmother anymore."

"She died a year after her accident."

"I'm sorry," he said.

"I'm sorry, too. It's been four years now and I still miss her."

Brad picked up his tea and sat in the chair opposite Jo. "You said you 'moved' to Boulder?"

"From California. I was almost finished with my junior year at UCLA when she broke her hip."

"Why didn't you go back to UCLA after your grandmother died?"

Jo smiled. "That's a story all by itself."

"I'm in no hurry."

He couldn't be serious. But then she realized that he was, so she plunged ahead. "My grandmother didn't improve as fast as we'd thought she would but after the first two months she no longer needed constant care, so that left me with a lot of time on my hands.

"One day I noticed that the ice-cream parlor in the shopping center across the street from her apartment complex was going out of business. I mentioned the closing to my grandmother, and she told me what a blow it would be to her friends. The ice-cream parlor was kind of an informal gathering place for her more militant friends, the ones who wouldn't be caught dead in the arts-and-crafts kinds of places senior citizens are supposed to enjoy. To make a long story short, I took over the business. Only instead of selling ice cream, I decided frozen yogurt was the path to fame and fortune."

"And?"

"It depends on whether you count your riches in friends or silver."

"I take it that means frozen yogurt wasn't the hit you'd anticipated?"

"To put it mildly. At least, not with the crowd I get. Some of the yogurt shops closer to the campus do pretty well, and I've managed to pick up some of the college group when they drift in my direction, so business has improved a little since I opened." She smiled. "Occasionally I even make a convert in the over-sixty group. But for the most part, being in frozen yogurt in this part of Boulder is a labor of love. I manage to keep my head above water, which is more than a lot of other shop owners around here can say," she added with an unmistakable note of pride.

"Have you considered selling the shop and going back to school?"

"There are times when it's all I think about," she admitted.

"But?"

"I would feel that I was abandoning friends who had nowhere else to go." She saw what she interpreted as a look of admiration in his eyes and recoiled. "Wait just a minute. Before you start thinking I'm some sloppy sentimentalist or an altruistic do-gooder, I think you should know that I get a lot more from these people than I give."

"Regardless, it adds up to the same thing. You don't have the heart to turn your friends out in the cold so you continue what is basically a losing proposition." He shook his head in gentle reproach. "Not very businesslike. You'll never get a key to the executive washroom with an attitude like that."

Jo realized he was teasing her, but still she felt a flash of anger. "What makes you think I want to come anywhere near the executive washroom?"

"Unless I miss my guess, you majored in business at UCLA." It was a guess founded not so much on intuition as on logic, which told him that she must have had some kind of background knowledge or she'd never have had the confidence to jump into the ownership of anything at such a young age. "Every business major I've ever known has had a dream that went along with the degree."

"Well, since I intend to switch my major to social science should I ever go back to school, that observation no longer applies to me."

Brad studied her for a moment before abruptly standing. "Are you hungry?"

Jo was too surprised at his sudden change in manner and conversation to answer immediately. She looked up at him for several seconds before nodding, not aware until he'd mentioned it that she was indeed hungry.

"Me, too. As a matter of fact, I'm starved. How does Italian sound? I haven't had any really good Italian food since I left Boulder." He held out his hand to help her up. "Please tell me the Leaning Tower is still selling their incredible pasta," he said. "I've been thinking about a great big plate of lasagna all afternoon and I'm not sure I could survive the disappointment if I had to settle for eating someplace else."

Jo laughed. "I think you'll be around a while longer. The Leaning Tower was still in business three days ago, and I doubt anything's happened to it since."

"Three days ago?" A frown appeared. "If you were just there three days ago, I couldn't possibly ask you to go again tonight."

Jo shook her head in wonder as she tugged her hand free of his grasp. Florence hadn't warned her about the charm that went along with Brad's stunning eyes and his sensuality. How...why had Karen ever let him go? "Something tells me if I continue with this discussion, I'll wind up begging you to take me to the Leaning Tower." She looked down at her cotton skirt and sandals. The skirt had a circle of strawberry topping and a smear of chocolate yogurt; her sandals were new and comfortable but utilitarian. "Give me a minute to clean up."

His gaze swept her. "You look fine." Actually, he noted with a bit of surprise, she looked more than fine. Jo Williams had a spark about her that would always make whatever she wore, whatever trappings surrounded her, seem incidental and unimportant.

Jo gave him a look that told him she thought he was a few cents short of a dime and headed for her bedroom. "There's more tea in the refrigerator. Help yourself," she said as she closed the door.

Brad decided to take her up on the offer, picked up his glass and walked toward the kitchen. He smiled when he opened the refrigerator. A friend had once told him he could tell more about peoples' personalities by looking in their bathroom medicine cabinets than by talking to them for an hour. After considering the statement, Brad had disagreed. To him, the refrigerator held the more revealing clues.

Jo's was no exception. Sitting side by side on the top shelf were diet colas, a package of doughnuts, low-fat cottage cheese, broccoli and chocolate milk. She was obviously a person in conflict with herself. Sensible at war with impulsive. Fat doing battle with thin. He chuckled to himself when he saw which side seemed to be winning. While the broccoli was still in its original wrapper and beginning to show signs of wilting, the doughnuts looked fresh and were almost gone. He thought about his hasty conclusion. *Fat* was definitely not the winner where Jo was concerned. She had a trim, well-proportioned body—almost athletic in appearance.

Brad filled his glass with tea and then returned to the living room. Ten minutes later he was in the middle of a magazine article about the expansion of Boulder's thirty-year-old pharmaceutical plant when Jo opened her bedroom door and announced she was ready.

He glanced up to see that she had changed into a yellow muslin dress that made her hair seem streaked with sunlight and her skin a golden bronze. He acknowledged the transformation with an appreciative smile.

Unexpectedly, Jo blushed. That she had reacted to Brad's smile at all made her blush even more deeply. Could it really have been so long since a man had looked at her in open admiration that she fell apart when one did? "Shall we get this show on the road?" she asked, reaching for her purse and heading for the door, hoping if she ignored the flush covering her neck and cheeks, he would, too.

Brad got to his feet to follow. Sensing her discomfort over his unspoken compliment, he turned the conversation away from anything personal. "While I was sitting here waiting for you, the thought occurred to me that it's possible I've blown the food at the Leaning Tower way out of proportion."

"Memories can be dangerous things..." she said before realizing how poignantly applicable her statement was. With forced cheerfulness, she went on, "So this time we won't take any chances. Just in case you've erred on the side of memory, we'll kill a few brain cells and numb a few taste buds on the Tower's house wine before we order dinner." Jo stepped out into the hallway and came face to face with Amy, who was dressed in an electric-blue silk dress and wispy three-inch heels.

Amy looked from Jo to Brad and then back again. She seemed flustered. "How lucky I caught you before you left," she said in a hurry. "I was just on my way over to your place. I wanted to get that recipe for peach jam you promised to dig out for me. But I see you're leaving, so why don't I call you this evening when you get home? By the way, what time would that be?'' she added with seeming innocence.

Jo was caught completely off guard by Amy's bizzare behavior. ''I . . . uh . . . I'm not sure.''

''Oh, I don't need an exact time, just something approximate. I plan to stay up late tonight anyway.''

Jo looked at Brad. When he only shrugged in reply, she told Amy, ''I . . . we . . . should be back by midnight.''

''Great. I want to get an early start on my canning tomorrow.'' She offered Brad a quick smile. ''Well, have a good time.'' When Jo and Brad didn't immediately leave, Amy laughed nervously and backed across the hall as if returning to her apartment.

Jo turned so that Brad couldn't see her surreptitiously ask Amy, ''Are you all right?''

Amy nodded quickly in reply. ''I'll see you later,'' she said too cheerfully. ''Around midnight.''

Jo frowned in puzzlement as she gave Amy a questioning look. When Amy only continued to smile, Jo waved goodbye and headed downstairs. Behind her, as she was nearing the second-story landing, she heard a deep chuckle coming from Brad.

When they reached the sidewalk, he asked, ''Is your friend always so fiercely protective?''

Of course. The reason for Amy's strange behavior would have been obvious if she hadn't been so wrapped up in Brad's problems. ''I'm afraid so,'' she admitted. ''I seem to send out some kind of signal that makes people think I'm doomed if they don't run interference for me.''

''Perhaps it's your dangerously trusting nature.''

Assuming they would walk the five blocks to the restaurant, Jo automatically started down the street. After hesitating a few moments in front of his truck, Brad followed, quickly catching up. "What do you mean, 'dangerously'?" she asked as he came up beside her.

"Well, for one, did it ever occur to you that it might be more prudent to use a post-office box instead of your home address when you sent out those eight hundred letters?"

"Not *you*, too."

"Somehow it doesn't surprise me that I wasn't the first to mention it."

"There was a two-month waiting list at the post office for a box," she said, as if he would undoubtedly understand and agree with her reasoning.

"What about the shop's address?"

"I thought of that, but it seemed so impersonal."

Had he been told about Jo instead of meeting her himself, he would have said no one as naive and trusting could survive in the modern world. Now he wasn't so sure. "I'm only surprised you didn't keep the jewelry at your apartment so I wouldn't have to wait around for the bank to open." When Jo didn't immediately answer, his heart skipped a beat. "It is in the bank, isn't it?"

"Of course it is." But only because Amy had thrown a fit when she'd found out Jo was keeping the jewelry in the bottom of the closet wrapped in an old dresser scarf. Years before, when Jo had made the conscious decision not to live her life as if a thief lurked around every corner, she'd had no idea it would cause such intense reactions or bring out such strongly protective instincts in those around her. Since discovering how disconcerting her life-style was to family and friends, she'd reached the conclusion that someday she would have to find a middle ground, a place where she could maintain her faith in her fellow man but not be a source of constant worry to those who loved her. She just hadn't gotten around to it yet.

Brad stopped at the corner, a thoughtful look on his face.

"What is it?" Jo asked, following his gaze and seeing nothing out of the ordinary.

Memories assailed him, swarming around him like disturbed bees, some promising the sweetness of honey, others a stinging pain. "I grew up in that brown house down there."

Jo looked down Mapleton Avenue at the house across from the elementary school. Many of the homes in the Mapleton area were considered historic and architectural heritages. The brown one Brad had indicated was one of the largest and finest. "It's beautiful," she said simply.

"My great-grandfather came to Colorado a penniless immigrant. He made his fortune in the silver mines and then settled down in Boulder to build this house. As soon as it was finished, he set out to search for a bride."

"I thought it usually worked the other way around. Bride first and then house."

"If you could see a picture of my great-grandfather Tyler, you'd understand his reasoning."

Jo smiled. "Being handsome isn't everything."

Brad returned her smile and added a wink. "Especially not if you were rich back in those days."

They crossed the street and waited for the light to change so they could cross to the opposite side. "When did your family sell the house?"

Brad hesitated before answering. "I didn't know it had been sold until this morning," he said quietly. "Somehow, the possibility it was gone hadn't even occurred to me."

"That was a dumb question. I'm sorry."

He put his arm around her shoulders and gave them a gentle squeeze. Unexpectedly, her warmth penetrated the cold shell that had formed around him. "Don't be sorry. I should be past feeling surprised at anything my mother might or might not have done these last ten years." He looked down at her through narrowed eyes. "No…let me amend that. That she changed her mind about Karen and left her jewelry to the two of us surprises me. 'Stuns me' would probably be a better way of putting it."

"Florence told me Mabel was once quite different," Jo rushed to say. After everything she'd gone through to find Brad and give him the jewelry, she wasn't about to tell him the truth and ruin the one chance he might have to finally end the battle with his mother.

"There are times when I wonder if that other person I remember ever really existed—or if she simply managed to keep her true personality in check all those years because of my father."

Jo blanched at the bitterness in his voice. "The woman you remember was real, Brad. I remember her, too." There had been only a few glimpses of that earlier Mabel Tyler in the hours of conversation they had shared. But it had been enough to give Jo hope that the anger Mabel harbored might someday dim and allow her the freedom to love again.

"Perhaps—but then, it really doesn't matter anymore, does it?"

What had Mabel done to him so that, even in death, he couldn't forgive her? "You must know that if you let this feud continue, you'll end up just like her someday."

Brad removed his arm from around her shoulders and stuck his hands in his pockets. "Pop psychology, Jo? Somehow, I expected better from you."

"Why?" Her anger was immediate and intense. What right did he have to judge her that way? "You've only known me an hour. You couldn't possibly—" Damn it! He'd done it to her again. "All right. I admit I don't really know you any better than you know me, but—"

"You have a few facts and the opinions of a woman whose view of the world was warped forever when her husband died—and that's all you have. I'm not the same man who left here over eight years ago and I refuse to let you think of me as if I were."

"It isn't just what Mabel told me about you that formed my opinion. Florence helped, too. Besides, I consider myself a pretty good judge of character, and so far you've shown me that you're a stubborn, embittered person. You've said nothing since you arrived to make me change my mind about you."

Brad stopped and silently counted to ten. In a gesture that only hinted at his frustration, he raked his hand through his hair. "Do you make a habit of wending your way into the middle of people's lives unasked?"

Jo felt as if she'd been hit. She realized she had no right to feel offended, but his words still hurt. "I can see this dinner thing was a mistake," she said quietly, stepping away from him. "Why don't you go ahead by yourself? I'll go back to my apartment. We can meet again Monday morning at the Arapahoe National Bank." She turned to leave. "It's the branch on Arapahoe and Thirty-third."

Brad reached out and grabbed her arm. He gave her a beseeching look. "I know you're going to find this hard to believe, but I'm usually a much nicer person. If I promise not to bellow at you anymore tonight, would you reconsider having dinner with me?"

Something deep inside warned her she would be making a mistake to spend even another hour with him. It was a voice she often promised herself she would heed. When she didn't, no matter how determined she was not to become involved in someone else's problem, she invariably wound up right in the middle of it. Even strangers told her about themselves—in doctors' offices, on buses, in the yogurt shop. It didn't matter where she met them or how long she had known them, Jo invariably became privy to the most intimate details of their lives. It was long past time she called a halt. After all, she had her own life to worry about, as Amy was forever pointing out. The minute the bank opened on Monday morning she would give Brad his mother's jewelry and wash her hands of the whole Tyler clan.

"Please," Brad said softly, breaking into Jo's thoughts.

She stared at him. *Oh, Florence, you really knew what you were talking about,* she thought with a mental sigh. She'd wanted to be his friend since the idea of finding him had first occurred to her. "All right," she finally said. "But maybe we should set down a few ground rules first."

He gave her a lopsided grin. "Such as?"

A feeling of warmth spread through her as she responded to his smile. "I won't play psychiatrist if you'll stop flying off the handle every time I mention something about your past."

He let go of her arm. "That's it?"

"For now. We may have to add a few more rules as we go along, however."

"Do we need to shake on this?"

"I think your word would be sufficiently binding."

"Then consider it given. And none too soon." He made a gesture that indicated he thought they should be on their way. "If we don't get to that restaurant quickly, I'm afraid you're going to have to carry me. I'm about to pass out from hunger."

She eyed him. "I don't know about carrying you. But I suppose I might be talked into propping you up somewhere and bringing you a glass of wine and a piece of garlic bread. After I have already eaten, of course."

"Oh, of course. I wouldn't dream of asking you to delay your own meal on my account."

LATER THAT EVENING, when Brad brought her home, Jo asked him in for coffee. They had managed to avoid further arguments by sticking to safe subjects and had shared a pleasant evening filled with more laughter than heavy silences. Brad had told her about the construction trade in Wyoming and his plans for expansion, and she had told him about growing up in Colorado Springs and her life as a student at UCLA.

Standing at the door to her apartment, Brad told himself that after three days without sleep, it was well past the time he should have been in bed. But he was reluctant to end the evening. Jo's easy laughter had been like a balm to his tumultuous feelings. Finally, it occurred to him that coffee was just what he needed, since he'd almost single-handedly finished the bottle of wine they'd had with dinner.

"Have a seat," Jo said, moving toward the kitchen. "I'll only be a minute."

Brad settled himself comfortably on the sofa—too comfortably; before Jo returned with a tray carrying their coffee, he was fast asleep.

Jo considered waking him but didn't have the heart. Instead she pulled an afghan out of the closet and tucked it around him. She was on her way to her bedroom when she heard a knock on the front door. Rushing to answer it before whoever it was knocked again and woke Brad, she hit her toe against the coffee table and let out a groan of pain. Brad didn't budge. She realized he was so tired that even if she'd landed on him, he probably wouldn't have awakened.

When Jo finally made it to the door, Amy had her hand raised to knock again. "It's about time," she said. "I was beginning to worry."

"Everything's fine," Jo said, struggling to keep the pain from her face. "You can go to bed now."

"What's the matter with you?"

"I stubbed my toe." She looked down at the throbbing appendage. "I think it's broken."

"Here, let me see." Amy bent down and reached for Jo's foot. "Which one?"

"The big one."

Amy gently prodded Jo's toe, then glanced upward, her gaze taking in the living room as she looked at her friend. Slowly she stood. "I don't believe it," she hissed. "Another stray. Is he so broke he can't afford a motel?"

"Just tired. He fell asleep when I went into the kitchen to fix us some coffee. I couldn't bring myself to wake him."

"If I had any sense, I'd make you spend the night at my place." She sighed wearily. "For my peace of mind, would you at least tell me what a wonderful, all-American guy he is so I don't have to worry about you tonight and I can get some sleep myself?"

"Trust me on this one, Amy. He's special."

Amy studied her friend as if trying to decide what to do next. "I'll be right across the hall if you need me."

"Thanks." Jo almost had the door closed when she remembered something. "By the way, did you still want that recipe for peach jam?" she asked, her eyes sparkling with impishness.

"All right, so it wasn't one of my better efforts. It was the best I could come up with on such short notice."

"I hate to be the one to break this to you, but you didn't pull it off."

Amy clasped her hand over her heart as if she'd been wounded.

"I think it might have been the silk dress and spike heels that did you in."

"What is this? Are you intimating only frumpy people like to preserve their peaches?"

Jo laughed. "I wouldn't dream of touching that one."

"Coward." Amy made a haughty sound and turned toward her apartment with a victorious grin.

"Amy?" Jo said, her voice suddenly serious.

"Yes?"

"Thanks."

The grin changed to a warm smile. "Anytime. After all, if *I* didn't look after you, who would?"

Jo didn't give the answer that immediately sprang to mind, that there were whole lines of people who thought it their duty to take care of her. Instead she told her friend good-night and closed the door. As she passed a softly snoring Brad, she readjusted the afghan, which had slipped from his shoulder. When she realized her hand lingered on his arm longer than absolutely necessary, she snatched it away. Stray dogs and cats and lost souls...

Shaking her head, Jo walked into the bedroom.

CHAPTER FIVE

FLORENCE PICKFORD glanced out her fourth-floor-apartment window at the leaves rustling in the trees and absently wondered if the innocent breeze would turn into one of Boulder's infamous winds. With an altitude of more than five thousand feet and nestled between the Rocky Mountains to the west and vast grasslands to the east, the city was in a natural location to pick up the effects of atmospheric changes. This sometimes meant winds that reached over a hundred miles an hour, so the area around Boulder provided the perfect laboratory for the Center on Atmospheric Research, which had been built on a hill overlooking the city.

The center was the last place her husband, Edward, had been employed and the primary reason Florence now called Boulder her home. Edward had been a dear and loving man, but not someone who'd given much thought to the future.

Consequently, when he'd died ten years earlier, Florence hadn't been too surprised to learn she had little more than a small pension and social security to live on for the rest of her life. Worst of all, the pension had an effect she was sure Edward had never intended and would never have wanted. Because she would lose the pension money if she remarried, she was financially constrained to remain single...or to find someone with enough income to support two, an almost impossible task with inflation incessantly devouring fixed incomes.

When Edward had died unexpectedly of heart failure, nothing had mattered to Florence except her grief over the loss of her lifelong companion. But gradually, a different kind of grief had set in—loneliness. She and Edward had had a full and loving relationship and she missed the intimacy they had shared, as well as the companionship.

And then she had found someone who had put the sunshine back into her days and magic into her nights. Howard Wakelin had reignited passions she had learned it was best to try to ignore. Just looking at him across a room could fill her with a longing that would last deep into the night.

When they'd first met, their hearts had ruled their actions, and they had slipped into loving each other as easily and joyously as winter slips into spring. Not until later had reality reared its ugly head. No matter how they adjusted the figures, the bottom line always came out the same. If they were to get married, they would have to settle for eating one meal a day.

And to live together without marriage was unthinkable. Or at least it had been in the beginning. Since then, they'd both occasionally weakened—but never at the same time. The thought of how their children and grandchildren would react to ''old people'' living in ''sin'' always intruded. And they feared the scandal they would inevitably create among their own friends if they decided to live together without benefit of matrimony.

They had tried to shed the values of their youth and adopt the less stringent life-style of the current generation. But the codes and strictures they'd grown up with were so deeply ingrained it was impossible to cast them aside.

When the pressure of their situation and its resulting tension became too great for them to bear, they would stop seeing each other. But it didn't take long for the loneliness to become even worse than the strain and the threat of constant quarreling, so the separations never lasted long.

Most of the time Florence managed to cope with her life's ironic closing chapter, but there were days, like this one, when the frustration would become almost unbearable. Not even the brisk three-mile walk she'd taken that morning had succeeded in easing her mind the way it usually did.

She was just turning from the window when she saw Jo Williams approaching Yogurt, Etc. on a bicycle. Florence watched as Jo swung her leg over the bar, her skirt catching in the breeze and showing the length of her thigh. How marvelous it must be to be young in a time of such freedom. Even though Florence rejected the archaic guidelines of her own generation, those guidelines would not release her.

She continued to watch as her young friend wheeled the bicycle into the shop and disappeared behind the closed door. Jo and everything she represented was just the medicine Florence needed that morning. Without giving her decision another thought, Florence grabbed the jacket to her maroon sweat suit, left her apartment and dashed across the street.

JO WAS IN THE BACK of the shop mixing the ingredients for a fresh batch of frozen yogurt when she heard a knock on the front door. Wiping her hands on the terry-cloth dish towel she'd tucked into the waistband of her skirt, she headed out front. For an unguarded instant she thought it might be Brad. He had been gone that morning when she woke up. A note, written on a corner torn from a grocery bag, was the only indication he had ever been there. In a difficult-to-decipher scrawl, he had thanked her for going to dinner with him, apologized for falling asleep and said that if she needed to reach him, he would be staying at the Hilton. She'd noted with a twinge of regret that there had been nothing about seeing her again before Monday, when they were to meet at the bank.

A crazy mixture of disappointment and delight came over Jo when she saw who was outside waiting for her. "Florence—come in," she said, stepping aside to let her friend enter. "What are you doing out and about this early?"

"I couldn't stand being cooped up any longer, so I thought I'd come over to see if you needed any help this morning."

"I can always use your help...and the company. You can measure the ingredients for me while I do the mixing." She reached behind Florence to relock the door. "You couldn't have come at a better time. I have a hundred questions and you're just the person to answer them."

Florence studied her for several seconds. Her frown of concentration soon became a nod of understanding. "You've heard from Brad, haven't you?"

Jo made a face and rolled her eyes. "I hope you take this in the spirit in which it is intended, Florence, but I'm sure glad I wasn't one of your children. You're too darned clever to have ever had anything pulled over on you."

Florence's laugh was melodious and spontaneous. "I probably shouldn't admit this, but I love it when you use such outrageous flattery on me, Jo. It never fails to give me a lift for the rest of the day."

"Flattery has nothing to do with it."

"So tell me about Brad. How is he? Does he have children? Where is he living?" The questions tumbled forth like pebbles down the side of a hill, each setting the next in motion, until the momentum was overwhelming and impossible to stop. "How is Karen? Do they believe your story about Mabel leaving them the jewelry?"

Jo placed her palm against the swinging door that led to the back room and gave a push. Now, after having met Brad, she finally understood the special tone that crept into Florence's voice whenever she talked about him. Jo didn't bother to try to control Florence's enthusiasm; she simply began answering her questions. "Since I just met Brad yesterday and can't compare the way he is now to the way he was before, I can only tell you that to me he seems like he's getting along fine."

"He's here? In Boulder?"

Jo nodded. "And will be until Monday."

"And Karen?"

Jo would have given a week's profits to have the answer to that one. "Brad and Karen were never married, Florence." Joe handed her a measuring cup.

"*Never married?* I don't understand. If they never..." She thought about what Jo had said as she absently dipped the measuring cup into a bowl of frozen strawberries. "Then why did he stay away?"

"I wish I knew. Every time I tried to lead the conversation around to him and Karen last night, he outmaneuvered me. I went on and on about myself, thinking I might get him to open up about himself, but he never did." She shuddered at the memory. "I even told him that I got kicked out of the third grade for beating up on Tommy Paulson, that I sucked my thumb until I was five years old and that I wore braces in high school. And what did I get out of him in return? I found out he owns a construction company in Casper, Wyoming. Does that seem like a fair trade to you?"

Florence smiled. "Maybe I can even things up a bit for you. As far as I know, Brad never sucked his thumb or beat up on anyone. At least, if he did, he never got kicked out of school for it. I do know, for a fact, though, that he never wore braces."

"*That's* supposed to make me feel better?"

"He did, however, run away from home—twice."

"Somehow, with a mother like Mabel, that doesn't surprise me. Where did he go when he ran away?"

"Into the mountains, both times. He would come back on his own after a few days and take his punishment without ever offering a word of explanation."

Jo thought a minute about what Florence had just told her. "Damn it!" she said, closing the mixer lid with a resounding bang. "It just doesn't seem fair that one woman could cause so much grief."

"Brad would be upset if he ever found out you felt sorry for him. And I don't think you should. He always managed to find ways to cope. He's a very clever young man."

"A kid shouldn't have to succeed in spite of his parents, but because of them."

"In a perfect world, maybe." Florence thought of the mistakes she had made with her own children, how she had been too lenient with them when she should have been stronger and too hard when she should have simply put her arms around them.

A sheepish grin appeared on Jo's face. "If you'd like to tell me I'll be singing a different tune when I have children of my own, you're entitled."

"I wouldn't dream of it. You'll be telling yourself often enough when the time comes."

"We haven't talked about anything but Brad this morning," Jo abruptly announced. In only a matter of weeks, he had become the primary focus of her life, and she was beginning to find it more than a little disconcerting. It was time to get on with other things. "How are Howard and his granddaughter getting along?"

"As far as I know, they made it through their first twenty-four hours together without any major problems, and today should be a piece of cake for them both. Howard's oldest grandson, the one who lives in Denver, is going to stop by with his family this morning to pick up Sandy and take her to Estes Park with them for a day of horseback riding."

"She should enjoy that. Sandy's about the right age to be going through every young girl's love affair with horses."

When they finished discussing Howard and Sandy, they moved on to the upcoming local election and then to the Erma Bombeck column they had both read in that morning's paper. An hour later it was time to open the shop for the day, and only half of the yogurt had been made.

Thankfully, the Saturday-morning crowd was lighter than usual. By putting the peach and strawberry flavors on special, and with Florence to help her serve customers and mix yogurt, Jo was able to catch up on the other batches before noon.

"I can't remember the last time I had so much fun," Florence said as she wiped spilled nonpareils from the table nearest the counter.

"I've enjoyed your company, too. You've made the morning fly by." Jo grabbed the broom to sweep up the chocolate bits that had fallen to the floor.

"It's more than your delightful company I'm talking about, Josephine. I love the feeling of being useful. When you have only yourself to be responsible for after a lifetime of caring for others, it's difficult not to feel like a piece of life's excess baggage."

Jo was too stunned by Florence's deeply personal statement to answer immediately. She'd known Florence found her situation frustrating at times, but she'd had no idea her friend felt so completely isolated from the mainstream of society. But then, in a city where a college provided a third of the population nine months of the year and made the median age of the residents twenty-five, she shouldn't have been so surprised.

Florence's life had never seemed any worse or any better than the lives of most of the older people who came into the shop. Jo knew money was a problem for Florence and for just about all of her friends, but it was also a problem for a lot of people who weren't old or retired.

Jo tried to figure out what there could be about spending the morning working in her shop that would make Florence feel so good about herself. Her thoughts led her to try to imagine what it would be like to wake up each morning and know there was virtually nothing she had to do that day. The idea took her breath away.

Jo had always assumed people retired because they wanted freedom from work. But now she realized true freedom required money—to travel, to start a small business for the enjoyment of it or to indulge in a truly fulfilling hobby. Without money, retirement could be a prison.

"Florence, I'd love to have your help whenever you want to give it," Jo said, praying she didn't sound condescending. If only she could offer her a real job. But there was hardly enough work or profit to keep one person busy.

"You'd better be careful of such offers, Jo. You're liable to have me here more often than I already am."

Jo was about to answer when the bell over the door announced a customer. It was Howard Wakelin. "Come in and let me get a good look at you," Jo said, leaning on her broom. "I want to see if Sandy's worn you down yet."

"It's going to take more than an eleven-year-old to do that." Although he was talking to Jo, his gaze, as usual, drifted to Florence.

"Did Sandy get off all right?" Florence asked.

He nodded. "And she won't be back until late this evening. I've been calling your apartment to see if you'd like to attend tonight's performance of *Macbeth* at the Mary Rippon Outdoor Theater. The Mackeys couldn't go, so they gave me their tickets."

"If it were anything but *Macbeth*," Florence said. "I'm in a wonderful mood and I'd like to stay that way."

"Perhaps the performance will be bad enough to give us a laugh or two."

"You know there's no chance of that."

"Does this mean you're turning me down?"

Before Florence had a chance to answer, the front door opened again. Jo turned at the sound and felt her heart leap to her throat. Brad had found her shop.

He was dressed in a faded pair of jeans and a short-sleeved plaid shirt that made his shoulders look even broader and his hips narrower than they had looked the night before. "This isn't the same town I left eight years ago," he declared. "There are a dozen yogurt shops and almost as many new shopping centers. I damn near got lost twice while I was looking for you."

"I'm in the phone book," Jo said, trying to keep the inordinate pleasure she felt at seeing him again out of her voice. "You should have at least tried to call before you ran all over town."

Brad caught a movement out of the corner of his eye. He turned toward the counter and saw Florence Pickford staring at him. An immediate smile lit his face.

"How are you, Brad?" she asked warmly.

"I'm doing all right," he said before going to her and taking her in his arms. They held each other in silence for several emotional moments. "It's been a long time, Florence. I've missed you."

She placed her hands on his arms and looked up at him. "The years have done well by you. I thought it was impossible, but you're even better-looking than you were when you left."

He slipped his arm around her shoulders and turned to face Jo. "What do you say to something like that?"

"Me? I'd say 'Thank you.'"

"There's someone here I want you to meet, Brad," Florence said, indicating Howard. "He's a good friend of mine and he knew your mother." Brad looked over at the man standing by the front window. "Howard, this is Brad Tyler, Mabel's son. Brad, this is Howard Wakelin."

"I'm pleased to meet you," Howard said, coming forward to grasp Brad's outstretched hand, his gaze openly curious.

"I take after my father," Brad offered as explanation for the lack of resemblance to his mother.

"I regret I never had the pleasure of meeting him," Howard said. "Florence has often told me what a fine man he was."

Brad smiled. "Thank you." He turned to Jo. "I'm sorry if I've interrupted something. I just stopped by hoping you'd be free and I could get you to show me around town. But I can see that you're busy, so I won't keep you from your work any longer."

"You wanted me to show you around town?" she repeated, dumbfounded. If anything, he should have been the one showing her around.

"I have a wonderful idea," Florence broke in before Jo had a chance to say anything more or Brad had a chance to leave. "Why don't you let Howard and me take care of the shop the rest of the afternoon? That way, you and Brad could spend the entire day together. I'll even close up for you. You can stop by my apartment to get the keys on your way to work in the morning."

Jo had never been so blatantly shoved into someone's company. She looked from Florence to Brad and then back again, unsure of what to say.

"Is there some problem with Florence's suggestion?" Brad asked.

"No..."

"Well, then?"

"Are you sure you want to do this, Florence?" Jo asked. "And what about you, Howard? I know this isn't the way you'd planned to spend your evening."

"I'll take any opportunity I can to be with Florence," he replied, the note of seriousness unmistakable in the flowery statement.

If it hadn't been for her earlier conversation with Florence, Jo would never have thought of leaving. But now she sincerely believed she might be doing her friend a favor. "Then I guess it's settled." Jo reached behind her to untie her candy-striped apron. She walked over to Howard and looped the apron over his neck, wrapping it around him and tying it with a smart-looking bow. "If you have any problems," she said, giving the bow a final pat, "just close up and I'll take care of them tomorrow."

"I can't imagine a problem either Howard or I couldn't handle," Florence said. "Now you two get out of here and don't you dare worry about us. We'll be fine."

Brad bent down and gave Florence a kiss. "I'd like to take you to dinner tomorrow night—we have a lot to catch up on. Do you think you could fit me in?"

"Oh, I'm confident something could be arranged. What time did you have in mind?"

"Seven-thirty?"

"I'll be ready. You can pick me up at the apartment building across the street—I'm in number 413."

Jo looked over at Howard. "Why don't you try talking her into going to the play tonight, after all? It wouldn't hurt if you closed early. There's never much business past seven, anyway." To Brad, she said, "I'll be with you in a minute. I just have to get my purse."

When Jo disappeared into the back room, it became obvious that Howard had something he wanted to say to Brad. Still, several seconds passed before he cleared his throat and said, "I'd like to offer my condolences about your mother. It must have been difficult to learn about her passing so long after she died."

A dozen replies came to Brad's mind. He settled for the simplest. "It's never easy to learn someone you once loved has died, but I doubt knowing any earlier would have made a difference. My mother wouldn't have welcomed me back had I come home any sooner." His words were spoken with a profound sadness.

Florence blinked away the sudden tears that threatened to spill over her eyelashes. She thought of a line from a Tennyson poem she had learned as a child... *a sorrow's crown of sorrow is remembering happier things.* Mabel had missed so much with her son. How terribly wasted were those years when she had clutched her bitterness to her like a precious cloak. And how much Brad had missed—the company of a mother he loved, the city he'd so often said he wanted to live in, his friends.

Jo immediately sensed the change in mood when she returned. "Is everything all right?" she asked.

Brad smiled. "It will be, as soon as we're on the road."

She looked at Florence and then Howard. "This is your last chance to back out. Are you sure you want to waste your Saturday cooped up inside this shop?"

"Right now we're sure," Howard said, giving her a teasing smile. "But I can't say how we'll feel if you hang around here much longer."

Jo turned to Brad. "Then I guess we'd better get going before they change their minds."

CHAPTER SIX

A HALF HOUR after Jo and Brad had left the shop they were several miles from the city, driving through Boulder Canyon. "I thought you wanted me to show you around town," Joe said, rolling down her window and relaxing against the seat to let the warm July air catch her hair and caress her face.

"I discovered something this morning—it was harder for me to come home than I had thought it was going to be. I needed some company today. I hope you don't mind."

Jo swallowed. His frankness had caught her completely off guard. Between Florence and Brad, she was having quite a day. "Of course I don't mind," she said, sitting up straight again. She felt she was walking an emotional tightrope with Brad. He was cool and aloof one moment, then open and vulnerable the next. She decided not to beat around the bush any longer. "What happened between you and Karen, Brad?"

Stalling for time, he reached for a pair of sunglasses that were in the glove box. He wiped the lenses on the front of his shirt, checked for dust and then wiped them again. Finally satisfied they were clean, he put them on, taking several seconds to adjust them on the bridge of his nose before he glanced over at Jo. When he saw she was still patiently waiting for his answer, he said, "It's a long story. And not that interesting."

"I have all day."

They traveled another mile. The echo of traffic reflecting off the steep canyon walls was the only sound that broke the silence between them. When a turnabout appeared on the side of the road, wide enough for them to park, Brad pulled the pickup to a stop, got out and went around to open Jo's door. "Let's walk," he said. When she'd climbed down, he took her hand and led her across the street to where a stream flowed under the roadway.

Jo looked down at the flimsy sandals she'd worn that day and wondered how long they would last on the rugged trail Brad had chosen for their walk, but she said nothing. She followed a few steps behind him. They were almost a hundred yards from the truck when she heard the sounds of cascading water. It was another hundred yards before a waterfall came into view. "How lovely," she said, coming to a halt to admire the scene.

Brad retraced his steps to stand beside her. "Did you know that Boulder has the distinction of being the only city in America to get its water supply from a municipally owned glacier?"

"No, I didn't know," Jo answered, smiling at the distinct note of pride in his voice. She shifted her feet to take the pressure off her little toes where the sandal straps had begun to cut into them.

A look of wonder and deep longing filled Brad's eyes as his gaze swept the hillsides. "I hadn't realized how much I missed Colorado until I came back yesterday," he said quietly, as much to himself as to her.

"I felt the same way when my family left Colorado Springs to move to California. I could hardly wait to get back."

He reached for her hand and started down the trail again. When they came to a spot where both the waterfall and the rushing stream were in full view, he stopped and bent down to brush the pine needles from a rock. He motioned for Jo to sit down.

The cold granite felt wonderful after the hot climb. Jo situated herself so that she could rest in a supine position. She closed her eyes and let the dappled sunlight shine on her face. The air smelled of pine and rock and moist earth. "This is nice," she said. "I don't get out like this very often. Thanks for bringing me."

"Thank you for coming," he answered, sitting down beside her.

"Did you come here often when you lived in Boulder?"

"This was my thinking place. Whenever something was really bothering me, sooner or later I'd wind up here to work it out."

"I had a place like that, too. Only mine was a favorite tree that I would climb when I wanted to get away from everyone. It was in our front yard, but no one ever thought to look for me up there. Have you ever noticed that people rarely look up?"

"As a matter of fact, I have. After the construction crew has knocked off work for the day I can be checking on things up in the beams, and as far as anyone on the ground is concerned, I'm invisible."

"You can overhear some interesting conversations...."

"So I've discovered." They slipped into an easy silence.

Her eyes were still closed against the sun when Jo felt something touch her cheek. She reached up to brush it away. Her hand struck Brad's and she saw that he had been tickling her with a pine needle. She smiled. "Don't worry, I won't fall asleep on you."

He stared at her. "You have beautiful skin."

Jo frowned, puzzled at the odd turn in their conversation. "If you happen to like freckles," she said.

"I do . . . a lot."

She felt a pleasurable warmth spread through her midsection. She knew it was insanity to attach more meaning to Brad's casual compliment than he had intended, but for some reason, her mind hadn't mentioned that to her body. She sat up and straightened her skirt. "If I could figure a way to manage it, I'd be happy to give you a few dozen of mine. Especially the ones on my nose."

Brad was relieved she'd made light of his clumsy attempt to flirt with her. He couldn't imagine what he'd had in mind when he'd started the whole thing. No . . . that wasn't quite true. He *could* imagine what he'd had in mind. Jo was a beautiful woman. And undoubtedly deep in a relationship with someone else. All of which made him wonder. "Am I keeping you from seeing anyone tonight? A boyfriend or anything like that?"

"Define 'anything like that.'"

"I just meant—"

"Never mind. Actually, you've managed to catch me between boyfriends." Did a year in which she hadn't dated any guy more than three times qualify as "between" men? she wondered. Boulder was a fantasy come true for any woman looking for ruggedly handsome, brilliant but slightly immature young males. After a steady diet of them when she'd first moved to town, she'd grown weary of the sameness. Now she found that she even preferred television to a night of "singles" conversation.

"What really surprises me is that you're not married," he said.

"Why in heaven's name would that surprise you?"

Brad suddenly realized how wide an opening he had just created and where it could lead, and he did some quick backtracking. "Whether you're married or not married is none of my business. I apologize for bringing it up."

"Don't apologize," Jo said. "I'm quite willing to tell you whatever it is you want to know about me—if you'll tell me about Karen."

Brad leaned forward, resting his elbows on his knees and staring at the ground. "I can't understand your relentless fascination with my life."

"Frankly, I can't either. I've thought about it a lot since last night, and the only conclusion I've been able to come up with is that it's like being told that Cinderella and Prince Charming didn't live happily ever after. Wouldn't you want to know why?"

He turned to look at her. "Quite honestly, no."

"Well, that only means we're curious about different things."

Brad picked up a stick and began drawing circles in the soft soil between his feet. "With the exception of private detectives, I haven't talked to anyone about Karen in almost eight years."

"And yet I have this feeling that she's as much a part of your life now as she was then."

"Oh? And what makes you think that?"

"The way you react whenever her name is mentioned."

"It's because she's unfinished business—something like a book that's left partially read. Our relationship never had its ending chapter."

"Why did you hire private detectives?"

Brad let out a resigned sigh. It would be easier just to get it over with and tell Jo what she wanted to know rather than continue to skirt the subject. "Three days before I was to graduate from college, I flew home to try to talk my mother into attending the graduation ceremony. We spent the next two days arguing about my plan to marry Karen as soon as I was established in a job." Restlessly he stood up, walked several paces and tossed the stick he'd been holding into the stream. "Acrimony would be a gentle word for the bad feelings that were created between my mother and myself in those two days."

Jo blanched. Eight years had passed and still the telling brought him pain. "For a mother and her son to go through something like that must have been terrible—for both of you."

He gave a disparaging laugh. "Even after everything that was said between us, I still left with the hope that someday I could get her to change her mind about Karen."

Suddenly Jo wasn't so sure she wanted to hear what came next.

"When I arrived back in Iowa, Karen wasn't there to meet the plane. I called our apartment, but there was no answer. So I waited, figuring she must be on her way. After three hours I gave up and took a cab home—we'd been living together almost a year and a half by then. All of her and Tracy's things were gone. There wasn't a clue that either of them had ever been there. It was as if they'd never existed."

"Tracy was Karen's daughter?"

A bitter smile pulled at the corner of his mouth. "I hadn't realized until they were gone how much I'd come to think of Tracy as mine, too."

"Did you ever find out how—or why—Karen left?"

"Only the why. Or what I've always assumed to be the why. One of the detectives I hired traced a man who'd been seen at the apartment back to my mother. It was just like my mother to do something like that. Finding the weakest link was a typical method of attack for her." He shrugged. "While I was in Boulder trying to make peace with her, she sent someone to Iowa City to convince Karen she wasn't good enough to be a Tyler. My mother probably had it all worked out so that Karen would wind up thinking that leaving me was the one way to prove how much she really loved me."

"So you're convinced Mabel was behind the reason Karen left?" No wonder the feud had lasted all these years. It was amazing how clear a picture became when the missing puzzle pieces were popped into their places.

"I'm sure of it."

"And you never found Karen?"

"No. Never." He shoved his hands in his back pockets. "But that's history. I've built a new life for myself and I'm sure Karen has, too."

Jo wondered if he truly believed Karen was history or if he was simply trying to convince her that he did. "Except there's the last chapter you spoke of—the one left unfinished."

"Since then, I've learned life doesn't always tie things up in neat little packages for you."

"Are you trying to tell me Karen is nothing more to you now than a poignant memory?"

"No, what I'm trying to tell you is that you're making more of this than there is. Aren't there things in your past you would change if you could?"

She considered his question. "Nothing that haunts me the way Karen does you."

"You're not painting a very flattering picture of me—a man who dwells in the past, someone who doesn't have enough strength of will to get on with his life." For a reason he didn't yet understand, it was becoming increasingly important to prove to Jo that she was wrong, that he didn't have a lingering obsession with Karen. "I prefer to think I'm made of stronger stuff."

"Have you been married? Have you even been engaged to anyone since Karen? I'd even settle for one long-term commitment over the last eight years."

His spark of irritation set off a fuse of anger. He stood there in silence, staring at the ground, not trusting himself to speak. Finally, after several moments had passed, he looked at her, this time in an openly sensual way. "If you want to know about my love life, Jo, just ask." The words were spoken in a deceptively quiet tone. "I'm not shy about such things." Slowly, purposefully, his gaze swept over her, lingering infinitesimally longer at the swell of her breasts and at the top of her thighs, provocatively outlined beneath her clinging skirt. "Do I look like the kind of man who would remain celibate for eight years?" he asked.

"What has how you look got to do with whether or not you can commit yourself to someone?" she asked, furious at her inability to hide the effect his lengthy perusal had aroused. She sat up and pulled her skirt over her knees. "Since when has being ugly been a prerequisite to becoming a priest?"

He responded to her goading on gut level, without
considering the consequences. Grabbing her by the arms,
he brought her up to stand in front of him, then took her
face between his hands as he kissed her. His lips were
hard and unyielding as he poured into the kiss all of the
frustration and confusion she had reawakened in him.

But where he had sought to prove his freedom, he only
demonstrated his lingering bondage to the past. If there
hadn't been a grain of truth in what Jo had said, he
would never have responded the way he just had. He
started to release her when a more powerful emotion took
over and stopped him. For an instant, in his mind and
because of desperate longing, Jo became Karen. His
years of loneliness disappeared as he became aware of the
feel of her body against his. His hands left her face, and
he reached for her arms to bring them up to wrap around
his neck.

Jo sensed the change in Brad as she felt his anger give
way to desire. His hard lips became soft and coaxing, his
hands stroked the length of her back, as gently and sen-
suously as they might have touched her breast. She'd had
no right to spur him on the way she had. And it was
wrong for her to encourage him by responding the way
she was now. Just as she was about to pull away, Brad's
lips brushed against hers, once, twice, three times, teasing, pleading, building a hunger in her that left her sigh-
ing his name. She touched the corner of his mouth with
her tongue, and with a soft, low moan, he stopped the
teasing and took her offering. Jo made an attempt to
fight being swept away emotionally but found she
couldn't summon the strength—or the desire—to resist.
It had been a long time since she'd been kissed with such
passion; she'd forgotten its pervasive power.

Brad felt the hesitancy in Jo and then the release, and a warning sounded in him. The realization of where he was, whom he was with and what he was doing came crashing down around him. It was not Karen he was holding in his arms; it was Josephine Williams, a woman he'd known less than twenty-four hours. He let go of her and took a step backward. "I don't know what to say," he told her, shrugging helplessly. "Considering the circumstances, 'I'm sorry' seems rather inadequate."

She couldn't look at him. She was embarrassed, both by the way she'd responded to his kiss and by her stupidity in provoking the incident in the first place. Not knowing what else to do, she sat down on the rock and began fiddling with her sandal. "I should never have worn these on this trail," she said. "Normally I have better sense than—"

Brad crouched down in front of her, took her chin in his hand and forced her to look at him. "Pretending that nothing happened between us won't make it go away."

She tried to pull her chin from his grasp but he held her tight. "You don't owe me an apology," she reluctantly admitted. "I owe you one."

He released her. It was too soon for him to touch her again. His heart still raced and his body burned from the feel of her. "Instead of stumbling around trying to decide who owes whom an apology, why don't we share the blame? Then maybe we can forget what happened and get on with our day."

Jo doubted she would ever forget what it had felt like to be in his arms. She attempted a smile. "You're not even going to make me promise to stop badgering you with questions?"

He returned her smile. "Badger away—there aren't any more secrets." He felt as if a weight had been lifted from his shoulders. With her willingness to put what had happened behind them, the day seemed brighter, the sun warmer. The sound of rushing water intruded into his thoughts. "You wouldn't happen to have any fishing poles, would you?" he asked. "It's been ages since I've gone fishing."

She blinked in surprise. Every time she felt on solid ground with him, he did or said something completely unexpected. "I don't, but Howard Wakelin does. I'm sure he'd let you borrow one of his."

"Ever been fishing in Boulder Creek?"

"Nope."

"Ever have any desire to go fishing in Boulder Creek?"

"Truthfully?"

Brad laughed. "Then how about a trip to Central City?"

Central City was an old gold-mining town, kept alive and healthy by modern prospectors who sought their fortunes in the pockets of eager tourists. It was a place few locals ever visited. "Why Central City?"

"I did some calling around this morning and learned an old friend of mine, Carl Vizenor, owns a candy shop up there. I thought I'd pay him a visit while I'm in town. It's been a long time since we've seen each other."

"Here I'm supposed to be spending the day showing you around, and we wind up going places I've never been."

"Do you like antique stores and museums?"

A gleam lit her eyes. "They'll do in a pinch. Most of all I like candy shops."

"Well, then, let's go." He reached for her hand to help her up.

"Wait a minute, I want to take off my shoes." She unbuckled the straps of her sandals. "If I don't, they'll never make it back to the truck and through Central City, too."

"You can't walk all the way back to the truck barefoot."

"Wanna bet?" She held her legs up and wiggled her toes. "These feet are a lot tougher than they look."

He'd bet half a year's salary that her feet weren't the only thing tough about her. Jo had an indomitable spirit that he found enormously appealing. Most of the women he knew were careful not to let their strengths show. Jo wore hers with unaffected pride, and he liked that. "You should have said something before you let me haul you all the way down here."

He'd given her the perfect opportunity to put what had happened between them into proper perspective, and she wasn't about to let it pass. If they could joke about the kiss, they could shrug it off once and for all. She gave him an innocent look and said, "But if we hadn't come, I might never have discovered what smouldering fires burn beneath that cool exterior of yours."

Without missing a beat, Brad winked at her. "Don't count on it," he said, his voice low and husky.

Jo felt the effect clear down to her toes. She threw up her hands in surrender. "You win."

He stared at her long and hard before a slow smile brought one corner of his mouth up into a rakish grin. "I usually do," he said softly. "You'll find you should be prepared to finish whatever you start with me."

Jo had a feeling there was more than a grain of truth in his teasing.

THE RIDE UP TO Central City took twice as long as it should have because of the number of times Brad stopped the truck to get out and refamiliarize himself with his beloved mountains. It was early evening when they finally arrived in the town. "Would you like to get something to eat before we visit Carl?" Brad asked, pulling into a parking place.

Jo got out of the truck. "Why don't we see what Carl has to munch on first?"

"According to the friend I called, Carl has candy in his shop—nothing else."

"Sounds good to me." She looked up from straightening her skirt and found him staring at her. "What's the matter?"

"I don't understand why you're not fat."

"It's my metabolism. I can eat anything, anywhere, anytime, and never gain a pound."

"I'll bet you have friends who hate you."

"One in particular—Amy. She's just the opposite. If she even smells a cake baking, her clothes are too tight the next day."

After locking the truck, Brad joined Jo on the wooden sidewalk. He glanced down the street to an overhead sign that read Carl's Handmade Candy. Now that the meeting was imminent, he was surprised to discover how nervous he felt about seeing his friend again. Although they hadn't attended the same college after high school, they had maintained a correspondence throughout the four years. However, the last time they'd actually seen each other was during the trip he'd taken home to try to talk Mabel into attending his graduation. If the two of them had drifted so far apart in the ensuing years that they no longer had anything in common, he would just as soon not know about it. Carl was a memory Brad didn't want tarnished.

"Ready?" Jo prodded.

"What?"

"Isn't that Carl's shop down there?" She pointed to the overhead sign, confused at Brad's apparent hesitancy to walk the final half block after coming so far.

He slipped his arm around her shoulders and started walking toward the shop. "I suppose you hear a truffle calling your name?" he teased, shoving aside his fear of seeing Carl again.

"You mean to tell me you don't? The roar is nearly deafening."

God, it felt good to be with her. Even when she was after him to talk about things he didn't want to tell her, she made him feel more alive than he had in years. He reached for the door and held it open for her to enter first. She came to a stop halfway across the threshold.

"I believe I've died and gone to heaven," she said, taking a deep breath.

He put his hand at her waist and gave a push. "Not yet, you haven't. You still have ten million calories to consume right here on earth." A glance around the shop told him Carl was not in. Disappointment mingled with relief.

"Do you always know precisely the right thing to say to make a young woman's heart sing with joy?" Jo said as she walked over to the glass counter to look at the trays of chocolate-covered nuts, caramels and assorted truffles. When she'd finished with the first counter, she moved on to the second. "They have *honeycomb* here," she exclaimed, spotting the yellow cubes sitting on a tray. She turned to see that Brad was absorbed in reading the varieties of saltwater taffy that were contained in the oak barrels scattered around the store.

"May I help you?" A young girl in a blue apron came out of the back room and stood on the opposite side of the counter watching Jo.

"Yes, you can. I'd like that piece of honeycomb right there." Jo pointed to the largest cube.

When the candy was weighed and paid for, Jo broke off a corner and handed it to Brad, who had come up to stand beside her.

"What is this?" he asked, holding her hand while skeptically examining its contents.

"Trust me, you'll love it."

Reluctantly, Brad let her put the piece of candy in his mouth. After a few seconds of chewing, he made a face. "It's nothing but burned sugar," he said.

"I know. Isn't it great?"

He slipped the candy from his mouth and looked around for a trash container. "You need an appointment with a nutritionist."

Jo ignored him and popped another piece of honeycomb into her mouth. "Where's your friend?"

"It must be his day off."

"Oh, no, it isn't," announced a booming voice from the back of the store.

Jo turned at the sound and saw a man the size and shape of a professional football player come striding into the room. He headed straight for Brad, lifted him up in a bear hug and swung him completely around before putting him down again. "It's a good thing you showed up here today," he said, clasping Brad by the shoulders. "Phyllis called and said you were back in town and asking about me. I'd have been mighty riled up if you hadn't gotten in touch." He let go of Brad's arms and stood back to look at him. "So, how the hell are you, anyway? You're sure looking great."

"I'm feeling that way, too." In his joy to see his friend again, Brad grabbed Carl and gave him another enthusiastic hug. "Damn, you're a sight for sore eyes."

"Well, nobody said you had to stay away so long." For a few moments the two men were absorbed in their reunion, as they laughed and touched and came to know each other again. Then Carl looked over at Jo. "And this must be Karen. Hot damn—she's everything you said she was, Brad." He bounded toward Jo to sweep her up in his ample arms. "Only I don't think you did her justice when you said she was pretty." He set Jo down again and took a step backward, his gaze covering her from top to bottom. "This woman of yours is downright beautiful."

CHAPTER SEVEN

Jo GLANCED OVER at Brad. The joy had left his face. She quickly looked back at Carl. "I hate to correct a man of such magnificent judgment...." She gave him her brightest smile, trying to keep his attention on her in order to give Brad time to recover. "However, there are a couple of things you've gotten wrong about me. My name is Josephine Williams—Jo to my friends—and I'm not Brad's 'woman.' Other than that, I'd say you pretty much hit everything right on the head."

Carl turned to Brad. "Karen couldn't come with you this trip?"

The awkward silence that followed lasted only a few seconds, but it seemed like hours. "Karen and I never got married, Carl." Somehow, the second telling was easier.

"Well, I'll be damned. All that heartache and none of the reward. I can see we've got some real catching up to do." He glanced at the regulator clock on the side wall. "Give me another hour to close up shop and then we'll go up to the house for some dinner."

"I didn't come here to bum a meal from you," Brad said. "Let me take you and Susan out to eat."

"She'd make me sleep on the porch for a week if I even so much as suggested such a thing. Susan started cooking the minute we heard from Phyllis that you were back in town."

"The two of you were pretty confident I'd show up here today."

Carl laughed. "One way or the other. I was going to give you another hour before I set off down the hill to bring you back." He walked with them over to the door. "If you don't want to do the tourist thing while you're waiting for me, the Teller House Bar still serves a good drink. How about if we plan to meet there at seven?"

"Seven it is," Brad said, stepping out onto the sidewalk.

They had walked a half block before Jo glanced up at Brad and said, "How could you let so much time pass without contacting Carl? It's obvious the two of you were good friends." She couldn't imagine doing what Brad had done. Her friends were as much a part of her as the air she breathed.

"It seemed the best thing to do at the time."

"Didn't you miss him—and Susan?"

Brad shot her a warning look.

"I thought we were past that," she said.

"Just because I told you about Karen doesn't mean I gave you carte blanche—"

"As I recall, the exact words were, 'Badger away—there aren't any more secrets.'"

"I take it back."

"You can't."

"You are without a doubt the most exasperating person I've ever known."

She looked up at him, unable to keep a smile from forming. "Carl did better, but I take compliments whenever and wherever I can."

They turned the corner from Main onto Eureka Street. "What do you want to do for an hour?"

Jo stopped and stared down the narrow street lined with hundred-year-old buildings. "I suppose we could go for a walk. What's down this way?" She pointed to her right.

He shrugged. "You have to remember, it's been a while since I've been here."

"Then I guess we'll just have to go exploring."

Forty-five minutes later, they were standing in front of the Teller House. "I do know something about this place," Brad said, feeling a complete failure as a tour guide after he'd been unable to answer even one of Jo's questions about the town.

"Is there some special significance I should attach to the fact that you didn't know anything about the city hall, or that charming little church we passed, or even the opera house, but you can tell me all about a bar?"

"Teller House is much more than just a bar," he said, managing to sound wounded. "This place is loaded with history. It was a fancy hotel in its heyday—President Grant and his family even stayed here. During one of his visits, they paved the walkway from the stagecoach to the hotel steps with silver ingots."

"*Real* silver ingots?"

Brad held the door for her to enter. "Thousands of dollars' worth."

"I don't suppose there's much chance they forgot any."

"That's highly unlikely."

Carl got up and came across the room to join them. "I finished up early," he said. "Susan's waiting dinner on us so we'd better be heading up the hill."

CARL AND SUSAN VIZENOR'S house was a ninety-year-old Victorian that Carl had taken pains to restore to its original beauty. The two-story wooden structure was tucked into the side of a hill and had a small fenced yard, with an Irish Setter puppy running excitedly around. Susan met them at the door, her arms held wide. Her smile of welcome transformed a rather plain face into one of beauty. She hugged Brad for a long time before she let him go to take Jo in her arms.

Jo was all prepared to explain that she wasn't Karen Patterson when Susan said, "I've always loved the name Josephine. If Carl and I ever have a daughter, that's the name I've picked out to give her."

"I was named after my grandmother," Jo said, pleased that Carl had thought to call ahead to forewarn Susan. Being mistaken for Karen once was enough to last Jo a lifetime. She'd be on her guard to make sure it never happened again.

The inside of the house matched the outside. Comfortable yet elegant, it was furnished in a pleasant combination of modern and antique pieces. Lace curtains hung on the windows, and the floors were highly polished hardwood, with area rugs in each room. Jo glanced up the stairs and spotted a child she guessed to be between two and three years old, peering down at her through the banister railing. He had softly curling blond hair and big brown eyes and was dressed in seersucker pajamas. She gave him a secret wave, assuming he was upstairs and wearing pajamas because he was supposed to be in bed. He smiled as he brought his hand up and wiggled his fingers at her.

"You might as well come down and say hello, Jason," Carl said, noticing his son.

Brad moved to stand beside Jo. "He looks just like you, Carl."

Jason came to a halt three steps from the bottom, waited for his father to walk over to him and then leaped into his arms. "It's hard to believe Susan had anything to do with him, isn't it?" he said, shifting Jason to his hip. He bent and gave his wife a kiss of appeasement at her immediate scowl.

"I've told him that if he keeps talking that way, he can spend nine months carrying the next one himself."

The last of Brad's fears that seeing Carl and Susan again would prove awkward disappeared as the three of them slipped into the easy repartee that had marked their friendship all through high school. The evening became a special kind of homecoming as they relived the past and caught each other up on the present.

They were careful to make Jo a part of the conversation, explaining private jokes and insisting she tell them about herself even when she tried to protest that the night belonged to them. Several times during dinner and afterward, Brad reached for her hand and gave it a gentle, reassuring squeeze. It was a natural and unconscious gesture but it implied an intimacy they didn't truly share. She tried not to think about how the silent communication must look to Carl and Susan. She knew they were reading more into Brad's bringing her to visit them than there was, but she felt that saying anything to clarify the situation would only belabor the point.

After dinner they all helped with the dishes, Brad and Jo clearing and Susan and Carl loading the dishwasher and wiping down the kitchen. When Jason called down for a drink of water before they were finished, Brad volunteered to take it to him. He'd been gone more than fifteen minutes when Susan suggested Jo go after him.

She found Jason's room at the top of the stairs. Brad was sitting in a rocking chair with the little boy curled up on his lap. They were both engrossed in a large, brightly illustrated storybook, and as soon as Brad finished reading one page, Jason would turn to the next. Instead of interrupting them, Jo watched for several minutes. For an only child and a thirty-three-year-old bachelor, Brad had an incredible rapport with Jason. He obviously liked children; it was a shame he had none of his own.

Brad looked up from the book and saw Jo staring at him. "I can't leave until we find out if Magic Mouse is going to make it home all right," he said. "Why don't you come in and join us?"

"First I'd better let Susan know what's going on, so she won't think we've both disappeared." When Jo returned to the kitchen, she found Carl cutting a pie and took a minute to help him bring the pieces into the living room. By the time she was headed back up the stairs, Brad was on his way down.

"Jason gave up the ghost," he said.

"Before or after you had a chance to find out what happened to Magic Mouse?" She stood at the bottom waiting for him.

"After, thank goodness." He came to a stop on the step above her. "You've been terrific tonight, Jo," he said softly. "I know it's been boring as hell for you to sit around listening to us rehash old times."

"I like Susan and Carl." She smiled. "And the dinner alone was worth the trip."

"What time do you have to open the shop tomorrow?"

"I usually get there by nine on Sundays."

Brad looked at his watch. "We should probably be taking off pretty soon, then."

"Not before you have a cup of coffee and a piece of my strawberry pie," Susan said, coming out of the kitchen carrying a tray of cups and saucers. "Heaven knows when we'll see you again."

"Now that you know where I live, there's no reason you can't come to see me."

"Be careful, we're just liable to take you up on that offer," Carl said.

"I'd love to have you. There's plenty of room and the refrigerator's always full."

Jo forced a smile as they walked together into the living room. Knowing she was not included in the invitation set her apart—even though she realized that it was only right not to include her in a gathering of old friends. After this one evening, she would probably never see Susan and Carl again. And after Monday, Brad would disappear from her life. The smile left her eyes.

FLORENCE GAVE a final sweep of crumbs into the dustpan and stood back to survey the shop. It was important that when Jo returned to open in the morning, she would find everything precisely as she had left it. The day had been long and exhausting—and Florence was positive she hadn't felt as good in years. Howard came up behind her and took the dustpan out of her hand.

"I've finished up in the back," he said. "How are you doing out here?"

"I'm finished, too."

He tucked a stray wisp of hair back from her forehead. "Feel like some warmed-up spaghetti at my place?"

She smiled. "I have some coleslaw and also a leftover piece of Ernie's birthday cake we can share for dessert."

"Sounds like a veritable feast. Now all we have to decide is where we shall partake of this sumptuous meal— my place or yours?"

They hadn't spent time in each other's apartments for months now, not since their last confrontation about living together. But tonight seemed special, and she was tired of denying herself Howard's company. "Why don't we make it mine?" she said.

"Yours it is."

Florence made one last check of the shop while Howard emptied the trash. When they were both satisfied everything was as it should be, they turned out all but the two lights Jo normally left on at night, locked up and headed across the street.

"Do you think it's a good idea that Jo is seeing Mabel's son?" Howard asked later when they were in Florence's apartment preparing their meal.

"What brought that up?"

"I was just thinking how easy it is to fall in love with someone and how complicated things can get if it isn't the right person."

There was a poignancy in Howard's voice that made Florence's throat tighten in anguish. She understood Howard's concern—too well. In their apartment building alone, there were thirty women who could return Howard's love unconditionally, without thought to finances or family. And yet, with so many to choose from, he had chosen Florence. Somehow they had found each other, and now they were trapped in a dilemma of their own making.

Their last argument, the one that had brought on the months-long separation, had started when Howard tried to talk her into going away with him for several days and, when they returned, telling everyone they were married. That way, he'd argued, they would still be able to receive her pension check and no one would be the wiser.

In the heat of the moment, she had been sorely tempted; she was tired of waking up alone in the morning and going to bed alone at night. In the end, she couldn't overcome knowing they would be living a lie, one that was sure to be discovered sooner or later.

She forced herself out of her reverie to answer Howard. "What makes you think Brad isn't the right person for Jo?" she asked.

"He seems troubled by something. And he is Mabel's son, after all. It would be surprising if some of her hadn't rubbed off on him."

"It's a shame you never knew Mabel the way she was before James died. If you had seen her then, you'd think Brad was the perfect choice for Jo."

"Do you have any idea how terrifying that is?"

"What?" She dished out their spaghetti and set the plates on the table.

"Knowing how completely old age can change someone. Who's to say we're not next? Is your life ending the way you thought it would? Or hoped it would?"

"You know it's not."

"Isn't it possible the frustration could eventually become bitterness? Isn't that what you've told me happened to Mabel?"

"I'm not like Mabel." Or so she prayed every night.

He took her hand. "No, you're not," he said softly. "You're kind and loving and there isn't a mean bone anywhere in that beautiful body of yours."

She flinched at his reassurance. He had just described the person Mabel had once been. "We'd better eat," she said, slipping her hand from his. "The spaghetti's getting cold."

WHEN BRAD AND JO drove past Florence's apartment, the lights were still on. She thought about having Brad stop so she could pick up the key to the shop, but she decided to wait until morning.

As they were passing the shop, Brad glanced at the sign. "What's the 'Et Cetera'?" he asked.

"In the beginning, it was going to be sandwiches."

"But?"

"It didn't take long to discover that the majority of my clientele couldn't afford yogurt, let alone sandwiches, so I never expanded."

"Wise decision."

"I do make them periodically."

He laughed at the pique in her voice. "I didn't mean to imply you didn't."

She had been struggling with an out-of-sorts feeling since they'd left Central City. That the evening was one of the most pleasant she had spent in ages only added to her puzzlement over her ill humor. Because she didn't know how to answer him, she said nothing, concentrating instead on finding her apartment key in the bottom of her purse.

They drove another block in silence. "Is something wrong, Jo?" Brad finally asked.

"No . . . I'm just tired."

He didn't believe her. She had been laughing and animated up until the time they had left the Vizenors'. Since then, she had been quiet and thoughtful. "Did Carl or Susan say something that upset you? Or did I?"

She met his glance and saw the genuine concern in his eyes. "No one said anything, Brad. I just get moody sometimes. If you knew me better, you'd know to ignore me."

He pulled up in front of her building and shut off the motor. Twisting sideways to face her, he laid his arm across the back of the seat. "I have so much to thank you for, Jo, I don't know where to begin."

Her heart gave a funny flutter in her chest. What he was saying sounded suspiciously like the opening of a farewell speech. "You don't—"

"Yes, I do. And if I have to sit on you to get you to listen, I will." He raked his hand through his hair and looked up to see Jo staring out the window as if she wished she were anywhere but there with him. He'd never felt so inarticulate before. Why was it suddenly so difficult to put his feelings into words, to tell her how much he appreciated all she had done for him?

"Brad—I have an early day ahead of me tomorrow." She glanced down at her hands, folded primly in her lap. "Since you insist on thinking you owe me a debt of gratitude, why don't you just say 'thank you' and I'll say 'you're welcome' and we'll call it a night?"

Damn it! What had he done to make her turn so cold? "All right, if you'll go out to dinner with me tomorrow night."

"As I recall, you already have a dinner date with Florence."

"Breakfast, then."

"I don't eat breakfast." At least, not all the time, she didn't. "Since tomorrow is out," she said before he could push her any farther, "why don't we simply plan to meet at the bank on Monday? We can say goodbye then." She climbed out of the truck. She was about to close the door when she noticed that he was getting out to follow her. "I can see myself in," she insisted.

"Humor me, would you, please? I want to be sure one of your other Brad Tylers hasn't decided to pay a visit."

Continuing to argue would have created an impossible scene. Jo forced herself to wait for him as he came around the truck. They entered the building and climbed the stairs in silence. When they reached the third floor, Jo assumed a cheerful smile and said, "See? No one lurking in the shadows. You can go home now."

He took her key, opened the door and switched on the light. His hand lingered in hers when he returned the key after quickly looking around her apartment. "I know it's against your nature, but I think you should be at least a little more cautious than usual for the next few weeks."

He was standing so close Jo could smell the faint trace of the after-shave he had used that morning. She retreated a step into the hallway. "I will." When she saw the look of skepticism he gave her, she added, "I promise."

He nodded in resignation. "Then I guess I'll say goodnight and plan on seeing you Monday morning."

She waited until he had left before going into her apartment. After closing the door, she turned out the light and went to the window, not wanting him to see her standing there watching him as he drove away. She couldn't fathom her peculiar behavior, nor did she seem to have any control over it. All she knew for certain was that Brad was the cause and that she was delighted he would be leaving in less than two days. Out of sight, out of mind. It had worked for others; it would work for her.

CHAPTER EIGHT

BRAD ARRIVED at the bank early. While he waited for Jo, he leaned against his truck watching the pedestrians who walked along Arapahoe, and he thought about how much a city could change in only eight years. Change and yet remain the same, as he'd discovered in his wanderings the day before.

Although Pearl Street had been closed off to traffic and turned into an open shopping area to try to revitalize a dying downtown, the aging hippies who had lingered on park benches and street corners when he had lived in Boulder were still a part of the scene. There were more shopping malls in the peripheral areas of town, but everywhere the streets were as filled with bicycles as they had always been. While the campus remained the core of the city, several large industrial plants were now bringing in groups of new residents with no connection to the university. Still, even in summer, Boulder was a college town. Bars and bookstores and specialty shops all catered to the young.

Out of the corner of his eye he saw an ancient-looking green Toyota pull into the parking space beside him. He glanced up to see Jo getting out of the car. She was dressed in a pair of jeans that hugged her hips and thighs and a flowered shirt that covered a bright red tank top. Her hair glistened in the sunlight and she walked with a sexy, self-confident stride Brad found enormously appealing. He left the truck and joined her. Although she seemed to be nervous, the moodiness was apparently gone.

"How was your dinner with Florence?" she asked, swinging the strap of her purse over her shoulder.

"Great. And your Sunday at the shop?"

"The usual. There was a little excitement around noon, when a family with ten kids came in after church. The twin boys decided to see how far a spoonful of yogurt would fly. Other than that, it was actually a pretty dull day." Late in the afternoon, when she had found herself jumping every time the bell over the door sounded and realized it was because she was hoping Brad had decided to drop by, she'd closed up and gone home to soak in a cool tub filled to the brim with bubbles. The bath had only increased her restlessness, so when an old boyfriend she hadn't seen in over two years called and suggested they go out for pizza, she had grasped the chance to get away for a while.

"Do you want to go someplace to get a cup of coffee before we go inside?" He had promised his foreman he'd make it back to Casper by that night—another problem had arisen with the sheet-metal contractor at the hotel and it required Brad's immediate attention—but he felt the need at least to try to communicate to Jo how much he appreciated all she had done for him.

"Actually, I'm in kind of a hurry this morning. There's a lot of running around I save up for my day off and if I don't get it done when I can, it really adds up." Her "running around" for that day consisted of a trip to the cleaners to pick up sweaters that had already been there for two months and the week's grocery shopping.

He shrugged. "Well, I guess we should get on with this, then." He followed her into the bank and over to a woman sitting behind a desk.

Jo told the woman why they were there and waited for her to release the lock on the vault door. After they had gone through the procedure for securing a safe-deposit box and were alone, Jo opened the lid and reached inside. She handed Brad a black velvet pouch.

He looked at the achingly familiar pouch and was instantly transported into a world of memories. They were good memories—of times before his father's death, when the three of them had still been a family. Mabel had loved her jewelry and worn it often, and she'd worn it with flair and style.

He opened the snap at the back of the pouch and spilled the contents out onto the counter beside him. Everything was there—his great-grandmother's pearls, the opal pendant, the rings and pins and necklaces of four generations of Tylers.

"I think the pearls are particularly beautiful," Jo said. "They remind me of pictures I've seen of turn-of-the-century dowagers who wore big long ropes of them looped around their necks."

"My favorite was this pin." He held up a large intricately made flower embedded with rubies, diamonds and emeralds. "Of course, I was five at the time. My tastes have changed somewhat since then."

"Thank goodness," Jo said. The pin was one of the ugliest she'd ever seen. "A woman would need a forty-inch bosom just to hold the thing up."

Brad chuckled. "From the photographs I've seen of my female relatives, they wouldn't have had any trouble." He'd meant to ask Florence if she knew what his mother had done with the family album, but it had slipped his mind. He would call her as soon as he got home. As it was, his only link to his family was the jewelry that was spread out in front of him on the counter.

"It's too bad Karen..." Jo left the thought dangling, wondering what had ever possessed her to bring it up in the first place.

"Yes, it is. She liked jewelry... and clothes. Only we never had the money for her to indulge herself with either. She used to talk about what she would buy when I was a famous architect."

Jo didn't know what to say, so she said nothing. After several seconds had passed, Brad put the jewelry back in its pouch and turned to her.

"Ready?"

When they were outside again, Brad caught Jo by the arm and turned her to face him. "I don't know how, but I'll find a way to thank you for all you've done."

"I'm just sorry things didn't turn out the way I thought they would have. I guess I'm an incurable romantic— forever stuck in happy endings."

"Don't change, Jo," he said softly. "The world needs more people like you. At least I do. You've helped me put some things into perspective—which was long over-due."

"There you go, making me sound like Wonder Woman again." She far preferred he think of her as an ordinary woman. Pedestal sitting had never been her style.

"Like it or not, as far as I'm concerned, you're special."

She'd heard that line from guys before and it hadn't taken her long to learn what it really meant: that she fell somewhere between being considered one of the boys and a kid sister. "I'd better be going, Brad...and you should, too. It's a long drive to Casper."

"Would you be offended if I kissed you goodbye?"

How was she supposed to answer something like that? What would he say if he knew what he had just done to her heart rate? Since when did any woman in her right mind turn down a kiss from anyone who looked like Brad? "Of course not. We're friends, aren't we?"

"I hope so." He bent and brushed a kiss against her cheek.

Jo felt an unreasoning urge to kick him in the shin. She didn't want to be his little sister. When she realized the implications of her reaction, she recoiled. If she didn't like the role he'd given her, what role had she had in mind to play? The thought hit her with the force of a runaway train. "Have a safe trip home," she managed to say with a mouth suddenly gone dry.

"I will." He went to his truck and got inside.

Jo stood on the sidewalk watching him as he drove away. He turned and waved when he reached the corner. She brought her hand up to wave back but knew he couldn't see her. After he was out of sight, she took a deep breath and walked to her car, wishing she had someplace to go.

WHEN JO ARRIVED BACK at her apartment later that day, she taped a note on Amy's door asking her to come over when she got home. The rest of the afternoon she spent cooking and freezing—something she did periodically to keep from living on a diet of fast food. She hated preparing a meal from scratch when she was having dinner alone. But if it was just a matter of popping something in the microwave, it wasn't so bad. She was on her second batch of lasagna when she heard a knock.

"What's up?" Amy asked when Jo opened the door.

As usual after a long day, Amy had begun the process of disrobing the minute she'd stepped inside the building. The jacket of her raw-silk suit was unbuttoned, her blouse was untucked and the straps of her heels were hooked over one finger. Jo had often told her friend it was a good thing she only lived three flights up. It was the only reason she hadn't been arrested for indecent exposure.

Although Amy was the general manager for a company that assessed the computer needs of small businesses, and consequently made a handsome salary, she insisted she had no desire to move to a larger apartment. Once, when she'd had one too many glasses of wine and she'd let the more tender side of her personality show, she'd admitted to Jo that their friendship was far more important than spacious closets.

Amy and Jo were the opposites that attracted. Amy was analytical and a bit of a gambler. After graduating from the University of Colorado with honors, she'd decided against joining one of the dozen well-known companies that had come to recruit her, and instead she'd taken a chance on a fledgling company that had little to offer but possibilities. The chance had paid off. In only four years she'd gone from being one of two employees to the manager of twenty.

Jo gave her hands another wipe on the towel she was carrying. "I feel like company tonight. Do you have anything else going?"

"You don't think I'd set a book—even if it is the latest Dick Francis novel—above the smells that are coming out of your kitchen? Besides, I'm dying to hear all about Brad Tyler. Give me a few minutes to get out of these clothes and I'll be perched on your kitchen stool watching you slave away."

Jo left the door open for Amy to let herself in when she returned and went back to her lasagna. Amy arrived ten minutes later.

"Good grief—isn't your air conditioner working?" she asked, fanning herself as she came into the kitchen.

"I've had the oven on all afternoon."

"That bad, huh?"

Jo stopped in midstride, a lasagna noodle held suspended between her two hands. "What's that supposed to mean?"

"You never go on one of these cooking binges unless you've had a bad day. With some women it's cleaning their cupboards; with you it's cooking." She reached over the counter to pluck a morsel of meat out of the sauce. "With me, thank goodness, it's neither." She licked her fingers and made an approving gesture. "I just brood."

"I forget how well you know me."

"So spill. What's bothering you?"

"I don't know."

Amy considered her answer. "Just a case of general 'down in the dumps'?"

"Something like that."

"Okay. If you can't put a name on what's bothering you, tell me about Brad Tyler." She picked up a piece of grated cheese that had fallen on the counter and popped it into her mouth. "Boy, is he a hunk—beautiful body, gorgeous eyes, neat hair. Hair might not be important to some people, but to me it's downright sexy. And Brad Tyler has about the sexiest hair I've ever seen on a man— thick and shiny, with just the right amount of curl."

"Tell me one part of a man's body you don't think is sexy."

Amy closed her eyes as if she were deep in thought. Then she opened one eye and grinned. "I can't do it. I've given it my utmost consideration and there isn't an element of male anatomy that I can disqualify." She swung around on the stool and let out a sigh. "All those men—and so little time."

"If anyone could hear you talk, they'd think you were a scarlet woman."

"*Scarlet woman?* I can't believe you said that."

Jo laughed, a little incredulous herself at her choice of words. It sounded more like something Mabel Tyler would have said. "I didn't. You imagined it."

"Oh, no, you don't. I've got you on this one and I'll never let you live it down."

Jo sprinkled cheese over the final layer of lasagna noodles and put the six small casseroles in the oven. "I'll tell you what," she said, sweeping the crumbs into the sink. "You forget 'scarlet woman' and I'll feed you three times next week."

"It's a deal," Amy quickly agreed. She went over to the refrigerator and got out two beers, then took Jo firmly by the arm and led her into the living room. "Now let's sit down, put our feet up and find out what's bothering you."

"I thought you wanted to hear about Brad."

Amy stared at her friend for several seconds. "Something tells me they're one and the same."

Jo set her beer on a coaster and leaned her head back against the chair. "And something tells me you're right."

"So talk. What has this guy got besides looks, fabulous jewelry and a wife?"

"Two out of three isn't bad...."

Amy thought a minute. "*No wife?* What happened—"

"To Karen?" Jo completed the question for her.

"I thought she was the reason for all this mess."

"She was." Jo told Amy what she had learned from Brad.

"So Brad blames Mabel for Karen's disappearance," Amy said when Jo had finished.

"And that's why he never came back to Boulder. I found out in bits and pieces yesterday that he spent the first year after Karen's disappearance working odd jobs and hitchhiking around the country looking for her. He was in Wyoming when he realized he was getting nowhere on his own, so he went to work for a construction company and saved all his money to hire private detectives. They came up empty, too."

"I think I'm beginning to understand why you're in a blue funk. You like Brad—and Brad still has a thing for Karen. Am I getting close?"

"I feel so stupid. Of all the men I've ever met, I have to pick one who's obsessed by a woman from his past. I know I could fight a real flesh-and-blood person for someone's attention. But what do you do with a memory?"

"Maybe it's not as bad as you think. Isn't it possible that coming here simply dredged up old feelings?"

"If you could have seen the look in his eyes when he talked about Karen you wouldn't have any doubt that he's still carrying a torch for her." She groaned. "The last thing I need in my life right now is to get hung up on some guy who's hung up on someone from his past."

"I'm not so sure you're right about Brad still carrying a torch for Karen. Put yourself in his place for a minute. You go along with your life thinking you've got everything squared away, when out of nowhere comes this letter that brings back everything you've tried to put behind you. This weekend must have been awful for him. Keep in mind, the past you laid on him wasn't one that anyone in their right mind would make an effort to remember."

"It's a moot point anyway."

"Why?"

"He never really looked at me as a woman."

"How do you know? When he left this morning, how did he act?"

"He kissed me."

Amy threw her hands up in exasperation. "What more could you want."

"*On the cheek*, Amy."

"Oh."

"See what I mean?"

"When is he coming back?"

"As far as I know, never."

"Hmm—it looks like you do have a problem after all."

"No words of wisdom?"

"Sure, two of them. Forget him."

"That's easy for you to say."

"Have you got a better idea?"

She sighed. "No."

"Then let's eat. Everything always looks better on a full stomach."

DURING THE FOLLOWING WEEK it proved easier for Jo to follow Amy's advice than she had ever imagined it could be. On Tuesday the hot-water pipe in the shop's bathroom burst, Wednesday Howard's granddaughter disappeared, Friday the refrigeration unit in the yogurt machine went out and Saturday her car stopped running. And almost daily she received letters from assorted Brad Tylers laying claim to their "inheritance."

Ernie Baxter, a retired plumber who lived in the senior-citizen complex across the street from the shop and who happened to be one of Jo's regular customers, fixed the bathroom in exchange for a month's worth of free yogurt. Sandy's disappearance turned out to be a case of misunderstanding. The note she had left Howard, telling him she was going to a movie with Florence, had become the victim of an errant puff of wind which had carried it from the dining-room table to the living-room floor and then under the sofa. The refrigeration-unit problem hadn't turned out as well. Although it was repaired promptly, Jo was stuck with an enormous bill that she had to put on her MasterCard. She and Amy read the letters from the various Brad Tylers and then Jo discarded them.

By the time Saturday arrived, she was pleasantly surprised to discover that she'd hardly thought of Brad all week. At least, not until the mailman came with a special-delivery package.

Florence showed up just as Jo was about to open the small box. "I love surprise presents," she said, and then laughed. "That's not quite true. I love all kinds of presents." She peered inside as Jo separated the tissue paper. "Why, it's Mabel's pearls," she exclaimed.

Jo took the pearls from the box. They seemed different somehow from the way they had looked when Mabel first gave them to her. And then she noticed they had been restrung and a new clasp had been put on them. She draped the single strand of matched beads over her hand and stared at their iridescent beauty. Pearls had always been her favorite jewel but she'd never been able to afford anything beyond a pair of earrings. "I can't keep them," she said, not realizing she had spoken the words aloud until Florence responded.

"I don't know why not. Brad obviously wanted you to have them or he never would have given them to you."

"Do you have any idea how much something like this is worth?"

"It's been a long time since I've priced jewelry, but I'd say it would probably be a tidy sum."

Jo started to return the pearls to their box and noticed a folded piece of paper on the bottom. Inside she found a note from Brad.

Jo,
This is small payment for all that you've done.
                                      Warm regards,
                                              Brad

Jo handed the paper to Florence, who read it, then gave it back. "It's just like him to do something like this, you know. He always was a thoughtful young man."

"But I can't possibly keep—"

"You would hurt him terribly if you returned the necklace. He thinks a great deal of you, Jo."

Jo frowned in puzzlement. "How do you know that?"

"He told me so when we went out to dinner last Sunday."

She'd completely forgotten that Brad and Florence had gone out together. It was on the tip of her tongue to ask what else he had said, but she thought better of the idea. Florence was too sharp not to guess the motivation behind the question. "I really don't know about this."

"At least don't do anything right away. Take some time to think about it."

"I guess that wouldn't hurt. After all, it doesn't matter whether I return them today or next week."

"Well, I'd better be going," Florence said. "I told Howard I'd accompany him to the airport to see Sandy off."

"I've noticed that the two of you have been seeing quite a lot of each other again lately."

"He's been using me as a buffer. Sandy's coming was more difficult than he'd thought it was going to be. There was a generation gap between those two as big as Colorado. Thank goodness they managed to work it out before it was time for her to go home." She picked up her purse and started for the door. "She's even talking about coming back for another visit next summer, only staying longer."

"I'm glad it turned out all right for them." Jo held the door for Florence and saw Ernie Baxter heading toward the shop with Mary McDonald. She waited for them to arrive.

"How's the pipe holding up in the bathroom?" Ernie called out.

"I don't know why you even bother asking. Everything you've ever done for me has been better than new." Jo let the door swing closed behind them and got on with her day.

THE FOLLOWING WEEK was almost too quiet. Jo found herself on edge by Friday, as if waiting for the proverbial other shoe to drop. Even though the pearls had been on her mind almost constantly, she still hadn't come to a decision about what to do with them. Every time she thought about the necklace she thought about Brad, which invariably led to remembering the two days they had spent together and how quickly she had come to care for him. She was suspicious of her feelings and tried to attribute them to an infatuation, a passing fancy for a particularly handsome man. Sometimes it worked. Other times . . . it didn't.

She gave the shop a quick once-over before closing up for the night. Business had been better than usual for a Friday, and she decided to celebrate by asking Amy if she wanted to go out for dinner and then to a movie.

She had dropped the key to the shop in her purse when the phone rang. Jo knew it was useless to try to get back inside before whoever was calling hung up, but it was impossible for her to ignore a ringing telephone. She dug for the key, opened the door and made a dash for the counter. By the time she'd picked up the phone, it had run six times.

"Hello," she said. Being out of breath made her sound angry.

"Jo? Is something wrong?"

"Brad?" she breathed.

"Are you all right?"

"Yes...I'm fine." She couldn't believe how good hearing his voice made her feel. "I had to run to catch the phone."

"I was afraid I'd missed you when you took so long to answer."

"Another minute and you would have."

"I was wondering...I just thought...do you have any plans for tonight?"

"I was going to ask Amy..." Suddenly she realized what he was asking. "Why?"

"I'm in Denver and my plane doesn't leave for another seven hours. I was hoping I could talk you into going out to dinner with me."

"You want me to come to Denver?" Her car was still in the shop, and even though Amy would gladly loan hers, Jo wasn't about to borrow anything that had a dashboard that looked like the controls of a 747.

"Actually, I'd prefer coming to Boulder."

Jo laughed. "Italian again?"

"I was thinking more along the lines of the Flagstaff House."

"What time?"

"I can be at your place in forty-five minutes."

That was faster than she could bicycle home and take a shower, let alone get dressed. "I'll leave the door unlocked so you can come in and wait for me in case I'm not ready when you get there."

"Don't do that. Just tell me how much time you need."

"An hour." She knew she'd probably need longer, but she was too excited about seeing him to ask him to come any later.

"I'll be there. And, Jo..."

"Yes?"

"Lock your door."

"I will." When he didn't say anything, she added, "I promise."

CHAPTER NINE

JUST AS SHE WAS PARKING her bicycle around the side of the house, Jo met Amy coming home from work. "Tell me which dress of mine you think I look best in," she demanded as they entered the foyer together.

"First tell me where you're going."

"The Flagstaff House."

"I kind of like the white one with the black trim around the collar. Why all the fuss?"

"Brad's back in town."

A slow smile lit Amy's face. "I see." She gave Jo a push toward the stairs. "Then this calls for something special." When they got to the third floor, Amy promptly unlocked her apartment door and pulled Jo in after her, not releasing her arm until they'd entered the bedroom. "I have just the thing." She reached into her closet and brought out a deceptively simple-looking forest-green dress. "You'll knock his socks off when he sees you in this."

"I don't know, Amy." Jo liked to think it was Amy's one-inch advantage in height that allowed her to wear certain clothes with the elegance of a high-fashion model, where she herself would feel like a gauche ingenue trying to appear sophisticated. But if she were honest, she'd have to admit that the end effect had a lot more to do with attitude than height.

Amy laid the dress over Jo's arm and guided her toward the front door. "I don't want to hear one word from you about not being the right type to wear something like this. You're a beautiful woman, Jo, and it's long past time you paid some attention to that fact."

Jo glanced at her watch. She had less than forty-five minutes to try to make the rest of her measure up to the dress. "I'm only giving in this easily because I don't have time to argue."

"I'll remember that delightful bit of information the next time I'm trying to get you to do something you don't want to do." She reached around Jo to open the door. "Now get going." Jo was almost at her apartment when Amy called out, "Wait a minute." She disappeared for several seconds. When she reappeared she was holding a pair of slinky-looking high heels and a matching purse. "I forgot to give you these."

"Wish me luck," Jo said, looking at the narrow black straps that were supposed to hold her feet securely to the flimsy sole and delicate high heel. "I have a feeling I might need it."

"You don't need luck. The trick is that once you're dressed, you forget what you're wearing and just be yourself. My dress and your personality—it's a combination no man in his right mind could resist."

Twenty minutes later she was sweeping one side of her freshly washed and dried hair back from her face and holding it in place with a gold comb. A quick application of makeup and she was ready to put on Amy's dress. She held the garment in front of her to determine front from back and felt her heart sink to her toes.

Although the sleeveless creation was modest enough in the front, the softly draped folds of material fell to her waist in the back, making it impossible to wear her normal undergarments. Jo had nothing against going bra-less in bulky sweaters or loose blouses, but she'd always considered herself a bit too well endowed—and far too timid—to wear anything that made her braless state ob-vious. Amy's dress not only missed the mark on loose and bulky, it downright screamed obvious.

She was heading for the closet and her black-and-white dress when the phone rang. It was Amy.

"I figured you'd probably reached the point by now where you'd need a little bolstering," she said.

"Amy, I can't—"

"*Oh, yes, you can.* Just remember what I said before. The trick is to put the dress on and then forget about it."

"All right," she said, not really convinced but decid-ing it was about time she did something adventurous. Besides which, she told herself, the dress was several cuts above anything she had in her own closet and was her one real chance to look special. "What have I got to lose?"

"That's the spirit. Call me bright and early tomorrow morning and let me know how the evening went."

Jo laughed. "Are you sure you don't want to wait up for me tonight? I thought mother hens were more in-quisitive."

"I would, but I have a date myself and I'm not sure when we'll get back from the concert."

Jo promised she'd call in the morning, hung up and glanced at the dress. Without giving herself time to think, she slipped the silky material over her head and adjusted it across her hips. Avoiding the mirror, she put on Amy's shoes and her own pearl earrings. Finally, when she could resist no longer, she braced herself and stared at her re-flection in the full-length mirror attached to the outside of the closet door.

Her breath came out in a whispered sigh of awe. Was that really her? She looked as she had always wished she could look, elegant and even self-assured—after all, what other kind of person had the nerve to wear anything as daring? She turned sideways and then turned again to catch a glimpse of her back. *Thanks, Amy,* she mentally told her friend as she whirled around to face the mirror. *I owe you one.* Only one thing could make her look better—Mabel's pearls.

BRAD GLANCED at the dashboard clock as he pulled the rental car to a stop in front of Jo's apartment house. It was fifty-five minutes since he'd called her—only five minutes to go.

He tried to take his time climbing the stairs but found himself quickening his step the closer he came to her apartment. He didn't attempt to analyze his strange behavior; instead, he let the incredibly good feeling he'd had since he'd talked to her guide his actions. When he left Casper that morning, he'd told himself he really should think about getting in touch with Jo someday; after all, he'd be flying to Denver from time to time and Boulder wasn't far. But he'd never thought it would be that very day. After sending her the pearls, he'd figured any reason for further contact was gone. Jo was a wonderful person and unusually fun to be with but hardly the type of woman he normally dated.

He smiled as he checked the time again before knocking. Three flights of stairs in a little over a minute had to be some kind of record, especially when he'd been trying to take it slow.

Jo was hurrying toward the door in response to Brad's knock when a panicked thought struck. What if he was wearing jeans? Although the Flagstaff House was one of the most elegant restaurants in the area, there wasn't a dress code. She'd gone there for dinner when the attire had ranged from long dresses and fur coats to ski pants and parkas. But it was too late now for her to do anything about the way she looked. She took a deep breath and reached for the knob.

Long years of practice at hiding his feelings was the only thing that kept Brad from gaping when he saw Jo. He'd realized all along that she was a beautiful woman, but nothing she'd done or said had even hinted at the stunning sensuality that lurked beneath the girl-next-door exterior. He glanced to where his grandmother's pearls lay against her full breasts. "The necklace looks . . . beautiful. I'm glad you wore it." The words were woefully inadequate, but under the circumstances, they were the best he could summon.

She reached up to touch the cool beads. "I'm still not sure whether I'm going to let you give them to me or not, but I couldn't resist wearing them tonight." She gave him a tentative smile and moved out of the doorway. "Would you like to come in for a while?"

Brad tried to ignore the image his mind created when he saw how freely her breasts moved beneath the softly clinging dress. The way she looked had caught him completely off guard and he needed time to get his wits about him again. And one thing he knew for sure—being alone with her in her apartment was not the place to do it. "I thought if you were ready we might get to the restaurant a little early and have drinks out on the patio."

"That sounds wonderful. I'll be just a minute." Jo returned to her bedroom to get her purse.

Brad swallowed as he watched her go, thinking how, with the slightest encouragement, the dress would slip from her shoulders and . . . *Damn it—what was happen-*

ing to him? If he didn't find some way to control his libido, he'd never make it through the evening. He felt as though he'd been transported back to his randy teenage years. No—the feeling was similar, but it wasn't the same. Jo had set fire to a complex set of emotions that went far deeper than good old healthy lust. "By the way," he said as she walked back across the room, "I'm not sure if I've mentioned this before, but if I did, it bears repeating—you look stunning."

The sudden flush that coursed from Jo's neck to her cheeks shattered the subtle tension that had existed between them, helping to set things in their proper order again.

"Thank you," she said, regaining her composure. When they were in the hallway, she glanced up at him and said, "You don't look half-bad yourself." Her fears that he might arrive casually dressed had been one hundred and eighty degrees off the mark. He was wearing an expensively tailored dark-brown suit with a soft yellow shirt and striped tie. This was the first time she'd seen him in anything other than jeans and a sport shirt. It didn't seem to matter what he wore; he managed to carry himself with the same confidence and grace. A question that was on its way to becoming a haunting refrain surfaced yet again. What could have caused Karen to leave him? Was there some hidden flaw in his personality? Or had the flaw been in hers?

ON THE WAY UP to Flagstaff House they discussed what had happened in their lives while they'd been apart. Brad talked about the frustration and expense he was going through in firing one sheet-metal contractor and hiring another, and Jo told him about the horrendous week she'd put in after he'd returned to Wyoming. By the time they'd traveled the narrow twisting road halfway up Flagstaff Mountain to the restaurant, they had finished working out their initial hesitancy over seeing each other again, and their friendship was back where it had been the Saturday they'd spent with the Vizenors.

Because of the narrowness of the path through the restaurant to the patio, Jo walked several paces ahead of Brad, giving him the opportunity to note the reactions of the men she passed. Not a male between the ages of seven and seventy missed seeing her. Some were more subtle than others, but all paid attention. Then, as she left their sight, they looked at him, curious to see what kind of man was accompanying the beautiful woman in green. When he caught up with her at the table, Brad wasn't surprised to see that she'd been completely oblivious to the commotion she'd caused. Intuitively, he sensed that knowing she had made heads turn would not please her, so he kept quiet.

They were seated at a table near the railing, where they could enjoy the spectacular view of Boulder beneath them and the rugged mountains to each side before going into the main restaurant for dinner. Jo had been to Flagstaff House several times in the years she had lived in Boulder, but her reaction was always the same. The majesty of the surroundings never failed to take her breath away.

"Do you suppose if you lived in a house with a view like this you'd eventually become insensitive to the beauty?" she asked.

"Probably like all things, after a while you'd begin to take it for granted."

She took a deep breath of the pine-scented mountain air. "Someday, if I'm lucky, I'll find out for myself."

"And what if you discover after a few years that you've become jaded and think no more of your hillside home than of the apartment you live in now?"

She gave serious thought to her answer. "If that happened, I'd find a way to get back what I'd lost."

Brad saw the determined look in her eyes and had no doubt that she would.

Their drinks came and Jo turned her attention to pointing out landmarks of Boulder that were new to Brad. As the sun slipped behind the mountains and the lights of Boulder began to dot the landscape, their conversation drifted into more personal things again. After a while, even the beauty around them was forgotten as their world shrank to a sphere filled by two people getting to know each other.

An hour passed before the waiter broke into their private world to tell them their table was ready. They followed him up the short flight of stairs into the main dining room. Once they were seated, Brad examined the wine list and then consulted with Jo. When she told him she knew nothing about fine wines, he suggested champagne.

"Now, champagne I love," she said, thinking that if she'd ever felt in a champagne mood, it was then. "But I have to warn you," she continued in a conspiratorial whisper, "I never seem to be able to stop until I've gone at least one glass beyond my limit."

Brad ordered a champagne for them from the wine steward. "And what terrible thing happens when you've passed your limit?"

"I fall asleep."

He laughed. "Then I guess I'll have to keep a close eye on you. I can just imagine the stir I'd cause if I had to fling you over my shoulder and carry you out to the car."

"Perhaps if your method were a little less on the caveman side, you might be able to pull it off." She tried to sound annoyed but failed.

His voice lowered in a sultry challenge. "Shall we give it a try?"

"You *want* me to fall asleep?"

Her response was innocent enough and entirely in keeping with their light-hearted banter, but the mental image it provoked made his heart skip a beat. When he pictured her asleep, he pictured her in bed...and she wasn't there alone.

Jo reached over to touch his hand. "Are you all right?" she asked, concern in her voice.

"What?"

"For a moment there, you looked so strange."

He turned his hand palm up, caught her hand in his and gently caressed her knuckles with his thumb. "I was just thinking how much I'm enjoying being with you this evening. Thank you for coming."

She felt a constricting band tighten around her chest. "I could hardly have let you wait around at the Denver airport for seven hours all by yourself."

He discovered he wasn't satisfied with the easy answer. "Is that the only reason you agreed to go out with me?"

She responded to the change in his mood. "No...I wanted to see you again," she said truthfully.

"I'm glad." Before Brad could say anything more, the wine steward arrived with their champagne, and immediately after that, the waiter returned to take their order.

Jo quickly scanned the menu and chose the first thing she recognized that sounded good to her—tournedos *au poivre*. Brad needed only a second longer to choose the Spanish red scampi.

When they were alone again, Jo nestled her chin in her hand and stared across the table at Brad. "You still haven't told me what you were doing in Denver."

He looked at her over the rim of his glass. She was not the most classically beautiful woman he'd gone out with since Karen, but there was something about her that made it difficult for him to remember any of the others. Being with her made the flickering candle on their table a mystical dancing flame instead of merely a poor source of light. With each sip of champagne, he was aware of the bubbles bursting in his mouth and caressing the back of his throat. Only at that moment did he fully realize how much she had figured in his decision to return to Colorado. "I thought it was about time Tyler Construction expanded its base of operation."

"Does that mean you'll eventually be working around here?" She struggled to keep her voice level.

"It's very possible. Someday I might even be moving the main office to Denver."

"What would that do to the business you've built in Wyoming?"

"I hope it wouldn't do anything. I have a top-notch foreman who's been with me since I started Tyler Construction. I would leave the running of the Casper office to him."

"Then you'd be living and working in Denver all the time?"

He smiled. Obviously he hadn't fooled her into thinking he'd only given his plans casual consideration. "*Most* of the time. There would be a lot of traveling involved if the business continues to grow the way it has up till now."

Jo pondered what he'd told her as she watched him refill her glass with champagne. "When I first went into business, I had a dream that one day I would own a string of yogurt shops.''

He saw in her eyes that he was the first person with whom she'd shared her dream. ''And what happened?''

''I came to understand that spending all my time checking my investments wasn't what I really wanted out of life.'' She ran her finger around the rim of her glass. ''And I had to accept something else about myself in the process. I'm the kind of person who invariably stops to smell the roses, and that doesn't fit the profile of an entrepreneur. Had I opened all of those shops, I probably would have failed in the long run.''

''Working six days a week the way you do now hardly puts you in the stargazer category.''

She stared out the window at the glistening bed of colored lights below them. ''I've only recently discovered something else about myself. Slowly but surely—without ever being aware it was happening—I've let the shop become my entire life.''

Brad didn't reply. Instead, he waited quietly for her to go on, sensing that any interruption would cause her to withdraw from her vulnerable position.

''I'm not sure yet how I feel about my great personal revelation,'' she said finally. ''It's certainly not the life I pictured for myself when I was in college. But then, I always go back to the same question. What's so wrong with what I'm doing?'' Her gaze met his. ''Do you understand what I mean?''

The wine steward came forward to refill Brad's glass, and in that brief interval, Brad saw the change in Jo as she mentally retreated from her moment of self-revelation. He immediately felt the loss as she closed a part of herself off from him, and he tried to bring back the intimacy.

"There are times when I think of the dream that I carried through school—I was going to be the next Frank Lloyd Wright—and how easily I let that dream slip away from me. I can't help but wonder if someday, when I've reached a point in my life where it's no longer possible to change things, I'll regret that I didn't go after my dream a little harder." He shrugged. "Right now, it's easy to tell myself that if I really wanted to design buildings instead of construct them, I would. But that won't be the case a few years from now. Someday my options will be limited and I'll have to face my decision to let the dream die."

"Maybe part of my problem," she said, "is that I don't know what I want to do with my life, so it's easiest to drift along with things the way they are now."

He reached over to touch her nose with the tip of his finger. "If you'd keep this thing out of the roses long enough, I'm sure you could figure out which direction you want your life to take."

She smiled. "But then, look how much I'd miss."

Brad tried to remember the last time he'd wholeheartedly put his energy into anything besides his business and was stunned to realize that not since Karen had there been any other focus in his life. After the first year, he'd started seeing other women, but he'd never really allowed any of them to get close or to become important to him. At the time he'd truly believed he was treating them fairly, but now he realized he'd given them all short shrift. "There has to be a middle ground somewhere...."

Their dinners arrived and the conversation drifted to less serious subjects. Jo talked about Amy and the time the two of them had been trapped by a late-spring snowstorm at a cabin in Estes Park, and Brad told her about a prank he and Carl had pulled on a stuffy neighbor when they'd been in the eighth grade.

When their plates were cleared and dessert offered, Jo adamantly refused, saying she couldn't eat another bite. Brad listened to the waiter recite the dessert menu, cocked an eyebrow at Jo and said he would be willing to share something with her. She laughed and told him he was a man after her own heart. After a lively discussion of the merits of each offering, they ordered baked apple in cream sauce. The beautifully arranged and delicately baked apple turned out to be the perfect ending to a perfect meal. When only one thin slice of apple remained, Brad took it on his fork, swirled it in the cream sauce and held it out to Jo. After she'd swallowed the last morsel, he picked up his napkin and dabbed a speck of sauce from the corner of her mouth.

"I was saving that for later," she protested.

Brad laughed aloud. God, he hated to see the evening end. A line from an old Jim Croce song that had been popular when he was in school suddenly floated into his head—something about wanting to save time in a bottle—and he understood exactly what it meant. If ever there had been hours he wanted to save and relive again and again, they were the ones he'd just spent with Jo. "If I don't get you home and myself on the way to the airport, you're liable to wind up with a houseguest again."

She knew he was teasing her, but she was at a loss for a correspondingly light answer. "I wouldn't mind," she said softly.

As much as he wanted to believe she was serious, he couldn't let himself. Had she been any other woman, he would have canceled his plane reservation and stayed the night. But she wasn't. Jo was too important, too special for him to treat like any other woman. "I appreciate the offer," he said, standing to leave. "But one night on that couch of yours was enough."

A feeling of relief swept over her. She'd been caught up in the magic of the evening when she'd made the offer and had doubted the wisdom of the invitation the instant it left her mouth. She told herself she was fortunate he'd misinterpreted her intentions and almost convinced herself that she meant it. "Well I guess we'd better get you on the road then."

Brad came around to hold her chair for her. A haunting trace of her perfume reached him as she stood up and stepped into the aisle. The soft lighting made the skin on her back seem to shimmer as she moved gracefully away from him. It was all he could do not to touch her, to run his hand along the flawless expanse, to press his lips to the soft ridge of her backbone and follow the line from her neck to the indentation at her waist. He shook himself out of his daydream and followed her.

As they left the restaurant and climbed the stairs to the parking lot, Brad placed his arm companionably around Jo's waist. The touch grew electric; she seemed to flow into his senses, and he became so intensely aware of her that time and place momentarily slipped away. It was as if she were wondrously new and yet had always been a part of him. How, he wondered, could he have ever mistaken her for Karen when he'd kissed her at the waterfall? Jo was nothing like Karen. He smiled. Jo was unlike anyone he had ever known, with an unfeigned innocence that gave him a glimpse back into a world he had left far behind.

His thoughts led him once again to that day at the waterfall. He remembered how her lips had felt pressed against his own and how her body had fit against his. An ache began to grow in his loins. When he removed his hand from her waist to keep the ache from becoming a raging hunger, Jo took his arm.

She heard what she thought was a sharp intake of breath as her breast accidently brushed against him but convinced herself she was imagining things when he simply reached in his pocket and withdrew the tag for the parking attendant.

CHAPTER TEN

THE FIFTEEN MINUTES it took Jo and Brad to drive back
to her apartment passed in relative quiet, compared to the
animated discussions they had shared over dinner. Brad
spent the time trying to cope with the feelings she had ig-
nited in him, and Jo struggled to keep from asking when
and if she would see him again.

They arrived at her apartment just as the wind began
to blow. The lonely sound echoed under the eaves and
nudged the windows of the old house. Jo felt in tune with
the wind and its forlorn cry as she climbed the stairs, for
the moment of her and Brad's parting drew closer with
every step. When they reached the door to her apartment, she turned to look at Brad. What words should she
use to end the evening? "Good night" was inadequate,
"goodbye" too final. And how inane it would be to say
she'd had a lovely time when the hours they had spent
together were the very substance of a young woman's
fantasy.

"Thank you," she said at last, because it had grown
awkward to stand there and say nothing. And then, not
knowing what else to do, she held out her hand and offered a tentative smile. "If you're ever stuck at the Denver airport again..."

Brad ignored her outstretched hand and reached up to
run a finger down her cheek to her chin. "I won't hesitate to call," he finished, gazing deeply into her eyes.

She felt on fire when he had touched her. "Even if you're not stuck . . ." she breathed.

He held her face and bent to give her a kiss that was brief and undemanding. She sighed and he lightly brushed his lips against hers again and then—with infinite restraint—yet again. He tasted the baked apple they had shared and smelled the sweetness of her breath and felt a seed of desire burst and grow in him until its tentacles reached every corner of his being.

Each kiss, though gentle and transient, sent her heart racing. She tensed in anticipation, willing him to kiss her more deeply to match the hunger he had awakened in her, but he moved on to her eyes, her nose and then her chin. He caressed her face with his lips and the tips of his fingers, tasting, touching, scorching her skin. Gently he tilted her head and kissed her throat; her pulse beat rapidly against the whispered pressure.

With a faint moan she brought her arms up and put them around his waist. In response, his hands slid down her back, fanning out against her skin and drawing her close. As he turned her face to meet his questing mouth, he kissed her, touching her teeth and the velvety inside of her mouth with his tongue and urging her to do the same to him.

She unbuttoned his jacket to run her hands up his chest and around his neck. The heat from his body burned through her dress, making her breasts ache to be touched. She caught her breath in expectation when his hand slid to her waist and slowly began to move higher. After agonizing minutes of waiting, she felt him lightly brush against the sensitive sides of her breasts. She moved to allow him freer access. His thumbs swept across her nipples, raising them to hardened peaks. He brought his hands forward until they were filled with the aching flesh that pressed softly against his fingers.

A primitive hunger tore through him, demanding release. It had been so long since he had experienced the wondrously consuming passion of really needing someone that he had feared it would never come to him again. He wanted Jo with every part of him. His fingers ached to feel the contours of her naked body; his lips longed to explore her hidden recesses; his mind refused to see her anywhere but in bed beside him.

Control became a two-edged sword for Brad, forcing him to choose between present and future—denying himself the world of passionate release he had so recently rediscovered or taking the chance that he might destroy the enduring relationship he wanted to build with Jo.

The instant the thought formed, the decision was made. In reality, there was no choice. He dropped his hands to her waist, kissed her lightly, then gave a soft sigh and gently pushed her away.

"This is insanity," he said, looking down at her, his voice husky with longing, his eyes leaving no doubt as to his feelings. After several seconds had passed, during which he fought to regain his emotional balance, he took her hands in his and kissed first one and then the other. "I had thought I was a few years beyond getting carried away on a woman's doorstep, but obviously I was wrong. I apologize."

"We could go inside," Jo said, the words spoken in little more than a whisper.

He looked at her long and hard. With four words she had shattered the control over his emotions he'd fought so hard to gain. "I should say no—but I can't."

Never before had Jo so deliberately encouraged a man. But never before had she wanted anyone as she wanted Brad. Rational thought was shoved aside; arguments against what she was about to do tried to surface in her fog of desire, but she resolutely ignored them. For once, she told herself, she was going to do something just because it felt right. If there were consequences to face, she would face them tomorrow. With trembling hands, she opened the rhinestone-studded clasp on Amy's purse and reached inside for her keys.

She held the brass ring up to the dim hall light to find her apartment key. *Oh, no,* she mentally groaned, *this couldn't be happening to her. Not now. Not tonight.* But denial failed to bring change. The same keys continued to rest in her hand.

She'd been in such a hurry to get ready, she'd transferred the wrong set from her purse to Amy's. Returning the useless keys to her purse, she told Brad, "I've locked myself out . . . the only place I can get in with these is my car. And *it's* behind a chain-link fence at Waldo's Garage."

Several seconds of silence were followed by the soft sound of laughter. Seeing how forlorn and embarrassed she looked, Brad folded her in his arms and kissed the top of her head. His passion had turned to protectiveness. "What are we going to do with you? You can't spend the night in the hall."

Jo laid her cheek against his shoulder. "I'll just have to wait until Amy comes home. She has an extra key to my apartment."

"Why don't we see if she's home now?"

"She's not. She had a date tonight."

"There's a light under the door. . . ."

"There is?" Jo turned to look. Sure enough, light spilled into the dark hallway from under the poorly fitted door. Reluctantly, she left Brad's arms and went over to Amy's apartment.

Amy answered after the first knock. "Jo... what..." She looked past Jo and saw Brad. "Is something wrong?"

"You might say that," Jo answered, her voice a mixture of embarrassment and frustration.

"But nothing serious," Brad added quickly, seeing the panic that flashed into Amy's eyes.

"I've locked myself out."

Amy looked from Jo to Brad and then to Jo again. "Oh, I see," she said, unsuccessfully trying to keep a grin from forming. She brought her hand up to cover her mouth but it did nothing to hide the sparkle of merriment in her eyes. "Wait right here. I'll get my key for you." When she returned, the grin had become a fullfledged smile that she was trying to control by biting her lower lip. She dropped the key into Jo's hand. "Just remember to give this back to me in the morning or next time you'll have to pay a locksmith."

"There isn't going to be a next time," Jo grumbled.

Amy glanced at Brad. "It was nice seeing you again."

"We'll have to try for a more conventional meeting someday," he said, deciding he liked Jo's friend and glad someone as practical and levelheaded lived across the hall.

They said good-night and Brad and Jo returned to Jo's apartment. When at last she had the door open, she stood there, unsure of what she should say or do next.

Brad spared her the need to say anything. "If I don't get on the road, I'll never get the car returned to the rental agency before my plane takes off." He touched the side of her face and gazed into her eyes. "I'll be back as soon as I can make the arrangements." As if afraid to rekindle banked fires by touching her lips, he pressed a kiss to her temple.

Jo didn't want him to leave but was grateful to have some time alone to think about what had happened between them that night. "I'll be waiting," she said. Before she could add anything else, he was gone.

She stepped into her apartment and switched on the lights. She hesitated a moment before going all the way inside, looking about her at the familiar surroundings. Everything was the same and yet, somehow, everything seemed different.

THE WIND BLEW for two days, lifting patio covers from their supports to deposit them in neighbors' yards and separating branches from trees to fling them through windows and on the tops of cars. Since it was impossible for Jo to ride her bike, she walked to and from work.

Unlike most of the residents of Boulder, she didn't mind the wind. Even the damage it caused seemed fair, in a peculiar sort of way. When man perversely insisted on building cities with no regard to the natural scheme of things, it hardly seemed right to complain at the consequences.

She would probably have saved money had she closed the shop and stayed home during the wind's wild race through town, but she needed something to keep her busy, so she went on as if everything were normal. Total receipts for the two days were less than fifty dollars, but she managed to catch up on some reading she'd set aside and congratulated herself for not spending all her time thinking about Brad.

On Saturday, as soon as she got home from work she stopped in at Amy's place to return the shoes and purse. "The dress is at the cleaners," she explained, joining Amy in the kitchen for a cup of coffee. "I hope you don't need it before Thursday."

"The way my life has been going lately makes me wonder if I'll ever need it," Amy answered.

"I take it all did not go well last night?"

"Did you ever go out with a guy who spent more time looking at himself than at you?" She reached for a packet of sugar substitute and dumped it into her coffee. "After three of the most agonizing hours of my life, I know everything about this guy and I'm willing to bet he'd have trouble remembering my name."

"That's why you were home so early."

Amy laughed. "I slipped out of the concert hall during intermission and took a cab home. It cost a small fortune but it was worth every cent."

"You just disappeared?" Jo thought of the number of times she'd felt like doing the same thing but hadn't had the courage. "What if he called the police?"

"How could he? He wouldn't know how to describe me." She took a sip of coffee. "But enough about me. I want to hear about you and Brad."

"There's not much to tell."

Amy peered at her through narrowed eyes. "Let's remember who it is you're talking to here, Jo. Now give."

Jo got up to pour herself another cup of coffee. She wasn't sure how to answer Amy because she'd begun to doubt that what had happened between her and Brad had been real. Nothing could be as perfect as she remembered their evening. No one could make her heart do strange things simply by looking at her across a table. She went to the refrigerator and added milk to her coffee before rejoining Amy at the table. "I like him," she said.

"And?"

"I think he likes me."

"If the look I saw in his eyes last night means anything, he more than likes you," Amy said.

Jo wanted to believe Amy but she was forcing herself to go slowly when it came to Brad and his feelings. The distant look that had come into his eyes when he told her about Karen was etched in her memory. "Maybe. I'll just have to wait and see."

Amy grew serious. "What is it, Jo?"

To talk to Amy about Brad would be giving voice to half-formed thoughts. But then, perhaps Amy and her pragmatic approach to things could help to give substance to the shadows. "I'm a little afraid I'm getting in too deep where Brad is concerned." She put her elbows on the table and rested her chin on her hands.

Amy waited patiently while Jo sought the words to express herself.

"The idea of undying love used to sound so romantic to me…until I realized I was falling for someone who felt that way about someone else. How can I compete with Karen? She'll always be young and beautiful to Brad. If they ever had hard times, or arguments that lasted until dawn, he's forgotten them. I'm not sure—no, I am sure—I don't want to be measured by that yardstick."

"Isn't it possible you're making more out of this than there is? Everyone—at least, almost everyone—has a lost love in their past. It's all a part of living to lose someone and then go on."

"But with most people, the loss is a natural conclusion to something—a relationship. Even unexpected death is followed by a ritual of saying goodbye…a finality. With Brad and Karen, there never was a real ending. It's like the wives of men who are listed as missing in action in a war. There's always that tiny bit of doubt that keeps you tied to the past.''

"I can tell you've been giving this a lot of thought."

Jo sat back heavily in the chair, her hands folded on the table in front of her. "I haven't been sleeping too well lately."

"Well, my friend, I think you've worked things out in a wonderfully levelheaded manner...." Amy reached for Jo's hand and gave it a commiserating squeeze. "But you forgot to tell your heart."

MONDAY THE WIND stopped blowing and business in Boulder returned to normal. Jo spent the day ridding her apartment of the fine dust that had crept in under the windowsills and settled everywhere. After the dusting, she tackled drawers that didn't need cleaning and a closet that did, trying to forget that Brad hadn't called. She was washing the living-room window when she heard the neighborhood dogs barking and looked down to see the mailman crossing the street.

She had picked up her bottle of window cleaner to finish the pane when she remembered that a letter was due from her parents. Rather than rummage through her purse, she dumped its contents on the table, grabbed her keys and went downstairs. She met the mailman on his way up the walk.

"Looks like we're finally going to have a nice day again," he said.

She'd learned not to tell people that she liked the wind. Invariably they looked at her as if they thought she was operating a little off center. "Yes, it does."

He separated her mail from the bundle he was carrying and handed it to her. "This Brad Tyler who's been writing to you lately manages to get around quite a bit, doesn't he?"

She smiled. "Actually, it's more than one Brad Tyler. A couple of weeks ago I wrote to about eight hundred of them."

His face fell. "And you expect all of them to answer you?"

She rushed to explain. "I was only hoping for one, but it turns out I was being rather naive." She glanced down and saw that the top letter was from a Brad Tyler in Kansas. "I suspect things will quiet down in a couple of days."

He finished filling the other boxes with mail. "Well, I'd best be on my way. Seems that everyone on my route is outside today and they're all eager for me to stop and talk a bit. Guess they're curious to find out how their neighbors fared with the wind."

Jo said goodbye, not doubting for a second who was the more curious, the mailman or his customers. She went inside and flipped through the mail as she climbed the stairs. There were five letters from Brad Tylers, an electric bill, a MasterCard bill and an advertisement for the local lumberyard. As soon as she reached her apartment, she tossed the stack of unopened mail on the table beside the mess from her purse, no more willing to face the bills than the letters, and then went back to washing windows.

Three hours later she sat down with a cup of coffee and opened the electric bill. It showed she was using less electricity than she had at the same time the previous year but that it was costing her more. With a disgusted groan, she laid the envelope aside and stared at the MasterCard bill. All it took was the memory of the refrigeration unit on the yogurt machine for the MasterCard envelope to be shuffled to the bottom of the stack. When she came to the letters, she considered throwing them away but curiosity got the better of her.

The first was from a man who claimed to be on his deathbed and in desperate need of the money coming to him; the second Tyler said he had a sick wife and constantly mounting expenses. The third letter brought a smile. It was from an eighteen-year-old who asked if he could be adopted after the fact. Jo set his letter aside to answer sometime when things were slow at the shop. She was about to tear open the next envelope when the return address caught her eye. This one was from Casper, Wyoming.

Her heart gave a skip as she opened the flap and shook out the single sheet of paper.

Dear Jo,
It's only been a couple of hours since I left you. I'm on the plane heading for Casper and can't seem to get you out of my mind. If there was a way, I'd turn around and come back to you, even though I know it's not in your best interests—or my own—for things to happen between us too fast.

What is it that's happening to us, Jo? I'm almost afraid to put a name to the way I'm feeling.

I don't know when I'll be able to get away again. I expect to be working nonstop with the new sheet-metal contractor to try to bring the hotel in somewhere close to schedule. If it turns out to be a while before I can get back to Boulder, know that I'm thinking about you.

Brad

Jo felt a warmth spread through her, destroying her fears and chasing away her doubts. The late-afternoon sun blazed through her freshly washed windows and outside a bird sang a joyous song. All was right with the world.

TUESDAY WAS the busiest weekday Jo had ever had in the shop. At two o'clock, when the crowds showed no sign of lessening, she put in a call to Florence and asked her to come over to take care of the counter while she went in the back to make more frozen yogurt.

Florence arrived five minutes later with Howard in tow. They slipped on aprons and had the backlog of customers taken care of before Jo had finished mixing the first batch of yogurt. As soon as Howard was able to handle the counter by himself, Florence went into the back room to ask Jo if she needed any help.

"I can't imagine where all these people came from," Jo said. She closed the freezer lid and started measuring the ingredients for the second load to go in the mixer. "Not once in all the time I've been open have I sold out on a weekday." Her nose itched and she stopped for a second to rub it against her forearm.

"If this keeps up, you'll have to hire someone to help you—at least part-time."

Jo thought she heard a hopeful note in Florence's voice and wondered about it. "I doubt this is going to keep up. There's probably some function going on around here that none of us heard about and we're just getting the overflow."

Florence watched as Jo expertly added ingredients to the mixer. "It looks like you don't need me here, so I'll go out front again and give Howard a hand. The condiment bins need filling and everything could use a good wiping down.''

Jo smiled. ''On the off chance this horde of customers continues, I don't suppose I could talk you into being my part-time employee?''

''Be careful what you offer, Jo. Someday, someone just might take you up on it.'' Florence gently closed the door behind her as she left the room.

Jo stopped her measuring in midstride, her mouth open in surprise. Florence's answer to what had been intended as merely a teasing rhetorical question had caught Jo completely off guard. After a lifetime of work and its restrictions, most people wouldn't voluntarily tie themselves down to the routine again, would they? She knew retirement without a sufficient income meant a bleak existence. And she knew money was tight for Florence—if it weren't, she wouldn't be living in an apartment house where the rent was subsidized by the government. But as far as Jo could tell, Florence seemed to get along on her income without any major problems.

The more Jo thought about Florence's remark, the more convinced she became that she'd read something into it that hadn't been there. Still, in the back of her mind, a voice kept insisting she was missing something. She promised herself she'd listen more carefully in the future. Although she and Florence were friends who had much in common, there were certain things that separated them, things neither of them could ever change. The world and how someone looked at it was necessarily different at twenty-six than it was at seventy-two. They might share the view from the same window, but what they saw could never be the same.

Jo PUT THE BROOM back into the closet and closed the door. She was at a loss to find some way to thank Florence and Howard for all the work they had done that day. Money was out. Both had been indignant when she'd offered to pay them for the Saturday they'd run the shop so she could go to Central City with Brad. Free yogurt wasn't even a remote possibility, since neither one cared for it.

She went into the front of the shop. "I have a problem," she announced. "And I want the two of you to pour yourselves a cup of coffee, sit down and help me figure out what I'm going to do about it."

Florence looked from Jo to Howard and shrugged. "I'm not in any hurry. Are you, Howard?"

He smiled. "There's a meeting of the Gray Panthers I have to attend two days from now, but I'm all yours until then. I think I'll pass on the coffee, though, if you don't mind."

Florence also said she'd pass on the coffee, so Jo poured three glasses of ice water and brought them to the table. "I owe something to some friends of mine and I need advice on how to pay them," she began, pulling over another chair and propping her feet on it.

"Now, Jo," Florence said, "we've already told you that we don't expect or want you to make a big fuss over the little bit of help we occasionally give you."

"Florence is right," Howard added. "After all, what are friends for if they can't be called on to help out in a pinch?"

"What the two of you have done for me recently is above and beyond the scope of friendship. There's no way I could have kept the shop open today if it hadn't been for your help. I'm going to make a nice profit from the work the three of us did today and it's only fair that I share it with you."

Florence stared down at her hands, which lay folded in her lap. Long seconds passed in expectant silence. Finally she looked up at Jo. "When you put a price on labor done in friendship, it takes away the pleasure," she said.

Jo felt like a small child who'd been gently reprimanded by a loving parent. With her insistence on paying them, she'd forced Florence to tell her something she should have realized on her own.

Howard jumped in. "However, I can't see that it would deny anyone anything if you were to take us all out for pizza."

If he had been sitting closer, Jo would have given him a hug. "What did I do to deserve friends like you?" she asked.

"My dear Jo," Florence said, her voice filled with love. "Don't you know how special you are? It's we who consider ourselves lucky to be your friends."

As always when she received effusive compliments from people she cared about, Jo blushed. She glanced from Florence to Howard. "What do you say we get out of here and go over to the pizza parlor?"

"The first round of beer is on me," Howard announced.

"Oh, no, it's not," Jo protested. "From beginning to end, tonight's on me. And I won't hear another word about it."

CHAPTER ELEVEN

JO LOOKED at the single piece of pizza that was left from the giant sausage and pepperoni they had ordered and shook her head. "I can't believe we ate the whole thing," she said.

Florence laughed. "Neither can I." She looked at Howard. "If you were a true gentleman, you'd insist that you ate most of it."

"I don't think I even had a third," he protested.

"How ungallant," Jo snorted.

He winked at her. "Not something your new beau would do, huh?"

"What new beau?"

Florence finished the last of her beer. "The exceedingly handsome one you were seen sitting nose to nose with at Flagstaff House last Friday."

"How—"

"You walked right by Ernie Baxter and his daughter without even seeing them. He said he tried to get your attention a couple of times, but you had eyes for only one man that night and it sure wasn't him."

"And now I suppose everyone knows...." Because she was still unsure of the developing relationship between herself and Brad, Jo had hoped to keep it quiet for a while longer. She should have known how impossible that would be if they went out together in Boulder.

"And everyone is happy for you," Florence said.

"Quite honestly, some of us have been a little concerned that you're already twenty-six and still living alone," Howard added. "You can take it from someone who's been there, life is twice as much fun when it's shared, Jo. We like you too much to want you to miss out on anything."

Florence gently poked him. "For crying out loud, Howard, Jo and Brad have had two dates and you're acting like they were getting ready to mail out invitations to the wedding. Give them some time to get to know each other."

"Amen," Jo said.

"*Then* we can start sending out the invitations." Florence chuckled, obviously immensely pleased with herself.

"What makes you think Brad and I are anything more than friends?" The incredulous looks they gave her let Jo know she'd never win with that line of reasoning. "All right, I'll admit we like each other—but there have been lots of men I've liked over the past couple of years and not one of them is still around. Brad's no different from any of them."

"We're not trying to back you into a corner, Jo," Florence said. "We're just happy for you, that's all. Brad is a fine young man—"

"Not like some of the other..." Howard caught himself several words too late to disguise his implication.

"Why do I get the feeling I'm being mothered?"

"Not mothered, dear—grandparented," Florence said. "It's rare that those of us who live in the apartment complex come in social contact with young people. Because of our isolation, we have a tendency to jump in with both feet whenever an opportunity arises for us to become a part of a young person's life."

Under other circumstances, Jo wouldn't have minded if everyone knew whom she was going out with. But where Brad was concerned, it was different. If something happened and they stopped seeing each other, she didn't want to have to explain anything to anyone. The hurt would be too great. "I'm probably being foolish about this, but I can't get over the feeling that if I don't protect what's happening between Brad and me from becoming common gossip, it will self-destruct."

Florence looked at her young friend and was transported back to the time when she was twenty and involved with a man her parents considered completely unsuitable. She had experienced the same protectiveness Jo was feeling, the same fear. "I understand," she said softly. "But if you ever feel the need to talk to someone, we'll be here."

"Thank you."

"And we'll even be here if you don't feel like talking," Howard put in.

Jo laughed. "Somehow, I can't imagine the three of us getting together and not talking." She stood up and took her sweater from the back of the chair. "How about walking to the corner with me?"

"We'll walk you all the way home, if you like," Florence offered.

Jo groaned. "I don't know where you two get your energy. I'm about ready to drop and both of you act like you've been sitting around all day doing nothing."

"It's all those days we do sit around doing nothing that wear us out," Howard said, handing Florence her purse.

A blanket of warm air surrounded them as they left the pizza parlor. It was one of those lazy summer evenings meant for doing nothing more strenuous than lying around and watching the sky for shooting stars. They strolled down the sidewalk toward home, matching their pace to the languid feel of the night. When Jo insisted they part at the corner, she headed north, Florence and Howard east.

"She's a lovely young woman," Howard said as soon as they were alone.

"I hope she doesn't get hurt." Florence had been thinking about Jo and Brad and she'd begun to feel a sense of foreboding about the two of them that she couldn't shake.

"You're beginning to sound like I did a few days back. What's happened in the meantime that makes you think there's a possibility she'll be hurt?"

"It's not what I think, it's what Jo thinks. I'd venture to say she's not even aware of it herself yet, but she's running scared where Brad is concerned."

"I thought you said he'd be perfect for Jo."

"That could be the problem. It's when two people are the most perfect for each other that loving can cause the greatest pain."

They walked the rest of the block in silence. When they reached the corner, Howard took Florence's elbow and turned her to face him. "Was it Jo and Brad you were talking about back there or was it us?"

"You're too clever for me," she said, avoiding his gaze.

He touched her chin and gently forced her to look at him again. "We have so much to give each other. Why are we wasting the little time that's left to us?"

She was tired of fighting him and herself over something she wanted as desperately as he did. There wasn't a night she crawled into bed that she didn't think what it would be like to have Howard there waiting for her, not a morning that she didn't wish him beside her. It wasn't the big things, the important events, that she regretted not being able to share with him; it was the little things, things that happened every day, the bits and pieces of life that were too inconsequential to remember for more than a minute or two but were the kinds of things that created a bonding, an intimacy, between two people. It was a lonely feeling to read something in the morning paper, look up and realize no one was there to listen to the simple comment she wanted to make.

How could she deny him when her heart cried out with the same question? "We've been over this time and time again."

"And we'll keep going over it until—"

"Until you have your way?"

"Is it just *my* way?"

Her heart felt as if it were breaking. "You know it's not," she said, blinking back tears of frustration and yearning.

"Stay with me tonight, Florence. Let me make love to you and then let me wake up in the morning with you in my arms."

"I—"

He touched his finger to her lips. "Answer with your heart this time, not your mind."

With all her heart she wanted to say yes. She looked into his eyes and saw the love he wanted to give her, she knew he could see the same love reflected in her own eyes. She thought of the years they had already wasted denying that love. They had treated their relationship as if they had an endless supply of tomorrows. As if somehow, something would magically happen one day to let them be together. Was it so wrong to take just one of the days left to them and spend it selfishly, lavishly on themselves? "How will I get from your apartment to mine in the morning without anyone seeing me?"

His face glowed with happiness. He brought her hand to his lips and planted a kiss on the parchment skin. "You'll just have to stay until dinner. No one would question you leaving then."

"My phone—"

"Would you rather we stayed at your place?"

She was seventy-two years old and she was allowing the remote possibility that a child or grandchild might call to keep her from spending the night with the man she loved. "No. . . ." She smiled shyly. "Your bed is bigger."

He cupped her face with his hands and stared deeply into her eyes. "I love you, Florence Pickford."

"And I love you," she breathed, tilting her head to meet his kiss.

He put his arm around her and they headed home.

IT WAS SUNDAY and the after-church crowd had come and gone, leaving Jo with bins to fill and tables to wipe down. She was trying carefully to pour coconut out of a bag when the phone rang, startling her and causing her to spill white flakes all over the counter. "Damn—" she grumbled, reaching for the phone. "Hello—I mean, Yogurt, Et Cetera, how can I help you?"

"Do you have any idea how provocative that sounds?"

"Brad!" It felt so good to hear his voice. "What sounds provocative? Yogurt, Et Cetera?"

"No, the how-can-I-help-you part."

"Oh. So tell me, how provocative does it sound?"

"How about if I tell you tomorrow?"

"Tomorrow? You're going to be in Boulder tomorrow?" She tried for a cool, sophisticated response but was unable to keep the excitement out of her voice.

IT'S A JACKPOT
OF A GREAT OFFER!

- 4 exciting Harlequin Superromance novels—FREE!
- a folding umbrella—FREE!
- a surprise mystery bonus that will delight you—FREE!

Harlequin Folding Umbrella— ABSOLUTELY FREE

You'll love your Harlequin umbrella. Its bright color will cheer you up on even the gloomiest day. It's made of rugged nylon to last for years, and is so compact (folds to 15″) you can carry it in your purse or briefcase. This folding umbrella is yours free with this offer.

But wait . . . there's even more!

Money-Saving Home Delivery!

Join Harlequin Reader Service and enjoy the convenience of previewing new, hot-off-the-press books every month, delivered right to your home. Each book is yours for only $2.50—25¢ less per book than what you pay in stores! And there's no extra charge for postage and handling.

Special Extras—Free!

You'll also get our free monthly newsletter—the indispensable insider's look at our most popular writers and their upcoming novels. Now you can have a behind-the-scenes look at the fascinating world of Harlequin. It's an added bonus you'll look forward to every month. You'll also get additional free gifts from time to time as a token of our appreciation for being a home subscriber.

Mail this card today for
4 FREE BOOKS
this folding umbrella and
a mystery gift ALL FREE!

"Well, not Boulder exactly. I have some business in Denver that will take a couple of hours in the morning, but after that, I'm free. I can be at your place sometime after lunch."

"Why don't I pick you up at the airport? That way you won't have to rent a car." And she wouldn't have to wait as long to see him.

"Are you sure you want to do that? There won't be anything for you to do while I'm in the meetings."

She gave up all pretense of neutrality. "All I know is I don't want to wait one minute longer than absolutely necessary to see you again." There, it was said and there was no way to take it back.

Brad tossed his pen on the desk, leaned back in his chair and smiled. "You sure know how to make a guy feel good, lady."

The warmth in his voice felt like a caress. "I got your letter," she said. "I wasn't expecting you to call this soon."

He'd worked every night that week and was spending his weekend in the office as well, just to be able to leave Casper and return to Colorado as soon as possible. Still, the one day, Monday, was all that he could afford to take. "I guess I couldn't stay away from you."

"What airline—and what time?"

He reached for a piece of paper in his desk drawer. "It's United, flight number 807, and it gets in at 9:22."

"Should I wear a carnation or something so you'll recognize me?" she teased.

"Trust me," he said, his voice low and husky. "That won't be necessary. I have every part of that beautiful body of yours memorized."

Jo was glad no one was in the shop to witness the sudden flush that went from her chest up her neck to her face. She picked up the empty coconut bag and began fanning herself with the thick plastic. "I was about to ask you what I should wear for our day in Denver but I think I'll decide that one for myself."

After a quick knock, Jack Hargrove came into Brad's office. Brad asked Jo to wait a minute while he found out why his foreman had shown up at work on his day off. "What are you doing here? I thought I told you to go home and spend some time with that family of yours before they forgot what you looked like." Since the problems had surfaced at the hotel site, Jack had been putting in almost as many hours as Brad.

"We're on our way to the park for a picnic. I just stopped by to see if I could talk you into coming with us."

"I wish I could—"

"Don't give me any of that I-wish-I-could crap. What's the good of being the boss if you can't get out of the office once in a while?"

It had been a long time since he'd done anything with Jack and Linda, longer yet since he'd seen their two boys. He looked at the stack of correspondence he still had to go through and the letters he had to read and sign. It was on the tip of his tongue to turn Jack down when he surprised both of them by saying yes. "I'll be with you in a few minutes," he said.

"It's a good thing you decided to give in easy," Jack said as he moved toward the door. "Linda warned me that I'd better not take no for an answer, and there was no way I was going to spend the day with her mad at me."

Brad smiled at the departing man and lifted the receiver again. "I'm sorry I kept you waiting, Jo."

"A picnic sounds wonderful," she said with a sigh. "I wish I could go."

"I wish you could, too."

"Have a wonderful time. I'll see you in the morning."

They said goodbye and hung up. After several thoughtful minutes, Jo went back to work, imagining how it would be to share simple pleasures like picnics with Brad. Although he'd been completely comfortable in the elegant surroundings of Flagstaff House, she had a feeling he would really come into his own at a picnic filled with games and rowdy kids. It was easy to picture him organizing a baseball game or a three-legged race.

When Jo realized the direction her thoughts were taking, she forcefully thrust them from her mind. The kinds of picnics she had imagined were family celebrations—as in married, as in children. Thinking about Brad in any context other than a wildly exciting date was not only foolish, it was dangerous.

JO SET HER ALARM for five the next morning but discovered it was unnecessary. After several hours of tossing and turning because she was too excited to sleep, she got out of bed early to start getting ready. She'd asked Amy for advice on her wardrobe again and, at Amy's insistence, wound up with another of her dresses. This one was buttercup yellow with a slim skirt split five inches above the knee in the front. It had a matching yellow jacket piped in black and was the kind of dress sold in shops that carried only designer labels.

Even the Toyota seemed in a good mood, responding immediately when she turned the key. The repair bill for the leaking water pump hadn't been nearly as large as she had feared, so she'd had Waldo add a long-needed tune-up to the total. She hit the freeway and automatically switched on the radio. There was a station in Denver she particularly liked that played nothing but love songs.

She sang along whenever she knew the words and hummed when she didn't. Forty-five minutes later, she was pulling into the multistory parking lot at the Denver airport.

The United terminal was crowded with recently disembarked businessmen who were in a hurry to leave and with puzzled outgoing passengers who had just arrived and were congregating in the middle of the aisle to stare at the monitors. Jo checked the screen for flight number 807 and learned it was arriving at the last gate.

Because she was early, she took her time walking down the long aisle. She liked airports. The almost frantic activity never failed to imbue her with a sense of excitement. Airports were a gold mine for people watchers and she had been a people watcher since she'd first poked her head out of her baby carriage. Every emotion could be seen on the faces of the passengers and crews as they hurried along the narrow concourse. There were tears and laughter at partings and reunions, fear in first-time flyers and awe in children. She passed a stewardess who looked bored and an old man who looked terrified.

The crowd thinned somewhat as she neared the gate where Brad's plane would arrive. Jo looked at the clock that hung suspended above the aisle and sat down. She still had ten minutes to wait.

Waiting had never been something she did well; today it was torture. Every time she heard the sound of a plane coming or going in the noisy terminal, her gaze flew to Brad's gate. She absently turned the gold bracelet on her wrist around and around, crossed her legs and glanced at the clock. Less than two minutes had passed, but it felt like twenty. A section of the morning paper that had been left in the next seat caught her attention. She picked it up and began reading. It didn't take her long to realize that not only wasn't she absorbing anything she read, she had no interest whatsoever in learning which mutual funds were expected to be the hot performers in the next six months.

Determined not to give in to her impulse to check the clock yet again, she was in the process of refolding the paper when she looked up and saw Brad standing in the middle of a crowd of people not ten feet away from her. He was intently watching her. She felt her heart give a funny beat as a thrill of longing coiled down her spine. Forgetting the promise she'd made to herself to take things slow and easy, she sprang from her seat, ran across the distance that separated them and flung herself into his outstretched arms.

"My God, I've missed you," Brad said, holding her tightly, reveling in the feel of her. He bent to give her a kiss. The reality of holding her was light-years beyond the memories he had carried with him since they'd last seen each other. Lost in their private world, they were oblivious to the flow of passengers who continued to debark from the plane and were forced to walk around them. Finally, it was a twice-repeated announcement paging a Miss Betty Karlson that intruded and restored time and place.

Reluctantly, Brad let her go. "Have you been waiting long?" he asked, gazing steadily at her face as if he were trying to satisfy some deep-seated hunger.

Not trusting her voice, she shook her head.

He slipped his arm around her waist and they headed down the concourse.

"How was the flight?" she asked, searching for something ordinary and safe to bring her feet back to the ground.

"Other than seeming to go on forever, it was fine."

"How long does it take to fly from here to Casper?"

Instead of answering her, he abruptly pulled her out of the flow of traffic and over to a quiet corner. As soon as they were in their sheltered nook, he stared at her with such intensity that Jo began to feel uncomfortable. And then he smiled that wonderful smile of his and her world righted itself.

"You're probably wondering if I've gone off the deep end, the way I'm acting," he said, raking his hand through his hair. "It's just that the craziest thing happened to me on the plane this morning. I started thinking that it was impossible for you to be as wonderful as I remembered. And as for how I had you pictured... well, no one could possibly be *that* beautiful."

"I'm not sure what you're trying to tell me."

"I'm just letting you know how wrong I can be at times."

She smiled. "I've been a little nervous about this meeting, too," she admitted.

He touched his lips to hers. "I wish we had the whole day," he said, frustration making his voice sound harsh. "But we don't." He took her hand and started walking again. "If there were any way I could get out of those meetings, I would, but one of them is with a man who's leaving for Europe next week and won't be back for a month and a half."

"Do your meetings have anything to do with moving Tyler Construction to Denver?"

"That's all they're about. Now that I've made the decision to go ahead with the move, I'm impatient to get the road cleared so I can get going on the actual work."

Jo had a feeling that Brad operated with the same driving intensity in his personal life as he did in business. "Have you picked a location?"

"I have a realtor scouting prospective sites." They had reached the first level of the parking lot. "Which way?" he asked.

Jo pointed to her car, conspicuous by its multiple dents and lack of shine when compared to the showroom pieces surrounding it. "It isn't beautiful, but we're old friends and we understand each other. I've promised it a new paint job if it gets me through one more winter."

Brad laughed. "I've never tried bribery with any of my vehicles." When they reached the Toyota, Jo unlocked the passenger door and asked him if he would like to drive. Brad declined and got inside saying, "I don't believe in coming between a woman and her car."

She walked around to the driver's side. Brad's gentle teasing presented a side of his personality she hadn't seen before. She'd decided long ago that she could never love a man who didn't have a sense of humor. She came to a halt, as if stopped by a brick wall. Love was a word she had told herself she wouldn't use where Brad was concerned.

Brad waited for her to continue walking and when she didn't, he got out of the car. "Is something wrong?"

She looked at him and tried to smile but failed. "No, nothing's wrong...." She grasped at the first thing that came to mind to try to explain her peculiar behavior. "I was just trying to remember whether I unplugged the iron before I left this morning."

"Is Amy home?"

"No, she's already at work."

"Is there anyone else..."

She'd picked a dumb way to avoid telling him what was really bothering her. "It's all right. I'm positive I remember putting it away now."

"We can go there to check."

"That's not necessary." She opened her door and got inside. "My brother's a fireman and he's constantly lecturing me about safety. Which means that every once in a while I get a little weird about whether I've unplugged something or not. Usually it's my curling iron."

Brad reached over and touched her chin. "It wasn't an iron that put that look on your face," he said. "What's really bothering you?"

She tried to start the car but he stopped her by putting his hand over hers, preventing her from turning the key. They stayed that way for several seconds. A battle was raging inside Jo. She usually didn't bother to try to hide the way she felt from anyone. Because of some quirk of nature, her emotions were as visible as her clothing. There was never any question about whether or not she liked someone; it was written all over her face. When had she become so fearful? But she knew the answer before she'd even raised the question. "I don't trust the way I feel about you," she blurted out.

"Give me your hand, Jo."

"You already have it."

"I need the other one for what I want to do."

She held out her hand to him. He took it and placed it on his chest. Her mouth opened in surprise when she felt how fast his heart was beating.

He gave her a few seconds to think about what he'd done. "It was the only way I could think of to prove to you that I understand what you're feeling."

She leaned her head on his shoulder. "How long do you think it will take us to get over this craziness?"

He ran the tips of his fingers along her cheek. "Three and a half weeks."

"Why three and—" She looked up and realized he was teasing her again.

"Actually, I'm hoping it's just a matter of getting to know each other better. Which is exactly what we're going to spend the day doing."

But not *all* day, she reminded herself. Reluctantly she sat up and started the engine. Before pulling out of the parking space she gave him a sage smile. "One thing I'd rather not learn about you until we've known each other a long, long time is what you're like when you miss an important meeting."

CHAPTER TWELVE

BRAD'S MEETINGS were in an office building on the Six-
teenth Street Mall, giving Jo the opportunity to browse
through the shops in Tabor Center, a complex filled with
upscale boutiques that she rarely visited because of her
limited time and finances. Although her own wardrobe
necessarily consisted of whatever she could pick up on
sale at the department stores in Boulder, she had learned,
because of Amy's influence, to appreciate quality and
style in clothing.

She stood inside the block-long greenhouse that held
Tabor Center and looked around. A restlessness came
over her. To spend her time waiting for Brad here was
tantamount to sending a kid to a candy store with a nickel
when nothing in the store cost less than a dime.

Leaving the center, she crossed to Writer Square and
then over to Larimer Street—one of her favorite places in
the city. Dating back to 1858, Larimer Street had been the
first seed planted in the ever-sprawling growth that had
become Denver. A single block of the sturdy Victorian
buildings had been preserved and designated a Land-
mark Preservation District. The shops and restaurants,
sunken courtyards and vaulted passageways where Jo
spent her time exploring made the hours pass as fast as
she could reasonably expect.

When she arrived at the meeting place Brad had suggested—the lobby of the Westin Hotel—at one-thirty, he

was already there waiting for her. He was sitting on a padded bench in front of a small waterfall, reading a section of the *Denver Post* newspaper. "How did your meetings go?" she asked, joining him on the bench.

"If everything else about the move goes as smoothly, we could be breaking ground in early spring." He glanced at her empty hands, primly placed in her lap. "I take it things didn't go as well with you?"

"What makes you say that?"

"You're not carrying any packages."

She smiled. "I made a tactical error. Before I'd stopped anywhere reasonable, I went into an art gallery and fell in love with a painting that was a trifling few thousand dollars over my budget. After that, everything else I looked at was shabby in comparison."

"So, another piece of Jo Williams emerges. You like fine art. Does that mean you also paint?"

She laughed. "I have the dubious distinction of being the only student in my high school who ever made the art teacher cry."

"He was that impressed with your work?"

"Careful, Tyler," she said, failing to suppress a smile that destroyed her attempt at gruffness. "You're treading on dangerous ground."

He dropped a conciliatory kiss on her forehead. "Don't feel bad. I was rotten at making paper airplanes."

"You equate paper airplanes with art?"

"Hey, if you're a boy, paper airplanes happen to be an important part of growing up."

She leaned toward him and tilted her head back for a kiss. He readily obliged. "I didn't know that," she said, taking his arm. "Did this lack of skill leave any permanent scars?"

"Only one." He pointed to his side. "Right about here."

"Maybe if we eat, it'll feel better."

"What has eating got to do..." He laughed. "You wouldn't be hungry by any chance, would you?"

"How clever of you to guess."

"While you were shopping—or rather, not shopping—did you happen to see any restaurants that looked particularly good to you?"

"Let's remember who you're talking to here—I saw twenty places."

"Then I will leave the choice of where we eat to you. Lead the way."

Jo took him to a family-run delicatessen where the lack of service was made up for by the exceptional food. They ate in the shop's backyard patio, accompanied by what was left of the noon-hour crowd—a rotund orange cat and a young man softly practicing his guitar. "How did you find this place?" Brad asked Jo when they were seated.

"Florence brought me here one day when we went shopping together. It's been a favorite of mine ever since." She bit into her sandwich. "I've really missed coming since I started keeping the shop open six days instead of five."

"What made you decide to stay open longer?"

"There were a lot of reasons—boredom and money being the biggest. I'll probably go back to five days again when winter rolls around."

Brad took a drink of his soda. "This might seem like a strange time for me to bring this up, but in a peculiar way it fits in with what you just said. I've been meaning to thank you for something since I arrived this morning."

"Oh?"

"I never would have gone on that picnic with Jack Hargrove and his family if I hadn't been on the phone with you when he came into the office."

"I don't understand the connection."

"I knew I wouldn't be able to get my concentration back, so—"

"You decided you might as well spend the afternoon with Jack and his family."

"Getting away was quite a revelation. I had no idea I'd become such a slave to Tyler Construction."

"I take it you had a good time?"

"It was much more than a good time."

"Does this mean you're going to cut back on the hours you put in from now on?"

"Probably not right away, but being reminded of what else life can hold has given me something to think about."

Jo put her sandwich back on her plate. "Every once in a while, something like that happens to me and I get a panicky feeling that I'm not doing everything I should be doing with my life."

"And what do you do about it?"

She listened a moment to the softly played guitar music. "I remind myself of all that I already have."

Brad's heart went out to her. For the first time he fully understood the trap she had laid for herself in owning her yogurt shop. Now that he knew her better, he could see how impossible it would be for her to abandon the friends who depended on the shop for social contact. To Jo, friends were the coin by which she measured her success in life. And yet there was a side of her that was bright and curious and hungered to reach out and explore the world beyond Boulder. "Does counting your blessings work?"

"Sometimes," she said.

"And when it doesn't?" he gently prodded.

Could she trust him with something she'd never fully admitted to herself? "I take a long hot bath...and pretend I'm not crying." She looked away, embarrassed. "And then afterward, I'm all right again."

"Until the next time."

"Why are you doing this to me?" she asked, an almost angry look in her eyes.

"Because I think the day will come when I ask you to leave Boulder, and I want to know what I'm up against."

Jo felt her throat go dry and her palms moist. She had to consciously remind herself to breathe. He had only said what she prayed he would say, but she was at a loss for words of reply.

"I didn't mean to scare you, Jo," he said, reaching for her hand. "I thought you'd realized by now how special you are to me."

She slipped her hand from his and folded her arms across her chest. "I wondered..." she began, looking at the brick wall behind him and then at her half-eaten sandwich, anywhere but at him. "I hoped..." she finally admitted. And then, "But what about Karen?"

He stared at her unflinchingly. "What about Karen?"

"Don't play games with me, Brad," she told him. "I saw the look on your face when you told me about Karen's disappearance. Unless you've somehow managed to truly forget her in the last two weeks, you're not ready to talk to me the way you just did."

"I'm not trying to hide anything from you, Jo. And I'll never insult you by pretending Karen was less to me than

she was. She left an emptiness in me that I'd come to believe no one could fill—until you."

How desperately she wanted to believe him. With anyone else she could have talked herself into going along for
the ride, but if she allowed herself that freedom with Brad
and things didn't work out between them, she would
wind up more alone than she had ever been. What would
she do if... But what would she miss if she never took the
chance? "Where do we go from here?"

The worry left his eyes, replaced by a loving warmth.
"I don't know about you, but I've always wanted to visit
an art museum," he said, purposely ignoring the true
meaning of her question. "Do you know if Denver happens to have one?" He stood and held out his hand.

There were moments in Jo's life when having the feel
of someone's arms around her became almost as necessary as breathing. Right then was one of them. She was
filled with an actual physical ache to be held by Brad.

Almost as if he could read her mind, he gathered her
into his arms the moment she got to her feet. "I wish I
knew a way to tell you how much you mean to me," he
said, looking deeply into her eyes.

"I think you just did." Her arms came around his
waist and she lightly touched her lips to his before letting him go. Reaching for her purse, she asked, "Are you
really interested in art?"

He'd become an expert on shrunken heads if it would
please her. "Other than the art associated with the architecture I studied in school, I've never had a chance to
find out. But I figure there's no better time than the
present and no one in the world to guide me better than
you."

Jo took his hand and they headed for the door. On
their way out they passed the guitar player. He glanced up

from concentrating on the intricate chords he'd been playing, smiled broadly and gave them a thumbs-up signal.

BRAD'S VISIT to the Denver Art Museum was the first time he'd ever taken the opportunity to see some of the actual paintings by such artists as Rembrandt, Degas, Renoir and Picasso. All his life he'd seen only copies of their work, never the real thing. Jo was amused that she had trouble persuading him to move from one exhibit to the next as he became fascinated with the difference in quality between the original masterpieces and the reproductions he'd seen all his life. There was so much Jo wanted him to see at the museum, and so many things she wanted to tell him about the exhibits, that she found herself constantly tugging at him to get him to move on. They were at a quilt exhibit when it dawned on her that she was behaving as though they would never again have the opportunity to return to the museum together.

After spending several minutes studying a particularly intricate design on a hundred-year-old quilt, Brad suddenly realized how long he'd stood there and looked at Jo suspiciously. "Why aren't you trying to load the tour bus?"

"It just occurred to me that we don't have to cram everything into one day. We could always come back here the next time you're in Denver."

"At last," he said. "I was beginning to wonder how long it was going to take for that thought to occur to you."

"Why didn't you say something earlier?"

"I wanted you to figure it out by yourself."

A disembodied voice interrupted them to announce that the museum would be closing in ten minutes.

The stricken look on Brad's face brought a smile to Jo's. "I'd say your first foray into the world of art has been a success."

He put his arm around her. "I think you're right. There's only one problem."

"And what's that?"

"After seeing the originals, I'll never be able to settle for a print of anything again. Which means either I have bare walls or a bare bank account."

"Since nothing in here is for sale, I think bare walls is closer to the mark."

"You're kidding. And here I had my heart set on the Rembrandt."

"I thought the Degas was your favorite."

"Not for the living room."

Jo laughed. It was a wondrously happy sound that precisely reflected her feelings. "Where shall we go next, now that we're being kicked out of here?"

"Would you like an early dinner? I noticed you didn't eat much of your sandwich at lunch."

She thought for a minute. She was subdued when she said, "I have a better idea. Why don't I fix dinner for us?"

They both understood that she was suggesting more than just a meal. The tension that had been building between them all day left no doubt in either of their minds that the only way for them to keep any distance from each other was to remain in public places. "Are you sure?" he asked, touching her chin and gently turning her head until she met his gaze.

"Afraid of my cooking?"

"You know what I'm talking about, Jo. Maybe you'd better take some more time to think about your invitation."

The surrounding air grew almost too heavy to breathe. "I don't need any more time—I know exactly what I'm doing."

He found the confirmation he needed in the direct way her eyes met his. "Then why in the hell are we still standing around here?" he asked, his voice husky with wanting her.

She watched his mouth as he spoke, imagining how it would feel to have his full lips touching hers. A desire more intense than she had ever thought possible swept through her. Her breasts ached with a need to be caressed; her stomach knotted in anticipation of all that would follow. For an instant her thoughts focused on what their lovemaking was going to be like. Waiting the forty-five minutes it would take them to drive to Boulder would be torture.

As Jo's thoughts progressed to the drive home, her eyebrows drew together in a puzzled frown.

"What's the matter?" Brad asked.

She pressed her hand to her forehead and let out a cry of utter disbelief. "This can't be happening," she groaned.

"What can't be happening?"

"I don't remember where I parked the car after I dropped you off."

"Is that all?" he said with a sigh of relief. He took the back of her head in his hand and pulled her toward him to give her a kiss, remarkable in its restraint yet filled with an exquisite promise of what would come. "If we have to, we'll call a cab. We can always find the car later."

She touched her tongue to her lips. "If you keep that up, we'll have to."

Again the disembodied voice spoke to them through the speakers mounted overhead. "The museum is now closing. We will open again at ten-thirty tomorrow morning. A complete list of the museum hours is available at the exit as you leave."

"I remember," Jo cried out.

"Good," he said, taking her hand. "But if you don't mind, I think I'd better drive this time." He grinned at her. "I'm not at all interested in turning up in Colorado Springs tonight."

She laughed. "I don't understand why not. Colorado Springs is a perfectly lovely city."

"Do you have an apartment there?"

"No."

"Then I rest my case."

Jo felt such extraordinary happiness she was afraid to move for fear that all this was only a particularly vivid dream and any sudden motion would wake her.

"Come on," Brad said, grabbing her around the waist and starting toward the exit. "As much as I like this place, I'm no more keen to spend the night here than I am in Colorado Springs."

They sprinted toward the front entrance. Jo held her breath and waited. Nothing happened. A slow, private smile filled her eyes. She wasn't dreaming after all.

THERE WAS A NOTE from Jo's landlady taped to the front door of her apartment when she and Brad arrived. As she unfolded the yellow piece of paper, she heard music coming from her apartment. Once again she'd forgotten to turn off the radio. If the day ever came that she had the money, she planned to buy stock in the electric company that serviced her home. If anyone's fortune was going to be made from her forgetfulness, it might as well be hers.

"I have to go downstairs to pick up a message from Amy," she told Brad. "I'd go later but Mrs. Kennedy says it's important.'' She shrugged helplessly. ''Which could mean anything from Amy having a flat tire to her needing emergency surgery. I promise I'll be right back.''

He caught her to him and gave her a quick kiss. ''Do you want me to go with you?''

She shook her head. ''Knowing Mrs. Kennedy, I'd say she got a good look at you through her curtain when we came in just now. I'd prefer that was all she saw.''

''Afraid she'll insist we keep the door open while I'm here?''

''Not exactly. More like afraid she'll be up for a visit. She's the most predatory female I've ever known.''

The proprietary gleam in Jo's eyes pleased him. He brushed his lips against hers once more before letting her go. ''Hurry back.''

She smiled and handed him the keys. ''An army couldn't keep me away.'' As she left, she heard Brad unlock the door and go inside the apartment.

It took Jo a frustrating ten minutes to get Amy's message out of Janet Kennedy. The platinum blonde did everything she could, short of coming right out and asking, to find out about the man Jo had brought home with her. Finally, realizing Jo was too much of a match for her when it came to Brad, the older woman broke down and gave her the message, which was merely that Amy had called to say she would be out of town on a business cruise for several days.

Jo gritted her teeth as she headed back to her apartment. It was just like Janet Kennedy to make a mountain out of a molehill. Explaining Amy's simple message in the note would have been far too logical for someone who thrived on puffing up her own importance at every conceivable opportunity. A smile tugged at the corners of Jo's mouth when she realized her fit of pique had far more to do with being kept away from Brad than with her landlady's pompous personality.

The nearer she came to her apartment, the less Jo thought about Janet Kennedy. By the time she reached the third-floor landing, a feeling of shyness had come over her. It was a feeling that doubled and then tripled with each step until it became so strong it actually brought her to a halt. She was amazed to discover that although she'd been away from Brad for only a short time, she was at a loss for words to say or actions to guide her when she returned. What would eventually happen that evening had been silently acknowledged by them both. But she wasn't sure whether that meant before or after the dinner she'd promised to fix. She didn't know if she should go in and put on an apron or take off her dress. Either course of action was fraught with embarrassing possibilities.

When she reached her front door, she waited outside for several seconds, shoring up her courage. While she stood there, the haunting refrain of a love song drifted out to her, keeping her company as she struggled with indecision. It was an old song, a particularly beautiful ballad that for some reason had never made it to the top of the charts but had endured nonetheless. It still managed to get occasional radio play ten years after its release. She concentrated on the compelling harmony and eloquent words until they drove out her fears. Filled with confidence again, she opened the door.

Inevitably, the first thing she saw when she took a step inside was Brad. The look on his face brought her to an abrupt stop. She felt the moment being forever frozen in time and place as she continued to stare at him. Even though she was standing directly in his line of vision, he was unaware that she'd returned. He was lost in a world of his own. The color had drained from his face, leaving him with a haunted look; his eyes were filled with a tortured, profound sorrow.

Words from the song echoed relentlessly through the apartment and in her mind.

To some, love comes as a whisper.
For others, it's a raging storm.
With us, it was a gentle knowing....

Jo's initial confusion about what she was seeing changed into a dread-filled understanding. The song on the radio had been *their* song—Brad and Karen's. With the understanding came pain—a pain so intense it sliced through her chest, making it impossible for her to catch her breath. She felt her stomach heave and was afraid she was going to be sick.

She let out a quiet cry as she turned to run from the room. The sound brought Brad out of his fog. The instant he saw Jo, he realized what had happened and leaped to his feet to go after her. She was ready to descend the stairs when he caught up with her. He grabbed her shoulder and, when she tried to pull away, wrapped both arms around her waist and drew her to him. He held her firmly, her back pressed against his chest.

"Let go of me," she cried, twisting in his grasp.

"Not until you listen to what I have to say."

She tried to pry his hands from her waist. His grip loosened slightly as he fought her, and she took advantage of the moment to gain her freedom. She turned to face him. "There isn't anything you have to say that I want to hear," she said, her voice cracking with the hurt inside. She backed away, as much to keep herself from breaking down and returning to his arms as to put distance between them.

"Stop!" Brad called out, his mind dark with horror as he saw her inch closer and closer to the stairs.

But she was only conscious of her driving need to get away from him and the pain that being near him brought. She didn't hear the panic in his voice.

He lunged for her just as she was about to fall. The force of his movement threw them violently against the wall. Too stunned by the impact to move immediately, they remained where they had landed for several seconds before Brad raised himself up on one elbow and looked down at her. "Are you all right?" he asked.

Jo tried to catch her breath as her mind struggled to understand what had just happened. Her head hurt where it had hit the wall and she gingerly ran her hand over the sore spot. "Why did you—"

"You were about to fall." He lifted himself carefully off her and slid down to a sitting position. "Are you all right?" he repeated urgently, worried by the dazed look in her eyes.

Her only reply was a soft, despairing moan as she drew her knees up to her chest and turned her face to the wall. "I'm fine," she said when it became clear that he would not leave until she answered. "Now would you please go? Can't you see that I don't want you here?"

"I'll leave if that's really what you want me to do, Jo. But before I go, there's something I have to explain to you...." His tone implored her to listen.

When she turned to look at him, her face was streaked with tears. "What could you possibly have to say? You lied to me. All the explanations in the world won't change that."

"How did I lie to you?"

Angrily she wiped the tears from her face. How could he go on pretending? "You told me you were over Karen. You let me trust in you."

God, if he only knew how to reach her. She was the one good thing that had happened to him in the last eight years and she was slipping from his grasp. *And he felt powerless to stop her.* "But I never told you I could erase her from my memory." Somehow he had to make her understand. "You know that Karen was a part of my life once—an important part. I've never tried to hide that from you. We lived together a year and a half, Jo. No matter where I go or what I do, there will always be things that remind me of her, just as songs and aromas and street signs remind me of other things in my past that have nothing to do with Karen. *But that doesn't mean I would choose her over you if both of you were standing here in front of me today.*"

He felt a sudden desperate need to hold her, as if with his touch he might be able to communicate the feelings he couldn't find the words to express. He reached for her but she moved away from him.

"It's bad enough when you lie to me, but when you lie to yourself, too—" she gave a strangled sob "—then I know we never had a chance."

"You're wrong, Jo. We did have a chance. We still do." He refused to believe he had lost her. He couldn't go through that again. After years of a loneliness that had systematically eaten away at his insides until he'd been left hollow, Jo had come along. She had filled him with her awareness and her passionate love for life, showing him that it was possible to trust and to care about someone again. After being given such promise, returning to the emptiness he'd known for all those years would kill him.

"There's nowhere for us to go from here, Brad. I'll never be able to forget the way you looked when you were thinking about Karen. She'll always be there between us."

"Only in your mind."

"It doesn't matter. Every time we made love, I'd be wondering if you were thinking about me or remembering Karen. I can't live that way."

"When we do make love, Jo, there will be no doubt in my mind who I'm making love to." This time when he reached for her hands she was too tired to fight and she didn't pull away from him.

"But there would always be doubt in mine," she said softly.

For a long moment they sat without speaking, their silence broken only by the sound of yesterday's love songs drifting into the hallway from Jo's radio. "I love you, Jo," he said, his voice filled with a heartbreaking sadness. After several more minutes had passed, Brad released her hands.

Fresh tears gathered in her eyes as she looked at him. "Would you still tell me you loved me if Karen were here with us?"

How could he make her understand that no matter what he did or said, Karen would forever be a part of his past? That no matter how much he loved Jo, Karen would still be a part of him? He could no more isolate or totally exorcise the meaning of Karen than he could any other memory. *Why couldn't Jo see that nothing about remembering Karen kept him from loving her?* His frustration built until it led to anger. "Since forcing me to choose between the two of you is impossible, you'll have to pick another criterion for judging me," he said, the anger making his voice sound harsher than he had intended.

"I don't need to judge you at all. I've seen more than I ever wanted to see. It will be a long time before I'll be able to forget what happened between us today."

Brad rose to his feet with a lithe, graceful movement. He reached for Jo and brought her up to stand beside him. "I'm glad to hear you say that," he said. "Because I have no intention of letting you forget a single thing about today. I want you to remember how you felt when you met me at the airport. From now on, whenever you hear guitar music, I want you to think of me. And whenever you visit a museum or look at a painting, I'm going to be right there beside you." He held her face between his hands. "You love me, Jo. And, God knows, I love you. What we have is too precious to let go without a fight."

"I don't have any fight left in me."

"Then I guess I'll just have to summon up enough for both of us."

Jo saw that he intended to kiss her and she started to turn away, but something made her stay. With infinite tenderness he pressed his lips to hers. It was all she could do not to put her arms around him. Gently he touched the corners of her mouth with his tongue, asking but not demanding entry.

With a sigh of mingled joy and pain, she opened her mouth to let him deepen the kiss. She couldn't deny herself this last moment with the first man she had ever truly loved. She felt her heart breaking anew at the poignancy of his kiss, the plea for her trust. But she'd never been someone who gave her trust lightly, and when trust was broken, it took a long time to mend.

With supreme effort, Brad released her. "I'll give you a few days before I call," he said.

She had to restrain herself from stepping into his arms again. "I'll get my purse."

He shouldn't have been surprised that she intended to take him back to the city. Her sense of rightness was one of the things he loved about her. "It's not necessary for you to drive me, Jo. I can get back to Denver on my own."

She experienced a crazy mixture of relief and disappointment. Driving him to an airport hotel to wait for his morning plane would have been torture, but she couldn't just turn him out so far away from his home, either. "Are you sure?"

He ran the back of his fingers down her tearstained cheek. "I'm sure."

"I hope things work out for you someday, Brad." Why did she continue to stand there and talk to him? What part of her wasn't already hurting enough?

"They will, Jo." He bent to brush a fleeting kiss across her lips. "After coming this close to happiness again, I have no intention of letting my life return to the way it was." He turned and left, not once looking back.

Jo stayed in the hallway for several minutes before she could summon the energy to return to her apartment. Once inside, she immediately switched off the radio. The emptiness of the place closed in on her, weighing her down until she could hardly breathe. After an hour of wandering aimlessly from one room to the next, she could no longer stand being alone and left. As she went out into the hallway she glanced at Amy's apartment. With all her heart she wished her friend was behind that door. If ever she needed Amy's elegantly clad shoulder to cry on, it was then.

After going outside she aimlessly walked the streets of Boulder until the eastern sky had taken on the purple of false dawn and fatigue forced her to return home. Back in her apartment again, she fell across her bed fully clothed. She drifted into a deep sleep and her dreams took her to the places her mind refused to let her go.

CHAPTER THIRTEEN

FOR THE FIRST TIME since Jo had owned the shop, she was late opening the next morning. In her exhaustion from the miles she'd walked, she'd slept through the alarm, not waking until she received a phone call from a worried Florence.

When she arrived at the shop fifteen minutes later, Florence was there waiting for her. "You look terrible," she said.

"I decided I'd better forsake a shower and makeup to get here and open the shop before someone turned in a missing person's report on me. Now you've had a chance to see me as I really am. Frightening, isn't it?" Her attempt at levity fell flat.

As soon as Florence had looked across the street that morning and seen that Yogurt, Etc. wasn't open an hour after it should have been, she had become concerned about Jo. Not only was it the first time Jo had been late to work since she'd opened the shop, it was the first time her smile hadn't been genuine. "Why don't we hang a sign in the window saying you've gone fishing for the day? Then we could go over to my place and bake a batch of chocolate-chip cookies and eat every last one of them by ourselves."

Florence's loving concern was more than Jo could take. She bit her lower lip to keep it from trembling. "Don't be nice to me, Florence," she whispered, leaning her head against the glass door that she was trying to open. "I can't handle anyone being nice to me today."

"If you can't handle anyone being nice," she asked gently, "what are you going to do if someone gets mean?"

Tears came to Jo's eyes. "You're right . . . but I can't close the shop. Everyone will ask me why, and I don't want to have to answer them."

"If you think there are going to be questions because you closed the shop, that's nothing to what you're going to hear if you keep it open looking the way you do now." Jo's confusion made Florence decide to take things into her own hands. She took the keys from Jo and unlocked the door, then hurried inside to find a pencil and something to write on. She found both in the back room. She was retracing her path to the front door when Jo stopped her and asked to read the note. It said, "Gone on much-needed minivacation. Check back tomorrow."

"I just wanted to make sure you hadn't given me a dramatic disease," Jo said, a hint of a smile in her eyes.

Florence made a face. "That's the last thing you need—trouble with the health department." She taped the notice to the front door. "Now, does anything need to be done around here before we take off?"

Jo thought a moment before shaking her head.

"Well, then, let's get out of here."

"Where are we going?"

"My place. Since I couldn't talk you into chocolate-chip cookies, I guess it will have to be breakfast. Once we get some food and a few cups of coffee down you, you'll feel like a new woman."

"I can't go over there, Florence."

Florence's look of surprise quickly changed to one of understanding. *Of course Jo couldn't go to the apart-*

ment complex. The two of them wouldn't even make it as far as the elevators before the news that Jo was in the building and not at work would be burning up the telephone lines. "All right—then we'll go to your place."

Jo hesitated. "You don't have to do this. All I need is a good night's sleep and I'll be fine."

Florence put her hand in Jo's. The contrast between them was startling. Florence's fingers were bent and stiff with arthritis; Jo's were straight and supple. Where the older woman's skin was covered with hated brown spots, Jo's was clear and smooth. But hours of conversation had long ago shown them that the differences between them didn't matter as much as their affinities. Who they were inside surmounted the barriers of age and time and allowed them to be friends.

And Jo desperately needed a friend.

"I'll just lock up and we'll be on our way," Florence said. "You do have eggs, bread and the like at your apartment?"

"I even have bacon—somewhere."

"Somewhere?"

"I know I bought a package a couple of weeks ago... and I know I haven't eaten any since then...so it's got to be somewhere."

Florence rattled the door to make sure it was securely locked and turned to Jo. "Well, today's the day that bacon's either going to be eaten or thrown away. Now let's get out of here before someone shows up."

JO PUSHED HER EMPTY PLATE away from her and took another sip of her third cup of the extra-strong coffee Florence had made. "You were right, Florence. A hot meal and some coffee has made a new woman of me."

"Now that you're fed, would you like me to leave so you can add sleep to that list?"

The last thing Jo wanted was to be alone. To be alone would mean reliving the day she'd just spent with Brad. "You don't have to rush off. If I go to sleep now, I won't be able to sleep tonight."

Florence sat down across the table from Jo. "Then perhaps you'd like to talk about what's put you into this agitated state."

She would be insulting Florence's intelligence if she tried to pretend nothing had happened. Besides, the news that she had stopped seeing Brad was bound to come out eventually. But she wasn't sure she could talk about what had happened between them so soon. The memory was too fresh.

Seeing the struggle Jo was going through, Florence gently backed away from her inquiry. "I discovered something interesting the other day," she said conversationally. "It seems Mabel didn't die the wealthy matron we'd all assumed she was."

The statement managed to penetrate Jo's depression. "What do you mean?"

Florence jumped on Jo's spark of interest. "It's a convoluted story, so you'll have to bear with me. I was with Howard the other evening when he was working on the checkbook for the Gray Panthers. He made a comment about being worried that they might not be able to meet their commitments this month, which confused me because of something he'd told me last month about Mabel and the money she'd left to the organization. I was under the impression that since the national board had decided to give our local branch all the money Mabel had left to them, we would be financially set for a long time to come."

"Are you saying national didn't keep back any of Mabel's money?"

"They sent every last dime—which came to a little less than three hundred dollars—to our Boulder chapter."

"Three hundred dollars?" The implication was staggering. What had happened to the small fortune James had left to Mabel when he died? And then there had been the money from the sale of the house, and the beautiful antique furniture Florence had said was sold at auction. "There must have been a whopping mistake somewhere along the line. I could believe her estate was worth three hundred *thousand* a lot more easily than I could three hundred."

"Howard did some investigating as soon as he received the check. He called the attorney who was in charge of probating Mabel's estate, and although there wasn't much the attorney could tell Howard beyond the bare facts, he did confirm that the check we received was in the right amount."

The more Jo thought about what Florence had told her, the more dumbfounded she became. "What could she have done with all that money?"

"I've been racking my brain trying to come up with an answer ever since Howard told me, but so far I've drawn a blank. Mabel lived every bit as frugally as the rest of us did. And I was as close to her as she would let anyone be, so I know she wasn't sneaking off to Las Vegas every once in a while to kick up her heels."

Jo leaned back in her chair and rubbed her hand across her forehead. "This doesn't make any sense." Somewhere in her mind there was something floating around that seemed to have a bearing on what Florence had just told her, but the harder she tried to snag it, the more elusive it became. It was something Brad had said. . . .

"Howard and I even discussed the possibility that she might have used the money to hire private detectives to look for Brad."

"You don't really believe that, do you? She always gave me the impression she never wanted to see him again."

"You have to remember you didn't meet Mabel until Brad had already been gone quite a while. For the first few years, she acted as though she expected him to come back any day."

Jo considered Florence's answer. "Then I guess private detectives could be a possibility. I've never checked their prices but I would imagine a full-scale search for someone could be expensive."

"But expensive enough to wipe out everything James had left her? Plus the house and furniture?"

"Maybe he didn't leave as much as you thought he did," Jo suggested.

"I know exactly how much he left because I went with Mabel every time she had to go to the lawyer's office to sign papers. Any private detective she might have hired would have to have been a first-class hustler to take what James left her on top of what she made when she sold her house and furniture."

"When did she sell the house?"

"She put it on the market about six months after Brad left the final time."

Jo frowned. What Florence was saying made no sense at all if Mabel really had expected Brad to return. Jo would never forget the look of loss she'd seen on Brad's face when he realized someone else was living in the house that his grandfather had built. Mabel wouldn't have sold a part of his heritage if she truly believed he would be returning. Unless... She sat upright. "Did Mabel get sick around that time?"

"She was healthy as a horse until the day she died. Why do you ask?"

Jo leaned against the back of her chair. "I just thought there might have been a chance she was concerned about upcoming hospital bills. What about when James died?"

"Just funeral expenses."

Jo got up and poured both of them another cup of coffee, hoping activity would help her remember whatever it was Brad had told her that kept nagging at her. She handed Florence's full cup to her and started clearing the table. While she loaded the dishwasher she tried running through the alphabet, seeking a trigger word. When that didn't work, she thought of all the places she and Brad had visited the few times they'd been together. The mental return to those happy times was a terrible mistake. A flood of poignant memories returned to drown her before she was able to clear her mind again.

"Howard is going to check with a Realtor friend of his to find out how much Florence sold the house for, so we'll have some idea of how much money is missing," Florence said, coming into the kitchen carrying the butter and orange juice Jo had left on the table.

Surreptitiously, Jo wiped away the tears that had formed when she thought of Brad. She sought respite in a safer subject. "Let's talk about you and Howard." Instead of the conversational reply Jo expected, there was only an eloquent silence. She glanced over at the refrigerator just as Florence shut the door and was taken aback by the look she saw on her friend's face. It was a mixture of happiness and sad resignation.

"We foolishly started something we shouldn't have and now there's no way for us to go back to just being friends," she said, telling Jo something she had told no one else. "And no way that we can continue the way we are."

It took several seconds for Jo to absorb Florence's statement. When the implication became clear, her jaw dropped, "You mean you and Howard..."

A flush instantly colored the older woman's cheeks. Too embarrassed to look at her friend, she stared at the counter as she nodded her answer.

"Florence, I think that's wonderful," Jo cried. "Howard is a fantastic man, warm and giving—and he has a terrific sense of humor. Not to mention he's good-looking. What more could you want?"

"Marriage."

Jo was left temporarily speechless by her answer. "He won't marry you?"

"He can't."

She leaned against the sink and folded her arms across her chest. "But I thought Howard's wife died."

"She did, almost ten years ago. But not until after a long illness had cost them everything they had. Howard just finished paying the last of the doctor bills a year ago."

"Then I don't understand."

"It's really very simple," she said, unable to keep the bitterness from her voice. "If we get married I'll lose my pension money, and Howard doesn't make enough for both of us to live on."

"Then don't get married. Live together."

A slow sad smile came over Florence's face. "It's so easy for you young people. You can't imagine how pervasive the strictures Howard and I were raised under still are and how impossible it is for us to escape them. Even if we could go against our upbringing, we still have to think about our children and grandchildren.''

''But they're a part of my generation. I'll bet if you asked them they would say the same thing I just did.''

''They may be a part of your generation, Jo, and I'm sure they wouldn't bat an eye at one of their friend's parents entering into a common-law marriage, but they'd draw the line when it came to their own parent or grandparent.''

''All right—so they might be a little upset in the beginning. I'm sure they'd come around eventually. Even if they didn't, what could they do to you?''

''They could refuse to come and see us or let our grandchildren visit.'' She shrugged helplessly. ''Even though I don't see my children very often, it would kill me to know I had done something that cut them off from me. And I know Howard feels the same way.''

Jo felt a rage building in her. She knew damn well that if one of Florence or Howard's children were in a similiar position, they would do whatever they pleased with the sure knowledge that neither of their parents would dream of cutting them off. ''I can't believe your children are so straitlaced they would want you to spend the rest of your life alone just because you and Howard didn't have a little piece of paper that said you were married.''

Because she needed something to do, Florence took the dishcloth from the counter and began wiping down the stove. Her back was to Jo when she said, ''They can't see any reason for us to get married. As far as they're concerned, Howard and I can be 'friends' apart as well as together. And as for any intimacy between us, well, that's not something we 'nice' old people engage in, so it's not considered a viable reason for marriage.''

"What do they think happens when you reach sixty—that you turn asexual?" Jo looked down at the bowl she still held. She put it in the dishwasher to get it out of her hands before she threw it at something. "So what are you going to do?"

"All we know is that we can't go on the way we are. So far, we've managed to keep our affair hidden from everyone at the complex, but that can't last much longer. All anyone has to do is see me going into Howard's apartment some night and then catch me coming out the next morning. One thing we both agree on is that we don't want our affair to become the subject of gossip. What we have is too special to let it be tarnished that way."

"And so you're just going to give in to all those small-minded people and stop seeing each other?"

Florence turned to face Jo. There were tears in her eyes. "Please try to understand. This isn't something either of us wants. Surely you know that if there were any way for us to change things, we would. But there isn't."

Jo took Florence in her arms. Her heart felt as if it were breaking anew as she held her friend, silently raging that she could offer comfort but no solutions. Finally, it was Florence who broke the embrace, stepping away to dab at her eyes. "I believe I came here to cheer you up, not the other way around." She tugged on Jo's hand, urging her out of the kitchen. "Let's go sit down, and then why don't you tell me what's happened between you and Brad that's made you think the sun will never shine again?"

"How did you know?"

Florence smiled. "What else could have put that look in your eyes?"

Jo poured their cold coffee down the drain and got them both a fresh cup before they went into the living room. At Florence's gentle insistence, she spent the next half hour telling her how, against her own better judgment, she had fallen in love with Brad. "So you see," she said, bringing her story to an end, "I've wound up right in the middle of an old-fashioned triangle. Me and Brad and Karen—don't we make a lovely threesome?"

Florence waited several seconds before commenting. "Jo, you didn't expect Brad to stop remembering Karen the minute he fell in love with you, did you?" she asked, a gentle coaxing in her voice.

"Maybe that's the problem—I didn't expect anything. I never planned to fall in love with Brad. It just kind of happened." She ran her hand through her hair and rested her head against the back of the couch. "He's been carrying a torch for Karen for eight years. I know it was stupid of me to think he could drop it just because I came on the scene," she added softly.

"Not stupid—"

"But how can I fight a ghost? How could I possibly compete?"

"How hard has Brad tried to find Karen?"

Jo was so lost in her own thoughts she didn't hear Florence's question. "I'd give anything to know where Karen is. At least that way there could be an ending," she mused aloud. She thought about what she'd just said. Was finding Karen really what she wanted? What would she do if it were indeed possible to give Brad the opportunity to choose? And how would she feel if he didn't choose her?

"Jo?"

"Huh?"

"I repeat, how hard has Brad tried to find Karen?"

"I'm sorry—I was somewhere else." She propped her feet up on the coffee table. "He spent a year looking for her himself and then he hired detectives. He told me he didn't give up the search until a couple of years ago, when the fourth detective he'd hired told him he was throwing his money away."

"Maybe it's time someone looked again," Florence said, leaving no doubt as to whom she thought that someone should be.

"You can't possibly mean me."

"You found Brad, didn't you?"

"By blind luck."

"I don't believe that for a minute. Besides, what have you got to lose? More to the point, look what you stand to gain."

"I wouldn't know where to begin." But already her mind was working. She had yet to take Alex Reid up on his offer of dinner. Not only was Alex a gold mine of ideas; he owed her a favor for telling Tony Erickson she'd had a crush on him. Then there was Carl Vizenor. Although Carl had never met Karen, Jo knew he had talked to Brad about her dozens of times. Jo felt a sense of excitement growing.

"You begin at the beginning, of course. For instance, what exactly do you know about Karen's disappearance?"

Jo thought back to what Brad had told her. She scanned the hours they had spent in conversation, sorting through them for information as if she were working a mental editing machine. This time she didn't feel pain at the memories, only promise.

And then there it was—the elusive puzzle piece she'd been searching for earlier. Jo almost groaned aloud. Some sleuth she was going to make. How could she have forgotten the one thing that had made the breach between Brad and Mabel unbridgeable? After the detective had told Brad that Mabel had hired the man who'd been seen talking to Karen, Brad had become convinced of his mother's involvement in Karen's disappearance. He'd never been able to forgive her.

"When did you say Mabel sold her house?" Jo asked quietly, her voice a complete contrast to the tumultuous way she felt inside. She couldn't believe she'd stumbled onto the answer to Mabel's missing money so easily.

"She put it on the market about six months after Brad left." Her eyes narrowed speculatively. "Why?"

"I'm not sure yet. Do you happen to remember where Mabel did her banking?"

"The Merchant's Bank of Eastern Colorado."

"Which branch?"

"Downtown."

"You wouldn't happen to know anyone who works there, would you? Preferably someone who would be willing to do you a favor?"

"I might—but first I want you to tell me what's going on in that clever mind of yours."

Although she was reluctant to give voice to ideas so newly formed and unsubstantiated, Jo saw the steely glint of determination in Florence's eyes and knew she'd met her match. "Mabel hired someone to investigate Karen. Or at least I'm assuming he investigated her before Mabel had him make contact with Karen. Brad found out about the man his mother hired and that's why he's blamed her for Karen's disappearance all these years. Now that I know as much as I do, I have to agree with Brad; it does seem a logical connection. Especially after he learned the man Mabel had hired was seen at the apartment the day before Karen disappeared."

Jo leaned forward, resting her elbows on her knees and clasping her hands together to keep from gesturing excitedly as she spoke. "Because all I've ever heard about Karen is what a wonderful person she was, I've just assumed—as I'm sure everyone else has—that when she left Brad, it was for some altruistic reason." Jo hesitated, almost fearful of speaking her next thoughts aloud. After all, what she was about to say had been unthinkable blasphemy only an hour ago. She took a deep breath. "What if Karen's real reason for leaving Brad was Mabel's money?"

CHAPTER FOURTEEN

FLORENCE STARED at Jo for long seconds, too stunned to speak. "I hate to say this, but what you're suggesting makes perfect sense."

"But making sense is a long way from proving anything," Jo said.

"What did you want me to ask my friend at the bank?"

"If they can find out what Mabel did with the money from the sale of her house."

"I'm not sure I understand what you're getting at."

"We know Mabel didn't keep the money, or at least we know she didn't have it when she died. Since the check for the house was undoubtedly made out to her, I'm assuming she would deposit it into her account rather than sign it over to someone. If she did deposit the check—"

"Now I'm following you," Florence said. "You want me to see if I can find out what happened to the money in Mabel's checking account."

"Do you think your friend will cooperate?"

"We'll never know until I ask." She stood up and reached for her purse. "If you need me, I'll be at my apartment for the next few hours."

"You're not going to the bank?" Jo asked, unable to keep the disappointment from her voice.

"First I'm going to make a batch of chocolate-chip cookies. You may be able to resist them, but Buster Hollister never could."

"Your friend is Buster Hollister—the *president* of the Merchant's Bank of Eastern Colorado?"

There was a twinkle in Florence's eyes when she answered. "Surely you know by now, Jo, that if you want something done right, you should always go to the top."

Jo jumped up and grabbed her keys from the table. "I'll drive you back to your apartment. I don't want you wasting one minute walking around town that you could be home baking."

AFTER JO DROPPED Florence off at her apartment, she returned home to call Alex Reid at his office.

"If I remember correctly," she said as soon as he came on the line, "the last time we saw each other you promised me a home-cooked meal as soon as I was going to be in Denver for the day."

"This has to be Josie Williams" he said with a chuckle. "There isn't another person I know who can see someone once after eleven years and then expect to be instantly remembered by the sound of her voice."

"I was right, wasn't I?" she demanded, deciding it was useless to fight him about the "Josie" anymore.

"You were right, and I'm suspicious. To what do I owe the honor of your upcoming presence?"

Jo vacillated between telling him the complete truth or a slightly modified version. "I need your help with something."

"Still looking for your Brad Tyler?"

"No...I found him." Such a long silence followed that Jo began to wonder if they'd been disconnected.

"You did?"

"Why do you sound so surprised?"

"Frankly, I thought you had about as much chance of finding him as—"

"Finding a needle in a haystack?" she finished for him, knowing he'd had an expression far more colorful in mind.

"Something like that."

"But enough of Brad and my incredible sleuthing job. I know you're busy, so I'll get on to the real reason I called. Since your brilliant advice worked so well the first time, it was only natural for me to think of you the minute I needed help again. And since I still haven't met Barbara or your two children, it seemed a perfect opportunity to combine business and pleasure."

Alex laughed. "Still using bulldozer tactics, I see."

"I take it that means yes?"

"How is seven-thirty this coming Saturday?"

"What can I bring?"

"Wine—lots of it. I have a feeling I'm going to need it. Now, you were right, I am busy. So unless you have something useful to add to what you've already told me, I'm going to hang up on you and get back to work."

"Alex?"

"Yes?"

"I think it would add an air of sincerity to the invitation if you were to tell me where you live."

Alex laughed and gave her detailed directions to his house, even offering to send her a map. She declined the map but wasn't surprised when one appeared in her mailbox two days later.

THE REST OF THE WEEK seemed to drag by, the only highlight being Buster Hollister's reluctant agreement to "see what he could do" about looking into Mabel's accounts. By the time Friday arrived and they still hadn't heard anything, it was all Jo could do to keep from asking Florence to call him. But she controlled the impulse when she considered the possible consequences of pushing a man who'd rather not be doing the favor in the first place.

Three hours before it was time to close the shop for the day, she saw Florence and Howard coming across the street and went over to meet them at the front door. "Did he call?" she asked, letting the door swing shut behind them.

"Yes...but you're not going to like what he said."

Jo felt her heart sink. "He's decided he won't help us."

Florence was surprised at the degree of dejection in Jo's voice. She'd known Jo was counting on the information Buster would get for them, but she'd had no idea how much. "Of course he's still going to help us. He just wanted me to know that this has been an especially hectic week at the bank and he hasn't been able to do anything yet."

Jo put her hand on her chest. "You scared me," she said. "I thought for sure—"

"Stop borrowing trouble," Florence scolded. "If Buster doesn't come through, we'll simply have to find another way to get the information. One way or another, we're going to learn what Mabel did with all that money. Now, when is it you're going to have dinner with that policeman friend of yours?"

"Tomorrow night."

"Why don't you let us close the shop for you?" Howard offered. "That way you could get an earlier start."

"I'll have plenty of time. Dinner isn't until..." She saw the flash of disappointment in his eyes and felt like a spoiled child returning a gift. "Are you sure you didn't have anything else planned?"

"Nothing we couldn't get out of," Florence said.

"Then I would really appreciate it if you closed for me. But only if you let me take you out to dinner on Sunday."

"I have a better idea," Florence announced. "Why don't we go on a picnic Monday? We could even take a drive up to Central City. I understand the crowds aren't too bad on weekdays."

Howard gave her a look that let her know he thought she'd been out in the sun too long. "I thought you hated tourist places."

"I don't think she's planning for us to stay very long," Jo said.

Howard looked from Jo to Florence. "Why do I have the feeling I'm missing out on something?" he asked.

"I'll fill you in on everything tonight," Florence told him. "Now let's get down to why I really came over here this afternoon. I want to try some of that new flavor you made up yesterday, Jo—'berrylicious,' I think Ernie called it. He's been telling everyone that it's something extra special and that we should all give it a try."

Howard shuddered. "You go ahead. I'm going to pass on this one."

Jo laughed. "Where's your sense of adventure?"

He gave her a long-suffering look. "I'm saving it for our trip to Central City."

IT WAS SATURDAY, fifteen minutes before Howard and Florence were due to arrive to manage the shop for the rest of the day. Jo was taking advantage of a lull in business to sweep and refill bins and wipe down the counters so that everything would be ready for them when they walked through the door. She was in the back room putting away the dustpan when she heard the bell announce a customer. "I'll be with you in a minute," she called out.

She grabbed the can of window cleaner and a roll of paper towels before giving the swinging door a push with her hip. "Sorry to keep you—" The rest froze in her throat the instant she saw who was waiting for her.

"I just happened to be in the neighborhood," Brad said. "So I thought I'd drop in for a visit."

He was wearing a pair of pleated tan slacks and a striped blue-and-tan sports shirt that was open at the collar. His sleeves were casually rolled back, showing muscular, deeply tanned arms. Jo swallowed. She thought of the times she had been held by those arms and how wonderful it had felt. "What are you doing here?" she blurted out.

"Didn't buy my being in the neighborhood?"

"What? Oh . . . I guess you already gave an answer of sorts, didn't you?"

"Should I have called first?"

"I thought we'd decided not to see—"

"That's not quite the way it was, Jo. You were the one who decided we wouldn't see each other anymore. If you recall, I never agreed."

"But nothing's changed."

"Meaning, I suppose, that you're just as stubborn about listening to reason now as you were the other night?"

"How I feel has nothing to do with stubbornness," she said, the set of her jaw giving away not only her stubbornness but her anger.

He came across the room to stand in front of her. The need to touch her was almost overpowering as he stood there looking deeply into her eyes. But he drew no closer than an arm's length and his hands stayed at his sides. "I tried to get here sooner—I was planning to spend the day with you, helping you around the shop—but things didn't work out the way I'd hoped."

Jo struggled to catch her breath. She was confused both by his showing up at all and by his reason for being there. "I don't understand. What made you think I needed help in the shop today?"

"Helping you wasn't the point, Jo," he said. "Being with you was. I figured this was the one place you couldn't run away from me." He shoved his hands in his pockets. "You're the best thing that's happened to me in eight years and I'm not about to let you go without a fight."

How could words have such power to hurt? She didn't want to be the best thing that had happened to him in eight years. She wanted to be the best thing that had ever happened to him. Why couldn't he understand that? But she already knew the answer. It was because he still thought of Karen as the one all-consuming passion of his life. "If I believed you had any real idea of what you just said to me, I'd be hurt. But I guess, in your own way, you were trying to tell me that you love me, so it seems a little silly for me to get upset."

But she was hurt and she was upset. Brad could see it in her eyes and in the way she held her mouth. How could she have misinterpreted . . . And then he realized what he had said and felt like kicking himself. He could hardly keep from seizing her in his arms and trying to tell her with actions what he had so miserably failed to do with words. "You were right about one thing. I was telling you that I love you. As for the rest, I feel as if I've taken two steps backward for the one I took forward by coming here today. But it doesn't matter because I intend to spend the rest of the night convincing you—''

"You can't, Brad. I'm not going to be here. I have…I have a date.'' She looked up and saw Florence and Howard heading across the street. "As a matter of fact, I'm going to be leaving in a few minutes.'' She was torn between wanting to stay with him and needing desperately to get away.

"I see,'' he said softly. "What you're trying to tell me is that I should call before I come to see you from now on.'' He felt her panic to get away from him and it made him feel physically sick. He loved her and wanted to return some of the joy she had given him, but all he seemed to do was hurt her. Still, he couldn't let her go. "Perhaps we could see each other later. After you come home from your date.''

"I don't think so. I won't be getting home until late. Very late.''

"Jo…'' Unable to keep from touching her any longer, he reached for her hand. "Please don't do this. Give me a chance—'' Behind him, the bell over the door suddenly jangled as Florence and Howard walked in.

Jo slipped her hand from Brad's. "I was wondering where you two were,'' she said, her attempt at cheerfulness putting an awkwardly false note in her voice. "I was beginning to think you'd changed your minds about coming.''

Even though Florence and Howard were actually early, the instant Florence saw Brad, she understood Jo's peculiar welcome. "Not a chance,'' she said brightly. And then, as if she'd noticed who was standing beside Jo, she added, "Brad, how nice to see you. What are you doing in town?''

"Hello, Florence," he greeted her, and then nodded to Howard. "It's good to see you again, Howard."

"If you have business with Jo, we could come back later," Howard offered.

"No, don't go," Jo said too quickly. "Brad was just leaving."

Brad turned to Jo. A look of confusion was replaced by one of dawning understanding. She was too anxious to get rid of him. He knew it wasn't because she hated him, and she sure as hell wasn't neutral where he was concerned. That left one answer.

Even though he always seemed to be saying the wrong things, and even though he hadn't yet found the way to convince her that he loved her, she had fallen in love with him. Suddenly it didn't matter that she had a date with someone else. He knew she would be thinking of him that night as surely as he would be thinking of her—as he was always thinking of her.

"As I recall," he said, casually folding his arms across his chest, "you were the one who was leaving. I don't have a thing to do until my plane leaves, and that's not for another nine hours. As a matter of fact, if Florence and Howard don't mind, I think I'll stay here and visit with them while they work. And then, if they don't have any other plans, maybe they'll agree to go out to dinner with me later." He gave Jo a pointed look. "Now, shouldn't you be on your way? After all, you don't want to be late. I know I sure hate to be kept waiting when I'm picking someone up."

She glanced at the clock. There was plenty of time to shower and get ready. And the drive to Alex's house wouldn't take more than forty-five minutes. But she'd already made such a big deal out of leaving that there wasn't a logical reason for her to stay. She turned to

Florence. "You know where everything is and who to call if something breaks down?"

Florence's heart went out to Jo. The turmoil she was suffering because of Brad was every bit as obvious as the love she was feeling for him. And it was such insanity that they weren't together. Anyone who cared to look could see that the two of them were meant for each other.

A cold coil of fear wrapped itself around Florence's spine. What if Jo did manage to find Karen? Brad had spent a third of his life loving that woman. When the moment came, would he be able to cast all those years aside for the few weeks he had known Jo? Forcefully, she pushed the thought out of her mind. "We know who to call and we know where everything is. Now get out of here and have a good time."

Jo untied her apron. She was consciously trying to make her movements appear casual. "I think you should get Howard to at least taste the berrylicious," she said, determined to hide her nervousness behind the ordinary. "It's been my best seller all week."

Howard laughed. "All right, all right. If it will make you happy, I'll give it a try."

She could delay her leaving no longer without causing the others to wonder about what she was doing. She looked from Howard to Florence. "I'll see you tomorrow. Thanks again for minding the shop."

Brad took Jo's keys off the counter and held them out to her. "Have a good time," he said.

Have a good time, she inwardly railed. *Have a good time.* As far as he knew she really was going out with another man and here he was, telling her to have a good time. The look she gave him was filled with fury. "I have every intention of having a wonderful time," she said, snatching her keys from his outstretched hand.

Brad was nowhere near as detached as he tried to make her believe he was. It took every ounce of his willpower to watch her walk out the door and not go after her. He was consumed by a physical ache to hold her in his arms, to feel her arms around him. He wanted to make love to her more than he had ever wanted to make love to any woman. It was a deeper, more complete desire than he had ever felt before. His nights, his days were filled with his need. But he was playing for higher stakes. He wanted more of Jo than temporary gratification. He wanted her beside him for the rest of his life. In the meantime, if it took him months of cold showers to get her there, so be it. They had a lifetime of making love ahead of them.

THE SMELL OF BURNING CHARCOAL wafted past Jo as she headed up the sidewalk to the Reids' front door. There was a baseball bat and a tricycle in the front yard and children's drawings taped on the bedroom windows of the brick ranch-style house. Jo had barely reached the porch when the door opened and a tall woman with shoulder-length auburn hair greeted her with a broad smile. She was elegantly thin everywhere but around her middle, where her waistline indicated she was well into what Jo realized must be her third pregnancy.

"You couldn't be anyone but Josie Williams," she said, holding out her hand. "I'm astonished. For once Alex has managed to describe someone the way they really look." She laughed. "And as you've undoubtedly guessed by now, I'm Barbara Reid."

Jo breathed a private sigh of resignation as she took Barbara's hand. Like it or not, she would forever be Josie to Alex and, therefore, to Alex's family. "I hope you don't mind that I invited myself for dinner," she said, giving Barbara the wine she had purchased on her way.

"I've been after Alex to call you for weeks. Your family and Alex's childhood are mentioned in one breath around here. It's long past time the rest of us met one of the famous Williams clan."

Jo laughed. "You do realize, don't you, that with that kind of billing I'm sure to wind up doing something really dumb before the night's over."

Despite her misgivings, Jo didn't do anything to tarnish the sterling reputation of the Williams family. The evening turned out to be even more pleasant than she'd anticipated. She discovered that Alex had the intelligence and good fortune to marry someone who was perfect for him. They fit each other's personalities like the seasons, each distinctly different, yet gently blending into the other. Barbara was one of those rare people who had the ability to skip the awkward beginning stages of friendship and make her guests feel completely at ease in her home.

After dinner, Barbara shepherded the loudly protesting children into another part of the house, leaving Alex and Jo alone in the den.

"I think it's a rotten shame you and Mike don't see each other anymore," Jo said, sitting down in a maroon wing-backed chair. "Barbara and Kathy would really like each other. And your kids are almost the same age..."

"Are you through lecturing me about this?" Alex asked, a teasing smile dancing in his eyes as he took the chair opposite hers.

"I suppose you're going to tell me that you and Mike have already made plans to get together."

"Next month. Barbara and I are going to leave the kids at her mom's and then we're going to California to spend a week with Kathy and Mike in San Francisco. Then, this winter, they're coming out here to stay with us for a week of skiing."

"I don't believe this," Jo said, rolling her eyes. "I've been trying to get Mike to come out here for years and every time I suggest it, he has some harebrained excuse why he can't come. Now all you have to do is ask him and he's out here in a flash."

"Mike said you might get a little testy when you heard he was finally coming back to Colorado for a visit."

Jo looked at him through narrowed eyes. "There is a way to pacify me . . ."

"Here it comes." Alex laughed as he leaned back in his chair. "If you're half as tenacious as you were that summer you had a crush on me, I don't see any way I'm going to get out of this, so I guess you might as well lay it on me."

"What makes you think I ever had a crush on you?" she demanded. She was surprised both by his knowing something she had never told anyone and by realizing that even thirteen years after the fact, she still couldn't admit how she had once felt about him. It seemed adolescent feelings had followed her into adulthood.

"Your diary—and the weird way you acted that summer."

"My diary. You didn't—"

"You're right, I didn't—but Mike did. He told me."

Despite all the years that had passed and all that had happened in those years, she felt a hot flush of embarrassment at the thought of someone reading her diary. "What a dirty rotten—"

"Not really, Josie," he said gently. "As I recall, you left your diary someplace where Mike found it. He did what any brother would do—he picked it up and read it. At first he thought the whole thing was kind of funny, but then after he thought about it he got protective. That's why he told me. He didn't want me doing anything that might encourage you or accidently hurt you."

Jo met his gaze and knew he was telling her the truth. He hadn't brought the incident up to embarrass her; he had wanted her to know she could trust him with her feelings now as she had been able to then. Obviously, she hadn't succeeded in hiding her nervousness as well as she thought she had. She relaxed visibly, settling more comfortably against the back of the chair, her former hesitancy gone. "There's someone I'd like you to help me find."

"I thought you told me you'd already found Brad Tyler."

Jo took a deep breath. "This is someone new...." She began her story. Fifteen minutes later, she'd finished telling him about Karen without directly mentioning the real reason she wanted her found.

"Let me get this straight," Alex said. "Mabel's missing money makes you think she was behind Karen's disappearance. And because Karen has had this money all along, you believe it's the reason Brad has never been able to find her."

Having her thoughts so skillfully summarized made them sound simplistic. "Doesn't it seem reasonable that even professional detectives might be misled if they thought they were looking for someone who didn't have money?"

"Life-style would make a big difference in the search," he agreed. He became thoughtful. "What exactly is it you want from me, Josie?"

"I need someone to guide me, to keep me from going on too many wild-goose chases in my hunt for Karen."

"Before I do that, I want you to level with me about your interest in these people."

He had her cornered. She didn't want to tell him the real reason she was looking for Karen, because of the big-brother attitude he still maintained toward her. If he knew she was in love with Brad, he would turn protective and insist she was only asking for trouble by trying to find Karen.

He leaned forward in his chair and placed his hand on her knee. "Never mind," he said gently. "The real reason you're involved in this is written all over your face. I just hope you know what you're doing."

She gave him a tentative smile, relieved she didn't have to keep anything from him. "I don't have much choice," she said softly, hoping he would understand. "I can't live my life wondering if I'm just a pretty good substitute for the real thing."

"Are you sure this guy is worth all the trouble?"

"Would I be here if he weren't?"

Alex got up and went over to a desk. He took out a tablet and several pencils and handed them to Jo. "Then let's get started," he said. He began a slow pacing back and forth across the room, his actions a complete contrast to the rapid-fire instructions he tossed out to her.

"First of all," he said, "you need to find the man Mabel hired and question him about the work he did for her."

"Shouldn't I wait to find out what we learn at the bank first?"

"If the detective turns out to be the talkative type, he could be a gold mine of miscellaneous information. Remember, these guys aren't bound by privacy laws the way I am. They can use any means, fair or foul, to get information, just as long as they don't commit a crime in the process. And even that doesn't stop some of them."

"I've got the picture. Then what do I do?"

"You should find out everything you can about Karen—her likes, her dislikes, how she felt about educating her child, whether or not she was a social snob, what her career goals were—anything that will give you a clue to where she might have gone with three hundred thousand dollars in her pocket." He stopped his pacing and looked down at Jo. "I don't suppose there's any way you could get your hands on the reports from the private detectives Brad hired?"

"Not without letting him know what I'm doing."

"What's wrong with that?"

"He'd never understand."

Alex considered her answer. "Is it that he wouldn't understand," he finally said, "or that you want to keep the option open as to whether or not to tell him if you do happen to find Karen?"

It was on the tip of her tongue to deny Alex's allegation when she realized that he was at least partially right. But even more than that, what controlled her decision was the fear of seeing Brad's love die the closer she came to finding Karen. There was no way she could get around it—not only had she decided to play a dangerous game, she'd chosen one where the odds were stacked against her. "Can't we just say that there are lots of reasons I don't want to involve Brad in what I'm doing, and leave it at that?"

"It's going to make the search twice as hard."

"That's all right." She shrugged. "Wasn't it your mother who used to say that nothing worth having ever comes easily?"

Alex groaned at the platitude. "What about Karen's parents?"

"According to Brad, they died in an automobile accident when she was in high school."

"Any other relatives?"

Jo shook her head. "Again according to Brad, her lack of family was one of the reasons she clung to him as tightly as she did."

He threw her a cynical smile. "But obviously not as tightly as he would have liked."

"Do you think I'm right about Mabel offering her the money?"

"I'd bet my badge on it."

"But it doesn't make sense. If she was a fortune hunter, there must have been much better catches than Brad. From what he told me, he and Karen lived hand-to-mouth the whole time they were together."

"Maybe it was simply a matter of Karen taking advantage of an opportunity when it arose." He stopped beside her and looked down at the notes she'd made. "I think you have enough there to get you started. As soon as you've gathered some information on Karen, we'll get together again and see where we stand."

"*We?*" she repeated pointedly. "Does that mean—"

"You know good and well what it means," he grumbled. "Now let's go find out what Barbara's cooked up for dessert."

Jo tore off the sheet of paper she'd been writing on and stuffed it into her pocket. When she stood up, she put her arms around Alex and gave him a kiss on the cheek. "I do believe you're not so bad, after all."

"Does this mean I'm forgiven for telling Tony Erickson you had a crush on him *and* for knowing what was in your diary?"

She laughed. "Not quite—but you're getting close."

CHAPTER FIFTEEN

JO STOOD OUTSIDE Carl Vizenor's candy shop in Central City and thought about the reason she was there. She and Carl had known each other a grand total of one day, yet she was going to ask him to give her intimate details regarding a friend he'd had for a lifetime—and then not tell that friend about their conversation.

She glanced down the street where Florence and Howard had disappeared into a store. The three of them were to meet again in exactly one hour. When they'd decided on the time, Jo had thought it seemed an eternity. Now that she was actually standing in front of Carl's shop, she felt rushed. As she stood there, she reluctantly acknowledged that the longer she hesitated, the harder it was going to be to go inside and talk to him, so she squared her shoulders and stepped through the door.

Carl looked up from behind the counter as she entered. "Jo—" he exclaimed, his face lighting up with happiness at seeing her again. His gaze quickly swept the area directly behind her. When he didn't find the person he'd obviously been seeking, he said, "Where'd you leave Brad?"

She shoved her hands into the back pockets of her jeans as she walked over to him. "As far as I know, he's still in Casper."

"Well, I'm glad you didn't let that keep you from stopping in to see me. As a matter of fact," he said, wiping his hands on a nearby towel, "your timing couldn't have been better. Susan should be getting ready to fix lunch about now. I'll call her and tell her to set a place for one more."

She couldn't let him go on thinking she'd come there for a social visit. "It would probably be better if we made lunch another time, Carl. I've come here to see you today because I have some questions and I don't know where else to look for the answers."

He gave her a quizzical look. "Questions?" He thought a moment. "About Brad?"

"In a way they're about him, but not directly. The person I really want to talk to you about is Karen."

A young boy came up to the cash register carrying a bag of saltwater taffy. "Excuse me a minute," Carl said. He went to doorway that led to the back of the store and called for someone to come out front to wait on customers. A plump gray-haired woman with a dab of chocolate on her chin responded to his call. He quietly spoke to her for several seconds and then returned to Jo. "Why don't we go next door and get a cup of coffee? That way we won't be disturbed while you tell me just what it is you want to know and why you want to know it."

His voice wasn't gruff, but it wasn't exactly friendly, either. Jo knew she was going to have to do some fast talking to get him to cooperate with her. Carl was the one weak link in her attempt to keep Brad from finding out what she was doing. If she couldn't convince him not to tell Brad, everything would fall apart. But she had no real choice about whether or not to confide in him. He was the only person she knew who would give her information about Karen.

Carl took her to a small restaurant that seemed straight out of another time. It had a long counter with stools and four tables that were covered with vinyl red-and-white-checkered tablecloths. The menus had been slipped into plastic pockets and were propped on metal stands between the salt and pepper shakers. They sat down at one of the tables, and Jo looked absently around, her eyes finally settling on the slightly wilted daisy bowing its head over an imprinted ashtray. Carl greeted the young waitress by name.

When their coffee had been poured in thick china cups and the waitress had returned to her station behind the counter, Carl looked directly into Jo's eyes and said, "Now why don't you tell me what this is all about."

Jo had rehearsed what she would say and all the words were still in her mind, but for some reason they wouldn't emerge in the order she had intended. "I've fallen in love with Brad," she blurted out. "And I believe he thinks he loves me...."

"But?"

Jo nervously swept the crystals of sugar that had fallen on the table into a small pile with the tip of her finger. "Karen is standing between us."

"Is that what Brad told you?"

Her eyes opened wide in alarm. "No—he would never say something like that."

"Then what makes you think he's still carrying a torch for Karen?"

So much of what she had to say required Carl to take her on blind trust. "A lot of little things—the way he looks and the way his voice changes when he talks about her, the hurt he still carries around with him." She shrugged. "I'm not imagining this, Carl." Her throat tightened with emotion, making her voice crack. "I wish to God it weren't true," she whispered.

"So what is it you want from me?" Carl asked gently.

She waited a minute to regain her composure. "I want you to tell me anything you can that might help me find Karen."

He took a sip of his coffee. "Let me get this straight. Even though you say you're in love with Brad, you want to find Karen for him?"

"It's the only way I'll ever be sure...."

"You realize the chance you're taking, don't you? There are lots of people who have fallen in love with someone who had another love in their past. But not too many of those people go around trying to resurrect that lost love."

"I have to know—" She couldn't finish.

"That he loves you more than he loved Karen?"

"It goes deeper than that. I don't want him to settle for me because he can't have her."

Carl finished his coffee and went to get them both a refill. After returning the steaming pot to its burner, he again gave his full attention to Jo. "Am I to assume that you're coming to me for this information about Karen because you don't want Brad to know what you're doing?"

"I figured it would be easier that way."

"On you or him?"

"Me," she answered truthfully.

He tasted his coffee before adding another teaspoon of sugar. "Brad and I haven't been close for years, but we've never had secrets from each other."

Jo's heart sank. Finding Karen without Carl's help would be next to impossible.

"I guess there's a first time for everything," he said. "What is it you want me to do?"

Jo caught her breath to stifle a sob of relief. "Just tell me anything you can about Karen that will help me find her."

He considered her request for several minutes. "I have a better idea. I'll let Brad tell you."

"But you said—"

"Susan is an incurable packrat. She has everything that was ever given to her, including letters she received from Santa Claus and the tooth fairy. Among her collection are a few dozen from Brad."

"Brad wrote to you about Karen?" She had been counting on old memories to guide her, never daring to hope for anything as concrete as Brad's own words.

"At least half of every letter he ever sent us was about her. That's why it was such a shock when he showed up here without her. But then, I guess we should have been suspicious that something was wrong when he disappeared for all those years without so much as a postcard." He stood up and spoke to the woman behind the counter. "Add the coffees to my bill, would you, Agnes?"

She looked up and smiled. "Bring me some fudge this afternoon and we'll call it even."

Jo followed Carl back to his shop, where he called Susan to ask her to dig out Brad's letters. When he hung up he turned to Jo. "She's right in the middle of baking bread and says it's going to take her about an hour before she can get up to the attic to sort through the boxes. She wanted me to tell you that she'd welcome your company while she's looking, if you don't have anything else planned for today."

"Tell her I would have loved to spend the afternoon with her but I came with friends and they're expecting me to meet them in ten minutes. Do you think she would mind mailing the letters to me if I promise to return them as soon as I can make copies?"

Carl smiled. "She'd probably agree to that...if instead of mailing them, you brought them back yourself and stayed for dinner."

Jo held out her hand. "I can't tell you how much this means to me, Carl."

He ignored her hand and gave her a warm hug instead. "I sure hope things turn out the way you want them to, Jo."

"Thanks," she said, returning his hug. "I do, too."

WHEN SHE ARRIVED at work the next morning, she found Brad standing outside the shop waiting for her. She parked her car in its regular spot near the road, and as she walked across the parking lot she could feel the strength of his gaze boring into her.

"How was your date?" he asked when she was close enough to hear.

Jo felt her throat grow dry as she approached. As always, the sight of Brad did strange and wondrous things to her. He was wearing a charcoal-gray suit that made the intense blue of his eyes seem transparent, giving them almost impossible depth. Seeing him took her breath away. Fleetingly she thought of how different they were physically and wondered what their children would look like—if they ever had any. The musing thought brought with it a desperate yearning and then a cold fear. What would she do, where would she go, if Karen turned out to be everything Brad remembered?

She offered him a tentative smile. "I had a marvelous time." When she saw the impact her answer had, she knew she couldn't let him go on thinking she'd gone out with someone else. In this, at least, she had to be honest. "But it wasn't a date. I spent the evening with an old friend and his family."

"I see," he said. And after several seconds, "I'm glad you decided to tell me the truth."

"Why?"

"Because it means I'm wearing you down. One of these days it has to occur to you that I wouldn't be coming here at all times of the day and night if I didn't really love you." He gave her a crooked smile. "Or unless I was a little crazy." He caught her chin and brushed a quick kiss across her lips. "And I'm sure as hell not crazy."

She was surprised he could come so close and not notice how thunderously her heart was beating. She ran her tongue over her lips and tasted a trace of the kiss he'd given her. A bolt of pure excitement shot through her. "I think the jury is still in deliberation on whether you're crazy or not. How long have you been standing out here waiting for me?"

He shrugged. "An hour or so. I haven't been paying attention."

"Why didn't you come to my apartment?"

"I wasn't sure of my welcome."

She stared down at the key in her hand. 'You don't have to worry about that anymore," she said. After her return from Central City, she had spent the better part of the night thinking about Brad and Karen and herself and had reached an unexpected conclusion. For her own peace of mind she had to find Karen, but until that day arrived she would selfishly gather and cherish whatever time she might have with Brad. She'd finally acknowl-

edged that staying away from him wouldn't shelter her
from pain if, in the end, he chose to go with Karen. And
this allowed her the freedom to give him her love, as
completely and for as long as she could.

Brad took her by the shoulders and turned her to face
him. "Are you saying what I think you're saying? You
aren't going to put up a fight about seeing me from now
on?"

She shook her head.

"What happened that made you change your mind?"

"Let's just say I decided to take our relationship one
day at a time."

He watched her for several seconds and sensed there
was something she wasn't telling him. It tore at him to see
the fear in her eyes, but he knew, after what they had
been through, that mere words would never convince her
of how he felt. He bent to kiss her. Tenderly he poured
all his feeling into the way his lips touched the corners of
her mouth, the bridge of her nose, her temple and then
her chin. His breath skimmed and warmed the sensitive
curve of her ear; his tongue pressed against her pulse as
she moved her head to one side.

She felt a warmth spread through her and ached to
have him kiss her deeply, with a passion to match the one
growing inside her. "Brad," she pleaded, not knowing
whether she had spoken his name aloud or only in her
mind.

A car pulled into the parking lot behind them, bringing time and place abruptly back into sharp focus. "Give
me your key," Brad said, stepping in front of her so that
she was sheltered from the people in the car.

She put the sliver of metal into his hand and watched
him reach around her to unlock the shop door. When
they were inside, he locked the door again, took her hand

and led her into the back room. As soon as they were beyond the possibility of prying eyes, he reached for her. "It may be impossible for me to do what I would really like to do with you right now," he said, his voice a verbal caress, "but I'll be damned if I'm going to let anyone or anything stop me from kissing you."

"We have an hour before anyone will notice I haven't opened the shop," she said, a sudden shyness coming over her.

"My God, Jo, don't tempt me. I've never been known to be a stickler for doing things in the conventional time and place—" he ran his finger along the side of her face to her neck and down the strap of her sundress "—but the first time I make love to you, it isn't going to be under the threat of a phone ringing or someone coming to the door and interrupting us." His finger slid along the bodice of her dress, stroking the gentle swell of her breast, creating a friction that was both exciting and demanding. "I intend to take hours learning your body... until it's as familiar to me as my own." He touched his lips to the base of her throat. "I want to know the feel of your breasts..." he murmured, "in my hands..." Slowly he moved lower. "With my tongue..." He used his chin to nudge down the top of her sundress until yet more of her breast was exposed to him. "And, ever so gently, against my teeth."

Jo ran her fingers through his hair, lacing them together at the back of his neck, bringing him closer as a liquid fire raced through her. She felt him opening the small pearl buttons on the front of her dress and mentally urged him to hurry. When only the flimsy lace of her bra separated her aching flesh from his touch, she gently urged his head down and pressed herself to him. The heat and moisture from his mouth reached her through the fabric and she felt a tightening response in her breasts. The ache, the longing, built in her until his touch created a pleasure so intense it bordered on pain.

Her head fell back and a soft cry came from her. Brad cradled her head in his hand and absorbed her cry as he covered her mouth with his own. The contact was electric as he tasted the sweetness she offered, his tongue petting and stroking hers until she matched the rhythm and motions of his lovemaking.

He was kissing her as he had dreamed of kissing her since the night they'd gone out to dinner. Except that in his dreams, he hadn't stopped with kissing. He had held her and then slowly undressed her, savoring each moment of discovery, lingering at each revelation. He had gloried in her uninhibited response as he intimately touched her and then eased her hips against his own. He had felt the heat of their bodies merging into one... he had heard the cries of passion spent.

Jo's hands dug into his arms, pulling him closer, unable to get enough of the feel of his body next to her. She strained against him, an ancient need driving everything else from her mind but her desire for him to put an end to the sweet torment he had created.

His hands tangled in her hair as the kiss deepened. He felt himself being swept away by the power of his need for her. He forced himself to step back from that need, to recognize how wrong it would be to let things get out of control.

The way he made love to her was his one chance of diminishing the pain and uncertainty she felt about Karen—a chance he had no intention of destroying. With an overwhelming certainty, he knew that this was not the time, no matter how desperately he wanted her.

He had a gift for her—himself. And in the way he extended that gift he wanted her to see what she had already given him. By coming into his life, she had freed him from the past, allowing him not only to love again but to glory in the promise of each new day. He was whole for the first time in eight years.

"I gave myself too much credit," he said huskily, breaking their kiss to hold her tightly against him. He buried his face in her sweet-smelling hair. "Another minute like the last ten and I would have blown my dispassionate image."

Jo felt her wildly racing heart beating against her ribs, heard its clamorous sound in her ears. She laid her head on his shoulder and forced herself to take deep, calming breaths. "I can't imagine anyone thinking you were dispassionate," she said, her voice as shaky as her legs.

"That's because you have no idea what I was like before we met. I have no doubt there are some who would say 'emotionless' was a better description where I'm concerned."

Jo tilted her head back to look at him. "Only someone who didn't know you."

The love he saw in her eyes rekindled the need he had managed to bank only moments before, creating a fire that burned more intensely than any he had ever known. "What time are you through in here tonight?"

"I close at six."

"There are some things I have to do in Denver today, but I'll meet you at your apartment as soon as I can get away."

"Do you want me to fix dinner?"

He smiled as he rebuttoned her dress. "Only if you think we'll need sustenance," he said, his voice deep with meaning.

Jo exhaled a ragged breath. "Today is going to last forever."

He pressed his lips to the base of her throat. "That's nothing to the way tonight is going to feel, my love."

FLORENCE LET OUT a small whoop of joy as she hung up the phone after talking to Buster Hollister. She hurried to the closet to pick out the dress she would wear that day; she could hardly wait to get over to the yogurt shop and tell Jo what she'd found out about the money from the sale of Mabel's house. As soon as she was dressed and had run a comb through her hair, she grabbed her purse and headed for the living room.

Her gaze was immediately drawn to a slip of blue paper that had been shoved under the apartment door. She smiled as she bent to retrieve the paper. It was so like Howard to leave romantic messages lying around for her to find, it never even crossed her mind that the note might not be from him. The night they had just spent together had been especially wonderful. In the beauty and tenderness of his lovemaking, Howard had made her feel like a young girl again. They had spent the evening in his apartment, dining by candlelight and dancing to the love songs of their youth. Later, they had shared a bottle of wine while they sat on his balcony watching for shooting stars. And then later still, he had taken her into the bedroom and made love to her until she was spent with an incredibly sweet pleasure.

The sun had been well up in the sky before either of them had awakened that morning. After fixing breakfast for them both, Florence had returned to her apartment to begin her day and Howard had gone over to the YMCA for his morning swim—but obviously not before writing her a note.

Florence unfolded the paper, surprised when it wasn't Howard's familiar broad strokes she saw there but a tight, looping script. The color slowly drained from her face as she read the note.

My dear Florence,

I feel it is my duty to tell you that what is going on between you and Howard Wakelin has come to the notice of your friends. At first we didn't want to believe you could be involved in anything so tawdry, but we were forced to face the truth when you were seen going into Howard's apartment the other night and not seen coming out again until the next morning.

It pains me to tell you this, but if you continue to behave in this manner, we will be forced to go to the manager and request that you be asked to leave. I'm sure after you've taken a moment to consider what you're doing and thought about the possible consequences to all of us who consider ourselves your friends, you'll know that we're right.

Would you want your grandchildren visiting a place where people behave the way you and Howard have been behaving? We have a responsibility to the community to uphold a wholesome image for the youth of Boulder, and if that means occasionally having to rid ourselves of undesirables, no matter how close they are to us, I'm afraid that's just the way it will have to be.

But I'm sure it won't come to anything so drastic. As we grow older we realize it's far more important to live out what years remain to us in a community of caring neighbors than it is to sacrifice everything we have for one person.

A Friend

Florence felt as if she were going to be sick. She carefully refolded the paper. Not for a minute did she believe there was a "we" involved in the letter. She was confident that what she'd received was the ranting of an individual, but she was just as confident that whoever it was had every intention of carrying out their threats. Her worst fears had come true. What had been pure and sweet between her and Howard was now tarnished. Someone with a small, closed mind had stepped into her life with the power to take her happiness and turn it to ashes.

CHAPTER SIXTEEN

JO LOOKED UP from the cash register just as Florence came into the shop. She smiled a greeting before returning her attention to the young man with the newly grown mustache. After counting out his change, she again assured him that she thought he would do fine at the university that year and told him he was welcome to come back to see her anytime he wanted to talk. When he left, his earlier frown had become a confident smile.

"It seems like the kids are moving back to town a little early this year," Jo said to Florence. "School doesn't start for another five weeks."

"You know how it is when you're a freshman...." Florence tried to match Jo's lighthearted mood but wasn't able to bring it off.

Jo studied her friend for several seconds. The strain in Florence's voice was subtle but unmistakable. "Is something wrong?"

Florence glanced at a woman and her two children who were sitting at a table near the front door. She desperately needed to talk to Jo, but she didn't want to tell her about the anonymous letter in front of anyone else. "We'll discuss what's bothering me later," she said quietly. "For now, there's other news I think you might be interested in hearing. Buster Hollister called me this morning."

The incredible sense of well-being that had been with Jo ever since Brad's appearance at the shop seeped from her like sand through a sieve. With the mention of Buster Hollister's name, the real world returned. "What did he have to say?"

Florence attributed Jo's lack of enthusiasm to nervousness over what she had to report. "It seems Mabel sold her house out of necessity—not spite."

Jo took Florence's arm and led her to a back table, where they could talk and not be overheard. "She was that far in debt?" she asked softly, incredulously.

"About a month before Brad was to graduate, Mabel took out a mortgage on the house. Buster said she told him at the time that Brad would be moving back to Boulder to take over the payments. He particularly remembers the conversation because Mabel asked that the money from the loan be combined with her savings, which included the funds she'd received from the sale of her stock, and that a certified check be made out for the entire amount."

"He must have been concerned that she'd met up with a swindler," Jo said.

"I should think anyone confronted with such bizarre behavior would have imagined there was a swindler lurking somewhere in the background. But somehow Mabel convinced him she knew exactly what she was doing—she could be quite persuasive when she put her mind to it. Anyway, he complied with her request. He told me he feels guilty to this day about doing so. Mabel wasn't able to make even one of the mortgage payments, and the bank was actually on the verge of foreclosing on the house when she finally found a buyer."

Jo shook her head. "And Mabel never said a word about any of this to anyone."

"She must have believed Brad would come back to her when he couldn't find Karen."

"And when he didn't, Mabel probably figured Karen had double-crossed her and that she and Brad had gone off together and were living it up on her money. No wonder Mabel became so embittered toward the two of them. What a terrible way for her to live out her life."

Florence's eyes narrowed suspiciously as she watched Jo. "That bitterness is one of the reasons I was so surprised when you told me she'd decided at the last minute to leave her jewelry to Brad and Karen after all."

Jo looked at the ceiling as if it had suddenly developed a compelling fascination. "People do change," she said unconvincingly.

"About as frequently as tigers change their stripes."

"Well, none of that matters now."

"There was one other thing Buster was able to find out that he thought might be helpful to us."

"And what was that?" Jo prodded.

Florence couldn't resist a teasing smile. "The name of the private detective Mabel hired."

Jo got up and threw her arms around her friend. After the spontaneous moment of exuberance had passed, she returned to her chair and became thoughtful again. When she looked at Florence, all the joy had gone from her face. "The closer we get to finding Karen," she said slowly, giving voice to her worst fears, "the less sure I am that it's really what I want."

"You know, you don't have to keep up this search."

"But how could I stop now?"

Florence threw up her hands in exasperation. "You just stop."

"If I did, it would haunt me. I have to know—" The telephone rang, interrupting her. "I'll be right back," she said, getting up to answer the summons.

She removed her earring as she picked up the receiver. "Hello," she said, turning to acknowledge a goodbye wave from the mother and her two children, the last of her customers.

"Jo, it's Brad."

Her heart gave a funny beat. "I wasn't expecting you to call—"

"I'm at the airport. My plane leaves in ten minutes, so I have to make this fast. There's been an accident at the hotel site—Jack Chapman's been hurt."

"Brad...I'm so sorry. What happened?"

"The best anyone can figure out, he was up on one of the beams inspecting a connection when he lost his footing."

"Is he...has there been..." She couldn't finish the thought.

"I've told you all I know. He's undergoing emergency surgery right now, so I should be able to get some answers as soon as I reach the hospital. I'll call you the first opportunity I have."

"Brad, if there's anything—"

"I have to go now, Jo. I just heard them make the last call for my flight." He started to hang up and stopped. "I love you," he said. And then with a loving sternness, "Don't doubt it and don't forget it. I'll be back for that dinner you keep promising me just as soon as I can get away."

"I love you, too," Jo said, but she spoke the words to an empty line. Slowly she replaced the receiver and turned to Florence. She bit her lip to keep the tears from welling up in her eyes. "I don't know what I'll do if he decides to go back to Karen,'' she said, her voice barely above a whisper. ''I'm scared to death that when all of this is over, I'm going to wind up in the same place Brad has been for the past eight years.''

''I hate to keep repeating myself, but you could still drop this whole thing if you wanted to.''

''Where's my choice, Florence? Living under a cloud of doubt isn't really living. I have so much to give Brad, but unless I can feel complete confidence in his love for me, our relationship just isn't going to work. And the only way I can feel that confidence is to find Karen.''

''How can I argue with that kind of reasoning?'' She started to get up. ''I'll find Howard and get him on this detective thing.''

Jo gently but firmly pushed Florence back into her chair. ''You're not going anywhere until you tell me why you came over here today looking like you'd lost your best friend.''

Florence flinched at the aptness of Jo's description. ''It'll keep for another time,'' she said, feeling drained and too close to the edge of her emotional stability to be able to talk about what had happened that morning.

Jo purposely walked over to the door and turned her sign from Open to Closed. She leaned against the thick glass door and folded her arms across her chest. ''You can tell me now, or you can tell me later. The choice is up to you. But I think you should know that I have no intention of letting you out of here until I find out what's happened to you.'' Florence had been a godsend when Jo had needed a friend. Now that the opportunity had arisen for Jo to reciprocate, she wasn't about to let it pass.

Florence sat perfectly still for several seconds, then let out a shuddering sigh and reached into her purse. With trembling fingers, she withdrew the piece of blue paper she had found on her apartment floor that morning. Wordlessly she handed it to Jo.

Jo unfolded the paper and began to read. The bolt of anger that shot through her quickly turned to fury. When she finished the letter she threw it onto a nearby table and clenched her hands. Never in her life had she been as angry as she was at that instant. "Do you have any idea who sent this?"

Florence shook her head. "It was shoved under my door sometime after I returned from Howard's this morning."

"Does he know?"

"Not yet. He was swimming when I found it and I haven't seen him since."

"I can't comprehend what goes on in the mind of someone who would do something like this."

Florence sighed wearily. "Jealousy... frustration..."

"You sound like you're defending—"

"Not defending, simply understanding what motivations could lead to the action. When people have too much idle time, they tend to blow small things out of proportion. Little hurts become festering wounds. Jealousies change into righteous causes. It's impossible to fight people when they get that way, because they have all the time in the world and limitless energy. In the end, they simply wear you down. The only way to handle them is either to give in or to sidestep them in such a way that they think you've given in."

Jo felt a cold fear grip her spine. "Which method do you intend to use?" she asked.

Florence stared straight ahead, her hands clasped in her lap, her face a rigid mask. "For Howard and myself, there is really only one choice. We can't go on the way we are. No matter how careful we were, it couldn't be careful enough. Every time we were seen going into each other's apartment, the length of our stay would be noted by someone. Every one of our actions, no matter how innocent, would be the subject of gossip."

"Why do you care?" Jo said, unable to keep the frustration from her voice. It was inconceivable to her that Florence would even consider letting anyone as small-minded as the person who'd written that letter control her life.

"Why do I care?" Florence repeated, far louder than she had intended. "I care because all the innuendo and snide remarks would eventually destroy the finest man I have ever known, and I won't let that happen."

"And you think refusing to see Howard is going to be easier on him?"

"Please try to understand, Jo," she said sadly, tears glistening in her eyes. "When you're young, it's impossible to imagine what your life would be like without options. Howard and I live where we do not only because all of our friends live there but because it's the only place we can afford. The rents are government controlled, according to income. Moving anywhere else would mean cutting into the money we have to use for food—and God forbid either of us should ever get sick and need medicine. And you must remember I'd be losing one of my monthly pension checks." Florence's voice implored Jo to understand what she was going through. "You can't believe this is an easy decision for me, or that it's one I take lightly."

Jo saw Florence's agony in her eyes and in the unbending way she held herself. "I'm sorry," she said. "Isn't there any way I can help you?"

Florence wiped away the lone tear that had left a shiny trail down her cheek. "You can help the most by continuing to be my dear friend."

Jo bent down and put her arms around Florence's rigid shoulders. There was no question that she would always be the friend Florence wanted her to be. But if it was the last thing she ever did, she would find a way for Howard and Florence to "sidestep" the gossips at the apartment complex rather than give in to them. Perhaps when she was their age she, too, would have to face a life without options, but she wasn't there yet. "For you, Florence," she said, "I'll even find a way to control my temper."

THE ONLY HIGHLIGHT of the next two days was a phone call from Brad the morning after his emergency flight back to Casper. He told her that Jack Chapman had undergone eight hours of surgery and that, although he was being kept in the intensive-care unit, the prognosis was good.

As for Jo's promise to Florence, keeping her temper in check turned out to be a promise that was far easier given than executed. For the next two days, Jo found herself studying all her customers who lived in the apartment complex with Florence and Howard, wondering if they were responsible for the letter. Finally it was Ernie Baxter who brought her peculiar behavior to her attention.

"Is something bothering you, Jo?" he asked after he'd fixed a leaking faucet in the counter sink.

She stopped in the middle of wiping a smear of chocolate yogurt off a table. "What makes you think something's bothering me?" she snapped.

"If I didn't know better, I'd swear you were trying to remove the paint from that table."

She looked down at the washcloth and realized she'd been at a thirty-second chore for several minutes. "I've had a lot on my mind lately," she said, consciously adopting a calmer tone.

"Anything I can help you with?"

Yes, she wanted to shout, *you can tell me who sent that vicious note to Florence.* Instead, she gave him a halfhearted smile and said, "Not this time, Ernie. It's going to take more than a plumber's wrench to fix what's wrong with me." The bell over the door sounded and Jo looked up to see the mailman enter, carrying a large manila envelope.

"Looks like business is kind of slow today," he said, handing her the envelope along with the rest of her mail.

"It's just the lull before the storm," she answered automatically. Even though he had been delivering mail to her since she'd opened the shop, their conversation had rarely gone beyond the superficial. Because he invariably hit the shop when she was between customers, she had the distinct feeling he was waiting for her to go belly-up as many of the other small businesses in the neighborhood had done. Either that, or sell out.

"Well, have a good day." He chuckled. "Even if it doesn't pick up."

When he'd left, Ernie said, "Someone ought to turn him in to the post office."

Jo smiled at his protectiveness. "I doubt he's won any personality contests down there, either." She looked at her mail, quickly sorting through the normal bills and flyers to get to the manila envelope. She was surprised at first to see that it was from Susan Vizenor. And then she remembered that she'd failed to give Carl her home address, so the shop was their only way of getting in touch with her.

She stared at the package for several seconds, as if she were again poised on the threshold of a world she wasn't sure she wanted to enter. Peripherally she felt herself being drawn in another direction, but it wasn't until Ernie touched her arm that she realized he'd been talking to her.

"I'm sorry," she told him. "What were you saying to me?"

"The sink is fixed, so unless you've got something else you'd like me to do, I'm going to be on my way."

"No...I mean, there's nothing else that needs fixing." She smiled. "At least, there's nothing right at the moment. That doesn't mean there won't be an hour from now." She put the mail on the counter. "What do I owe you?"

"A large berrylicious with sliced almonds ought to do the trick."

"You're going to have to come up with a dollar figure this time, Ernie. I still owe you two weeks' worth of yogurt for the last repair you did."

"Well, then, I guess you'll have to add some raisins along with the nuts."

Acknowledging that she was in an argument she wasn't going to win, Jo went behind the counter to fix Ernie his dish of yogurt. As soon as she handed him the overflowing creation, he gave her a jaunty wave and promised to be back the next day to see that the washer had solved her drip problems.

Jo waited until she was alone before she tore open the envelope from Susan. She took a deep breath as she reached inside. Attached to a stack of photocopied papers was a note.

Dear Jo,

I had access to a copy machine so I decided to save you the trouble of having to return the originals. I thought you might like to know Carl and I are keeping our fingers crossed that this all turns out the way you're hoping it will.

If either of us can be of any further help, please let us know.

Susan

Jo laid the rest of the papers on the counter. For long seconds she stared at them and then wiped her trembling hands on her apron. Hesitantly, almost reluctantly, she reached for the top sheet of paper.

Three hours later, after several frustrating interruptions by customers, she had finished reading the last of Brad's correspondence to Carl and Susan. Because Susan had arranged the letters in chronological order, Jo was given a gradually emerging picture of the woman Brad had come to love. She followed the progress of their affair from the first meeting—only casually mentioned in the closing paragraph—to the week before graduation as Brad was getting ready to leave Iowa and return to Boulder to talk to Mabel.

Jo felt drained as she slipped the papers back into their envelope. It was one thing to imagine how Brad must have loved Karen, another to actually read about that love in his own words. She was surprised to discover her resolve to find Karen subtly changing. No longer was it just her own peace of mind she sought, it was Brad's also. The unfinished final chapter he'd spoken about still needed to be written—for both of them.

IT WAS TWO O'CLOCK in the morning before Jo finished the chart she'd made up for Alex. She'd listed all the clues to Karen's personality she'd been able to glean from Brad's letters. Included was her dress size, her height and her hair color. Birthday and Christmas presents given and received were listed, as was the information that Karen hated cold weather and insisted on working extra shifts whenever midterms and finals came around, in order to allow Brad the freedom of not working at all so he could stay home to study.

Irrationally, Jo had hoped to find reasons to dislike Karen in Brad's letters. Instead, she found herself drawn to the mysterious woman. Seen through Brad's eyes, Karen was the kind of person Jo knew she would naturally have gravitated toward. Not only was Karen able to make the most of a bad financial situation by either working harder or creatively skimping on everyday expenses, she did so without complaint. She made all of her own clothing as well as her daughter's. And because she loved the theater but couldn't afford tickets, she worked on costumes for a local production company in exchange for season's passes.

The little sleep Jo managed to get that night was filled with images of Karen and Brad together and her on the outside. When Brad called early the next morning, as he had every morning since returning to Casper, she could hardly make herself pick up the phone and talk to him.

"How's Jack doing today?" she asked, knowing Brad had already been to the hospital and put in an hour's work before calling her.

"He's managing to stay awake a little more each day."

"Has he been able to tell anyone what happened yet?"

Brad chuckled. "I asked him about that this morning and he gave me a look that could freeze the fires of hell."

"You mean he knows but he's too embarrassed to talk about it?"

"After you've worked construction as many years as Jack has, you don't like to admit you're still capable of making stupid mistakes—especially not the kind that end up the way this one did."

"How is his wife doing?"

"She finally left the hospital for the first time last night after the doctor convinced her Jack was going to make it. But she must not have stayed away long because she was there again when I arrived this morning."

Jo heard a background noise that sounded like a door opening in Brad's office. "Have you decided what you're going to do about that meeting you have scheduled with the planning commission in Denver for next week?" she asked, trying to keep from her voice the desperate need she felt to see him.

"Hang on a minute, Jo—"

While she waited for him to return, unbidden mental pictures of Karen came into her mind. For what had to be the tenth time since she'd read Brad's letters to Carl and Susan, she wondered what kind of man he would have become if he and Karen had married.

A hunger gripped her that went beyond the physical. The longer she knew Brad and the more intimate they became, the more passionately she wanted to share her life with him. In quiet moments of panic, when she was forced to face the possibility that she might lose Brad when he and Karen met again, a part of her demanded she stop what she was doing and compromise her feelings. *After all,* she reasoned, *wouldn't living with doubt be better than living alone?*

"I'm sorry I kept you waiting," Brad said, interrupting her thoughts. "What was it you were saying?"

"I was just wondering about the planning-commission meeting next week...." She paused. "To be honest, I wanted to know when I was going to see you again."

"I wish I could give you a definite answer," he said, the frustration evident in his voice. "But we've had so much trouble with the hotel, we're weeks behind schedule. I had to hire an extra crew for the hospital we started last week, and without Jack to keep an eye on them, I don't know when I'll be able to get away." When she didn't immediately answer, he said softly, "Don't give up on me, Jo."

She had promised herself that at the very least, the weeks or months it took her to find Karen was time she and Brad would have all to themselves. The way things were going, it looked as if they wouldn't even have that.

"Jo?"

"I'm here," she said.

"I'll make this up to you," he promised.

A sad smile formed. "That isn't necessary," she answered, forcing a lightness into her voice. "I think I read somewhere that cold showers were supposed to be good for the complexion."

He laughed. "Then mine should be peaches and cream."

"I love you," she told him, serious again.

"Just keep telling me that. It's what gets me through the day."

They talked for another minute before saying a final goodbye. Jo's hand was still on the receiver when the phone rang again. This time it was Florence.

"I wanted to catch you before you left for work," Florence said. "Howard called this morning to tell me that he'd finally managed to track down the detective."

Jo felt a sense of foreboding. She didn't like the tone in Florence's voice. "And?"

"I'm afraid it's not good news. He died three years ago, and the files his daughter kept from his business were all destroyed in a flood that she had in her basement last winter."

Jo felt a perverse sense of relief. Perhaps she wouldn't be able to find Karen after all. But as soon as the first surge of well-being had washed over her, she was left with a tenacious need to continue the search despite the setback. "If you see Howard before I do, be sure to thank him for the work he did for me."

"What are you going to do now?"

"I guess I'll take what information I've managed to gather over to Alex and see what he recommends." She hadn't seen or talked to Florence since the day the note had been shoved under her door, and the older woman's conspicuous absence had started to worry Jo. "What did Howard say when you showed him the poison-pen letter?" she gently prodded.

"I haven't showed it to him yet."

"Does that mean you're going to ignore it?"

"Not exactly...."

"Then what exactly?"

"I've been giving this a lot of thought...."

"And?" Jo asked after several seconds of silence had passed.

"I've decided the best thing for me to do is make Howard think I don't care for him anymore."

"What?" Jo nearly shouted. "You can't be serious. Besides, Howard would never believe you."

"He'd have to eventually."

Jo picked up the phone and began pacing, dragging the long cord behind her. "I don't understand your reasoning, Florence. Howard is going to be devastated if you do this to him."

"Not nearly as much as he would be if I showed him the letter. If I can convince him that I'm the reason we've stopped seeing each other, he'll never have to bear the humiliation of buckling under to outside pressure. If he really knew what was going on, he would want to protect me from the gossip and ridicule, Jo, and there's no way for him to do that."

"And you sincerely believe that by dumping him you're going to make him feel better?"

"At least he'll be left with his pride," she said.

Jo felt as if she'd received a blow to the midsection. Everything Florence had been trying to tell her finally penetrated. Howard would be devastated by losing Florence, but he would be destroyed if he ever learned of the real reason they could no longer be together. "I'm so sorry, Florence," she said, her voice in a choked whisper. "I should have understood what you were doing."

"I don't want you to feel you have to apologize. Even when you think I'm wrong in what I'm doing, you're always there when I need you. I couldn't ask for more in a friend."

Jo stopped her pacing and returned the phone to its former resting place. She sat down heavily in a chair. "Whatever happened to 'they lived happily ever after?'" she said with a poignant sigh.

"The last I heard it was still being tacked on the end of fairy tales. I don't think it was ever meant to apply to real life."

Don't tell me that, Florence, she mentally cried. *I haven't given up on happily ever after... at least not yet.* "What do you want me to say to Howard when he asks me about you?"

"I've been thinking about that, too, and I've decided it would be easier all around if I stayed away from the shop for a while. That way, you can tell Howard you haven't seen me and that you don't know anything about what's going on."

Jo's heart went out to her. "You're the bravest woman I've ever known," she said.

"I'm not brave, Jo, just in love. The only thing I have left to give Howard is to try to shelter him from some of the pain we are both going to have to go through."

Jo's anger at the anonymous letter writer became so intense she could hardly speak. Rather than inflict that anger on Florence, she told the older woman that she had to hang up and finish getting ready for work. As soon as they said goodbye, and before Jo had time to reconsider her actions, she called Alex to arrange another meeting. With Florence's example of self-sacrifice for the man she loved, how could Jo do any less for Brad?

CHAPTER SEVENTEEN

ALEX LEANED OVER the antique oak dining-room table at his house and sorted through the papers Jo had brought him, looking for the one she'd made up on Karen's physical description. "Do you think Karen is really this beautiful or that we're seeing her through the eyes of someone in love?"

Jo flinched. She was having trouble getting accustomed to the unemotional method Alex had adopted in their search for Karen. Whether he'd become that way intentionally she wasn't sure, but he had taken off the kid gloves as soon as it became clear that they had a real chance of finding Karen. "If anything, I'd say he played down her beauty."

"And what about her integrity? I find it hard to believe that anyone who'd accept Mabel's money and then take off the way she did was the paragon of virtue Brad makes her out to be in his letters."

"I've thought about that a lot."

Alex stuck his pencil over his ear and leaned back in his chair. "And what conclusions have you reached?"

"I haven't. No matter how I look at what happened it doesn't make any sense for Karen to do what she did. She obviously loved Brad. And her behavior during all the months they were together proved she wasn't afraid of hard work or hard times." She frowned in puzzlement as she rubbed the back of her neck. "I keep coming back to the same thought. It just doesn't make sense that she would leave when she did—not when Brad was about to graduate and the financial pressure they had been under would be gone.''

"I think you're right about Brad's letters painting a pretty accurate picture of Karen. At least, my sources in Iowa City couldn't find anyone willing to say anything different about her.''

She sat up straight in her chair. "Sources? What sources?''

Alex took the pencil from behind his ear and tossed it on the table. "Don't get excited. I have a friend who's a policeman there and he owed me a favor, so I had him check into Karen's background.''

"Hold on just a minute," Jo said, her eyes wide with disbelief. "I thought you told me it was against the law for you to help me find Brad and that you could lose your job if you did. How come all of a sudden it's all right for you to look for Karen?''

"This is different.''

"Oh, I see," she said sarcastically. "I don't suppose you'd mind telling me just what makes it so different?''

Alex eyed her for several seconds. "You're starting to walk on the edge of this thing, Jo. I think you should take a few days off and consider whether or not you really want to find Karen.''

Jo felt as if a band had been placed around her chest and was being constantly tightened, making it almost impossible for her to breathe. "Then she really is as wonderful as Brad thinks she is?" she asked, ignoring his suggestion, knowing he was right but also knowing he would go along with whatever she decided.

"So it seems.''

Because she needed something to do to cover her disappointment, Jo got up and walked over to the window to look outside. "So what do we do now?"

"I have a hunch where Karen might have gone, but I want more time to study the information you brought me today before I do anything about it."

"What kind of hunch?"

"I'll tell you as soon—"

"*Alex*," she groaned, "don't do this to me."

"Sorry, Josie. But until I'm sure I know what I'm talking about, I keep it to myself. It's the way I work."

"And how long is it going to take before you're sure?"

"I'll call you in a couple of days."

"Promise?"

He laughed. "I promise—one way or another."

THE TWO DAYS stretched into four. By the time Jo arrived home late from work on the fourth day and heard her telephone ringing behind her locked apartment door, she was a nervous wreck. She found her keys and opened the door in record time. Once inside, she threw her purse on the sofa and made a dive for the phone.

"Hello," she said, landing in the chair with a whoosh of outrushing air.

"Josie?"

"Alex?" she said, trying to catch her breath.

"Are you all right?"

"I will be as soon as you tell me what you've found out." She kicked off her shoes and brought her feet up to curl them beneath her.

"It's incredible. In all my years on the force, I've never had an investigation go this smoothly. And I can't even tell anyone about it."

"What do you mean, 'investigation'?"

"I guess I'm putting the cart before the horse, aren't I?"

"Damn it, Alex. *Would you please stop fooling around and tell me what you found out?*"

"Karen is in California—in the Los Angeles area, to be more precise."

"You actually found her?" Jo said, her voice a stunned whisper.

"Well...maybe what I should say is that I've *almost* found her. There's still some legwork that has to be done."

"I don't understand."

"I've narrowed the field down to three candidates. They're all named Karen and have last names that start with 'P'. And they all fit Karen's physical description. None of them are married but two of them have daughters around the age Tracy would be now. The third Karen doesn't list a child, but that doesn't mean she doesn't have one."

"Whatever made you think to look in Los Angeles?"

"Two things. Karen's hatred for cold weather gave me the general direction. When I combined that with the keen interest she had in the little theatre in Iowa City, it came down to a matter of having a friend of mine check out the membership of the Screen Actors Guild. I made the assumption that since none of the detectives Brad had hired were able to find her, she had changed her name. I guess I should add that I found out the only reason Karen worked behind the stage at the theater was because she didn't have the time to spare from her paying job to be on it. According to those who knew her at the time, although she had never said so, they were convinced she was secretly obsessed with the idea of becoming an actress."

It all seemed so easy and so obvious that Jo found it hard to make herself believe they had really found Karen. "Are you sure?" she asked.

"I'd bet my—"

"I know—you'd bet your badge." In the short time they had been working together, Jo had heard Alex bet his badge on everything from a baseball game to the sex of his unborn child.

"I have a feeling you're trying to tell me something."

"*Alex*—please get on with it."

He chuckled. "There are times when all a policeman has to work with are his hunches, Josie. We learn to listen to that inner voice that develops after we've been on the force awhile and to follow up on it." He paused. "I have to admit, though, there aren't many times my hunches have turned out to be as good as this one."

"I'm confused," Jo said after she'd had a few minutes to think about what Alex had told her. "Assuming one of these three women is Karen, why hasn't she tried harder to hide her identity? Wasn't she taking a big chance figuring Brad would never go to a movie she was in?"

"My guess is that his discovering her is precisely what she was after."

The thought sent a chill slithering down Jo's spine. "Is she successful?"

"That depends on which one of the women is the Karen we're looking for. Two of them have had a few speaking roles in minor movies, but for the most part, they're bit players and probably always will be. The third one, however, is on the verge of making it big—or at least she is in my friend's opinion."

"So what do we do now?"

"As I see it, we have two choices. Either we can do a background search—"

"Or someone can go to see all three of them," Jo finished for him.

There was a long pause. "I hope you're not thinking what I think you're thinking."

"Why not? Who else is there?"

"Lots of people."

"Name one."

"My friend."

Jo considered her answer. It would be far easier on her if someone else talked to the three Karens. But a perverse part of her character refused to let her take the easier route. "This is something I have to do for myself, Alex."

"You're only going to wind up being hurt a lot worse than you need to be."

His answer stung. "The way you're talking makes it sound like a forgone conclusion that Brad will decide Karen is the one he really loves."

"I'm just being realistic, Josie. Brad and Karen were a part of each other's lives for a fairly long time. They had a hell of a start on building a life together, not to mention the fact that when Karen left, Brad spent the next eight years unable to commit himself to anyone else. When you consider that you've known him less than a month..."

"You can pour logic down me all night, Alex. It's not going to get me to change my mind. Finding Karen is something I started that I have to carry through to the end."

"And I suppose you think I'm just going to hand the addresses over to you?"

She knew by the way he asked that she'd already won. "When do you want me to pick them up?" she asked.

"Damn it, Josie, I don't like this."

"Neither do I, Alex. I'm beginning to wish I'd never started the whole thing."

JO SPENT THE NIGHT thinking about what she would say to Karen when they finally met. She no sooner finished composing a speech than she discarded it as sounding inane. By the time morning arrived, she'd gone beyond fatigue into numbness.

She glanced at the digital clock on her nightstand as she walked from the bathroom. In ten minutes Brad would be calling—the way he had every morning since he'd returned to Casper. Her heart felt as though it had lodged in her throat. How could she talk to him and not tell him she'd found out about Karen? The thought plagued her as she finished getting dressed. In the end, just before it was time for him to call, she walked over to the phone and removed the receiver from its cradle.

Instead of going directly to work, Jo stopped off at the travel agency located two doors down from her shop. She didn't even try to hide her stunned disbelief when she heard the price of a round-trip airline ticket from Denver to Los Angeles. It would effectively wipe out her savings, leaving nothing for cab fares or hotels, let alone meals, while she was in Los Angeles. The agent patiently explained that the price would have been cut by two-thirds if Jo had only called for reservations three weeks earlier.

Jo left the agency in a stupor. Since she was afraid Brad was trying to reach her at the shop, she went over to Florence's apartment to figure out her next move.

"Jo!" Florence exclaimed, opening her door. "What a nice surprise."

"I hate to bother you so early, but I need to talk to someone. Can I come in?"

"Of course you can." She stepped out of the doorway to let Jo enter.

"Alex found Karen," she blurted out even before she was all the way inside.

"Oh…" Florence said softly. "Now I understand why you're wandering around at this time of the morning." She walked the short distance into the living room with Jo. "Sit down while I make us some tea, and then you can tell me what Alex found out."

But Jo was too nervous to sit down, so she followed Florence into the small kitchen to talk to her while she made the tea. It took only a few minutes to relay the information Alex had given her the night before and even less to tell Florence about her experience at the travel agency that morning.

"Perhaps Amy would lend you what you need," Florence suggested, handing Jo her tea.

"I have no doubt she would—if she weren't somewhere between here and Bermuda on a business cruise."

"When is she due back?"

"Not for another week."

"What about Alex?"

"Since he doesn't want me to go in the first place, I don't think I stand much chance of getting him to finance the trip." Jo blew gently on her steaming tea to cool it. "Besides, he and Barbara are going to have their third child soon and they need whatever money they have for that. It looks like I'm going to have to take my car whether I want to or not. It'll take me twice as long to get there, but it won't cost nearly as much."

"Are you sure your car can even go that far?"

Jo gave her a smile that expressed more confidence than she felt. "I just had it tuned up and the tires are almost new. As for the rest, I can stay at budget hotels and take a cooler with food and drinks." The details of the trip formed as she spoke.

"Jo, be reasonable about this. You can't take off with barely enough money to see you to Los Angeles and back. What if something happens to the car?"

"I'll use my credit card."

"I thought you told me your credit card was at its limit when you charged the new refrigeration unit for the yogurt machine."

"I forgot." Silence hung heavily between them as Jo sat staring down at her hands, searching for a solution. She looked up at Florence, a gleam in her eye. "I'll pawn Mabel's pearls," she said, enormously pleased with herself that the thought had even occurred to her.

"And what about the shop? What are you going to do with it while you're gone?"

It was on the tip of Jo's tongue to tell Florence that she planned to hang a sign in the window saying she had gone on vacation when an idea occurred to her. "I thought maybe I could talk you and Howard into taking care of things for me."

"Oh, Jo...we...*I*...couldn't."

"This is really important to me, Florence. If the shop doesn't stay open, I won't be able to pay my bills." She tried for a tone that was somewhere between pleading and pride.

"It would be terribly hard on the two of us..."

Good, Jo thought. Breaking up with someone you love should be hard. Maybe if it was hard enough, the two of them would find another solution to their problems.

"Please, Florence. I can't tell you how much it would mean to me. The income could even make the difference between my keeping the shop and losing it." She flinched a little at the last, hoping she wasn't laying it on too thick.

"I would hate to see you lose the shop."

"Does that mean you'll do it?"

"I'll have to talk to Howard first. He may not want to be around me that long. I'm sure I don't have to tell you why."

"Do you want me to talk to him?"

Florence sighed in resignation. "No—I'll do it. When would you want us to start?"

"Would this afternoon be too soon?"

"When you make up your mind to do something, you certainly don't let anything slow you down, do you?"

Jo grew serious. "Maybe I'm just afraid that if I hesitate, I won't be able to go through with finding Karen at all." She took her cup and saucer to the kitchen. "I'm going to go home and pack, and then I'll go over to the shop and get things set up for you and Howard. If you need to get in touch with me, call and let the phone ring twice, then hang up and call right back."

"Who is it you're trying to avoid?"

"Brad. I can't lie to him about what I'm doing, so I have to avoid talking to him at all if I'm going to go through with this thing."

"What do you want me to say to him if he calls while you're gone?"

"Tell him . . ." If she couldn't lie, she had no right to ask Florence to lie for her. "Just say that there was someone I had to see and that I'll be back in a week." She was halfway out the door when she stopped. "I've never pawned anything before. Do you know what I'm supposed to do?"

Florence shook her head. "I can tell you how they do it on television," she offered.

Jo smiled. "I can see we're going to have lots to talk about when I get back."

Jo was in the middle of filling her cooler with supplies from her refrigerator when the phone rang. She was certain it was Brad trying to reach her, and it was all she could do not to answer.

She was on her way out the door when, at the last minute, she thought about taking along her sleeping bag and a pillow, on the chance that she might be able to stay in a campground on her way to and from California.

As she was locking her apartment she considered leaving a note for Amy but decided against it, as the two of them were scheduled to arrive home around the same time anyway.

After stopping at the bank to withdraw her savings, she went to the yogurt shop, where she hurriedly got everything ready for the day's business. When she was satisfied Florence and Howard would be able to start selling the instant they stepped through the door, she hurried across the street to drop off the key, never once doubting that her friends would come through for her despite their reluctance to be with each other.

Her first stop in Denver was the police station, to pick up the addresses from Alex. After listening to a fifteen-minute "big-brother" lecture about locking her car doors and not putting her trust in strangers, she headed for a pawn shop she'd passed on her way into the city.

Once at the pawn shop, she learned a lesson in negotiation she would never forget. When she left, she was in shocked amazement at the difference between the asking and selling price of pearls. She made a vow that she would sell her car if necessary in order to retrieve Mabel's necklace. There was no way she was going to let those pearls permanently leave her possession for the small amount of money the broker had given her.

Before she'd left her apartment, she'd spent a few minutes studying a map, trying to decide whether to follow the less rugged but longer southern route down to Albuquerque and then across to Los Angeles or the more direct route, which would take her over the Rocky Mountains and through the desert to Las Vegas. Because of her desire to finish with the confrontation between herself and Karen as soon as possible, she was more anxious than cautious and settled on the direct route.

She was somewhere in Utah with only a sky full of glittering stars for company when she saw a sign advertising a campground. She paid her fee, found her campsite and fixed herself a sandwich.

A brilliant sun woke her early the next morning. She stretched and yawned and reluctantly crawled out of her sleeping bag. She took a quick shower and made for the small store where she'd paid her camping fee the night before to get a cup of coffee and a doughnut. She was on the road again before most of the other campers had started to stir. It was late that night when she finally arrived in Los Angeles.

The next morning, she treated herself to breakfast at a restaurant near her motel. Not trusting her memories of the area, she spent the time she waited for her meal to study a detailed map of the Los Angeles basin she'd picked up at a service station on her way.

The three Karens lived miles apart—one in Santa Monica, one in Torrance and one in Beverly Glen. Jo decided to start with the Karen in Torrance and work her way north.

For all her supposed resolve and acceptance of what she would find, Jo was a nervous wreck when she pulled up to the small stucco house that belonged to the first Karen on her list. Palm trees flanked the driveway and a gaudy bright-pink plastic flamingo sat beside the front porch. Gut instinct told her this was not the kind of home Brad's Karen would live in, but she had to make sure.

Irrationally postponing what she had come more than a thousand miles to do, Jo sat in the car, unable to move until she noticed a woman in the next house peering out at her through front-room curtains. She took a deep breath but it didn't still the trembling in her hands or slow her racing heart. Finally, she ignored her nervousness, reached for her purse and climbed out of the car.

The woman who answered the door had her long blond hair swept up in a ponytail and was dressed in a workout leotard that left little of her lithe body unexposed. "Yes?" she said, impatiently wiping sweat from her face and neck with a white towel. "What do you want?"

"I'm looking for a woman named Karen Parker."

"That's me."

Jo swallowed. "If you don't mind, I'd like to come in and talk to you about someone I believe is a mutual friend of ours."

The woman's eyes narrowed suspiciously. "Look, honey, I have another half hour of exercises to do—"

"This won't take long."

"Why don't you just tell me who this person is that we're both supposed to know?"

This was not going as she had planned. "Brad Tyler."

Karen Parker thought a moment before her forehead wrinkled in a frown. "I've never heard of any Brad Tyler,'' she said, keenly studying Jo. "Just what kind of game are you playing, anyway?"

No one, no matter how consummate an actress, could have faked the reaction Jo had witnessed. "I must have made a mistake," she said, backing off the porch. "I'm sorry to have disturbed you."

"See that sticker?" Karen said, pointing to a drawing of a stylized burglar on the lower left-hand corner of her front-room window. "That means we have a neighborhood-watch program here. I wouldn't be thinking about trying anything funny around here if I were you."

Jo smiled. The smile turned into a chuckle. "I'll keep that in mind," she said, turning to leave.

She was still chuckling as she drove through the housing project. She didn't know whether it was because she felt as strung out as an old piano wire or because she was afraid of what she would find when she discovered the right Karen, but the more she thought about being taken for a potential thief, the funnier it grew. By the time she pulled onto 405 to head north, she had tears of laughter running down her cheeks.

She'd managed to bring her almost hysterical laughter under control and remove all traces of the tears by the time she reached Karen Peterson's apartment in Santa Monica. She arrived on the second-story landing just as a man in his late twenties with a quintessential California look about him was unlocking the door to 209. "Excuse me," she said. "I'm looking for a woman named Karen Peterson. I was told she lives in this apartment."

The man gave her a curious stare. "Are you a friend of hers?"

"No—but I think we might have a mutual friend. That's what I'd like to talk to her about."

He shifted the bag of groceries he was carrying to his other arm. "Well, she isn't here right now. She left last Wednesday for a shoot in the valley. I don't expect her back for another week."

Jo felt the disappointment all the way to her toes. She couldn't wait a week. "Are you her husband?"

He shoved his keys back in his pocket. "Boyfriend."

"Then perhaps you could help me. It's very important that I find out if Karen Peterson is the Karen I'm looking for."

He leaned his shoulder against the door frame and studied her for several seconds. "What is it you want to know?"

"How long has Karen lived in California?"

"I think she's been here about nine or ten years."

Jo's heart gave a funny beat. The timing was right. "Where did she live before that?" she asked, struggling to keep her voice even.

"Winter Haven, Florida."

Jo blinked. "Are you sure?"

"Reasonably sure," he said with a trace of irritation. "You get to know those kinds of things about a person when you've lived with them for a couple of years."

"Thank you for your help," Jo said turning to go. Now that she knew Karen Peterson wasn't Brad's Karen, she was anxious to be on her way.

"I take it that means my Karen wasn't the one you wanted?"

"Not unless she stopped off in Iowa for a couple of years on her way here from Florida."

He laughed. "Then it's *definitely* not my Karen you're looking for. She's never been north of the Mason-Dixon line."

Jo was almost at her car when the man came back out of his apartment, leaned over the railing and called to her. "By the way, good luck in your search," he said.

She smiled. "Thanks, but I don't think I'll need it from here on out."

CHAPTER EIGHTEEN

JO SAT IN HER CAR in front of Karen Porter's elegant home and passionately wished she'd worn a better dress and had spent more time on her hair and makeup that morning. If she could just have met Karen on an equal footing.... But then, reason should have told her what to expect. Hadn't Karen left Iowa City with three hundred thousand dollars in her pocket?

She finally left the Toyota, grim determination in every line of her body and headed up the brick walkway to the Tudor-style house. A middle-aged Mexican woman answered the door. "I'm here to see Ms Porter," Jo announced.

"And who shall I say is calling?" the woman asked.

"My name is Josephine Williams. Ms Porter doesn't know me, but we have a mutual friend. She hasn't seen him for a while—" she stopped to catch her breath and make herself slow down "—but I know she'd be interested in hearing about him."

"If you'd like to give me his name, I'd be happy to check with Ms Porter for you."

It hadn't occurred to Jo that she would have to communicate through an intermediary. "Brad Tyler," she said, realizing it was senseless to evade answering.

"Please wait here. I'll be right back."

Jo nervously shifted her weight from one foot to the other as she waited. She glanced around her at the meticulously manicured lawn and weed-free flower beds. Everywhere she looked she saw the signs of wealth. Obviously Karen had not squandered the money she'd received from Mabel but had found a way to make it grow. She was gazing out across the lawn when the front door abruptly opened.

"Who are you?" Karen asked, her voice a choked whisper.

"Josephine Williams."

"What are you doing here?"

Jo wondered at the almost frantic look in Karen's eyes. "I came to find you," she said.

"Why?"

"Can I come in? I'd just as soon not discuss what I came to talk to you about out here on the porch."

With social proprieties to concern her, Karen's tense posture seemed to relax slightly. "Of course," she said, stepping aside to let Jo enter. She closed the door and held her hand out to indicate that Jo should precede her into a room off the foyer. As soon as they were both inside and seated, she turned her full attention to Jo again. "Now, would you please tell me what you're doing here?"

Jo took several seconds to study the woman Brad had spent so many years loving. Although Karen was in her mid-thirties, she looked no older than Jo's twenty-six years. She had shoulder-length blond hair and dark-green eyes. She moved with the natural elegance of a dancer; even her smallest gesture was exquisitely graceful. Jo had no doubt that this was the Karen Alex's friend had said was on the threshold of making it big in films. "I'm in love with Brad," she said softly, abandoning her prepared speech in favor of an uncomplicated honesty. "And I wanted to see my competition."

Karen's composure cracked. "What do you mean, 'your competition'?"

"Brad has spent the last eight years trying to get over you."

"You can't—" Her hand went to her throat. "You can't be serious," she said.

But Jo could see that Karen believed her. She also saw that Karen was more than a little pleased about the news that Brad still loved her.

"I thought . . ." Karen shrugged.

Whatever Karen had been thinking she apparently decided to keep to herself. "I know why Mabel paid you to leave," Jo said, without any attempt at subtlety, "but I don't understand why you took the money."

Karen stared at Jo, as if trying to decide whether to let go of a long-held secret. "How much do you know about what happened?"

"Only that while Brad was in Boulder trying to talk his mother into coming to his graduation, the man she'd hired was in Iowa City offering you money to leave."

Karen reached into a porcelain box beside her and pulled out a cigarette. Her hands trembled as she picked up the lighter and lifted it to her face. "That wasn't the first time Mabel had sent someone to 'talk' to me about leaving Brad," she said, carefully placing the lighter in its original position before continuing. "In addition to the phone calls she made to me herself, there were three visits by that obnoxious detective she'd hired. Mabel was obsessed with finding a way to prevent me from marrying Brad."

"What finally happened that made you change your mind?" Jo managed to keep the anger she felt from creeping into her voice.

Karen plucked a piece of lint from her tan slacks, then ran her hand down the crisp pleat before gracefully crossing her legs. "It took some doing, but Mabel managed to convince me that if I didn't leave, she had the power to make my life a living hell for as long as she was alive. To understand why I left, you have to understand that despite everything, Brad loved his mother very much. After his father's death he assumed responsibility for her welfare. It was very important to him that Mabel and I get along.

"Brad's lifelong dream had been to set up his own architectural firm in Boulder, but he knew that because of the way things were between Mabel and myself, she really would have made our lives miserable if the two of us had tried to move back there together." She tapped her cigarette against the marble ashtray beside her, got up and walked over to the window. Holding the curtain aside, she stared off into the distance.

"So you decided the best thing you could do for Brad was to paint yourself out of the picture."

"At the time, I truly believed it was the most loving thing I could do for him . . ."

Jo would have had less trouble accepting the altruistic nature of Karen's actions if she had left without Mabel's money.

"I've regretted my decision every single day for the eight long years we've been apart. I was too young then to realize what a rare and precious thing it is to find true love." She turned from the window to look at Jo. "I'd give anything if there were some way I could change what happened." She walked slowly back across the room.

"I know you told me that you're in love with Brad, and the last thing I want to do is come between you, but surely you can understand how important it is that I see him again—just one last time, to tell him how sorry I am for leaving the way I did."

Jo saw her hopes and dreams slipping away. She didn't have the smallest lingering doubt that as soon as Brad saw Karen again they would be in each other's arms. Forgiveness would be the first step, reconciliation the second. She rose to her feet. "I'll tell him how to find you," she said, her words spoken in a monotone of resignation.

"Please do," Karen begged. "I promise you, all I want from Brad is his forgiveness."

Jo started to leave. As she neared the door, she turned and looked at Karen again. She tried to imagine herself in Karen's position but couldn't. The woman hadn't even bothered to ask Brad's whereabouts. How did anyone acquire an ego so large she was confident a complete stranger would do her bidding? "Why didn't you try to find Brad all these years if you were so concerned about his forgiveness?"

Karen bent and methodically crushed out her cigarette. "I was afraid."

"But you're not now?"

She gave Jo a slow smile. "Why should I be afraid now? Didn't you say Brad still loved me?"

How could she have been so stupid? She was going to lose Brad before the two of them had even had a chance to really get to know each other. She recoiled at the thought that she would finally have to pay for her impetuousness and tenacity—and the price would be devastating.

JO DROVE THE FORTY MILES back to her hotel in a mental fog. When she entered her room, she was struck by its emptiness and the way it echoed how she felt inside. She turned on the television for company, but it only accentuated her aloneness. She desperately needed a friend. Her parents were less than a hundred and fifty miles away, but they would never understand what she'd done or why she'd done it.

The bubble of pain that had risen inside her at Karen's house had continued to grow until it felt as if it were going to suffocate her. The hurt stole her power to think or to act, preventing her from making rational decisions about what she had to do next.

She paced the room in a random pattern, unable to sit down. Although she was exhausted, she couldn't go to bed, fearing the dreams that would haunt her if she ever fell asleep. Finally she went to the closet, took her clothes from the hangers and packed them in her suitcase. Ten minutes later, she was on Interstate 10 heading back to Colorado.

JO WAS ON THE OUTSKIRTS of Las Vegas when she realized with a start that she was beginning to listen to an insidious internal voice telling her that if she just closed her eyes for a few seconds, she would feel rested and able to finish the trip home without stopping. She rolled down the windows and turned on the radio, but neither action helped clear the fatigue. Reluctantly she decided she had no choice but to leave the freeway at the next off-ramp and look for some place to get a cup of coffee. Strong and black. If it took a gallon of the caffeine laced liquid to put her back on the road again, then so be it. Anything—just to get home.

She left the freeway and drove several blocks, passing run-down warehouses and homes with weed-choked yards before she acknowledged that she'd picked the wrong exit to try to find a restaurant. She was about to return to the freeway to try another off ramp when she saw a flashing neon sign in the distance. Another half block and she was able to make out the words—Kirk's Koffee Kup Kafé and Truck Stop.

The outward appearance of the restaurant was in keeping with the neighborhood, but the parking lot was full. A wry smile touched her lips. There was one point in favor of the place—none of the cars were ambulances. She decided she might as well stop rather than waste more time looking for something more presentable. She made a U-turn and came back, pulling into the first empty parking spot she found. The tiny Toyota ended up sandwiched between a cattle truck and a moving van in a field almost a block away from Kirk's Kafé. It was dwarfed by its companions, looking more like a spare part that had fallen off one of them than something that shared the same road.

When she left the restaurant a half hour later after a meal of pancakes and bacon and four refills of coffee, she noted that she still felt tired, but she was awake enough to continue her trip. She paused a moment on the sidewalk to stretch and look at her watch. Almost four. The sun would be making an appearance soon.

If she had any sense, she'd find a motel and try to get some sleep before tackling the desert. But her desire to return home was too strong. The emptiness that drove her demanded she surround herself with the familiar, like a wounded animal seeking the comfort of its cave.

Although she'd gone over the whole thing a hundred times, she wasn't any closer to a decision on how she should tell Brad about Karen than she had been when she'd left Los Angeles. How was she going to make him understand that it was her love for him that had motivated her actions? What she was really looking for, she finally admitted, was some way to stack the deck in her own favor.

Karen didn't deserve Brad. But would Brad see that?

Jo was lost in the depths of her thoughts and oblivious to her surroundings when she stepped from the sidewalk to head for her car. A cricket jumped and landed on her blouse. She couldn't restrain a cry of surprise before she realized what it was and brushed it aside. Embarrassed, she glanced around to see if anyone had witnessed her "female" reaction to the insect. It was then that she saw the two men who had followed her out of the restaurant.

They had stopped several yards away and were intently watching her. Her first inclination was to say something to them about the cricket, but then she noticed the looks on their faces and the words died in her throat.

The taller of the two men was dressed in faded jeans and an open denim vest that showed a thick black mat of hair and a silver Maltese cross hanging around his neck. There were tattoos on both of his arms. The shorter man wore a bandanna headband knotted around shoulder-length brown hair and a heavy piece of chain around his waist. As she watched them, the taller one smiled; the short one licked his lips.

Jo looked at the restaurant. Returning there was out of the question. The two men stood between her and the front door and she knew with a dread certainty that they would never let her pass. She glanced over her shoulder to where her car was parked. The cattle truck had moved, giving her a straight shot at the Toyota. Still, the remaining half block looked more like a half mile.

How could she have been so careless? Even someone who lived her life insisting on the basic goodness of hu-

manity should have had better sense than to wander alone
around a strange neighborhood in the middle of the
night.

Because she didn't know what else to do, Jo took several steps toward her car. The two men precisely matched
their steps to hers, as if they were playing a sinister game
with her. She felt her mouth go dry. Invisible fingers
crawled up her spine to tease the hair at the back of her
neck.

Don't panic, she sternly instructed herself, repeating
the words until they became an unconscious litany. She
calculated that she was a good ten yards ahead of the men
and, if necessary, could sprint the final distance and have
the element of surprise in her favor. If she could just get
inside the car and lock the door before they reached her,
she was positive she could get away. She shoved her hand
into her purse and frantically started digging for her keys.

She was still digging after her dash to the car. She
looked up to see the men closing on her. Her body broke
out in a cold sweat; her heart sounded like a thundering
drum roll. Seconds became hours as she watched the two
men approach, taking their time as if supremely confident of the outcome. She considered running from them,
striking out in the most promising direction, but she immediately discarded the idea, preferring the known safety
of her car to whatever she might find in the surrounding
area.

Damn it! She could hear the keys—why couldn't she
find them?

Finally, in desperation, she flung the cloth bag from
her shoulder and dumped everything out on the hood of
the car. Frantically she sorted through the contents,
shoving everything else aside in her search for the keys.

At last she found the brass ring under a package of crackers she'd taken with her from the restaurant.

With an expansive sweep of her forearm, she scooped whatever she could reach back into her purse before jamming the key into the door lock. A quick glance over her shoulder told her that the men had now realized they were about to lose their quarry. They broke into a run just as she opened the door. She scrambled inside and slammed her hand against the inside lock at the precise moment the taller man seized the outside handle.

The lock wouldn't go down. But neither would the door open. They were at a stalemate. With intense effort, she forced herself to wait for the leering giant to release his thumb to make another try at entry. When he did, she was ready. Her timing was perfect and the lock slid into place. She caught her breath in a strangled sob as she fumbled with the keys on the brass ring. Her hand was trembling violently when she aimed for the ignition, but she managed to get the key in on the first try.

One quick pump on the accelerator, a quarter turn of the key and the car came to life. Fists slammed against the top of the car and crashed into the side window. Curses filled the night air as she shoved the gearshift into reverse and the car jumped backward. The Toyota's tires spun in the loose gravel before catching solid ground and shooting the car across the narrow street. She was over the opposite curb, inches from a telephone pole, before she had the car under control again.

A fresh wave of fear rolled over her when she thought of how close she'd come to destroying her one chance to get away. With careful, deliberate movements, she pushed the gearshift into drive. The two men were standing on the opposite sidewalk watching her, laughing derisively. A sudden rage consumed Jo, extinguishing her fear. As she passed the men, she gave them a derogatory salute—something she had never done to anyone in her twenty-six years. It felt amazingly good.

JO'S ANGER was all she needed to keep her awake the next hundred and fifty miles as she crossed the Nevada desert and entered Utah. She was outside of St. George when she glanced down at the gas gauge and saw the needle pointing to empty. The tank did contain a reserve, but she had no idea how long she'd been using it and decided to stop for gas at the first opportunity, regardless of the price.

A half mile later, she found a combined market and restaurant with a service station. After pulling up to the unleaded pump, she shut off the car and reached for her wallet. When she didn't find it right away, she let out a disgusted sigh and turned her purse over, dumping its contents on the passenger seat. As soon as she arrived home, she decided, she was changing to a smaller purse.

It took several thorough searches before she was ready to admit that she'd left her wallet and checkbook in Nevada.

Now what?

She opened the glove box and gathered up the parking change she kept there. Two dollars and sixty-five cents— enough to get her approximately another sixty miles closer to home. A car pulled in behind her to buy gas.

Jo started the Toyota and drove it over to the side of the building to sit in the shade while she considered her options. Options? She laughed aloud. As if she had any. As far as she was concerned, there was only one thing a mature, self-reliant, independent woman would do under the circumstances—call her family for help.

The only problem was that she was no more inclined now to let her family know why she'd taken this trip than she had been the night before. But if not her family, who else could she call? There was always Amy. Under normal circumstances Amy would have been the ideal person to ask for money to get home. Only she was still out of the country. Then there was Florence or Howard. They would give her anything they had, but neither of them had money.

A thought struck. What about Alex? She discarded the idea immediately. She shuddered to think how he would react. Especially since he had been dead set against her going to Los Angeles in the first place.

That left Brad.

CHAPTER NINETEEN

JO DECIDED it didn't make any sense to postpone the inevitable, so she collected the change she'd found in the glove box and headed for the pay phone she'd seen at the front of the store. After talking to the operator and dropping the coins into their respective slots, she glanced at her watch. At least she wouldn't have to go through Brad's secretary. It was still too early for her to be at work.

Jo's heart gave a funny lurch when she heard the first ring. She felt a sudden urge to hang up, but then she heard Brad's voice, and more than anything else she wanted to hear more.

"Tyler Construction," he said.

"Hi," Jo said softly, leaning her shoulder into the stucco wall and closing her eyes, letting a mental image of him transport her from her dusty surroundings to a place beside a cool mountain stream.

"Jo?" A pause followed. And then, "Where in the hell have you been? I've—"

"Please don't yell at me," she said. They had so little time left and she couldn't bear the thought that it would be spent in anger.

Brad leaned forward in his chair, placing his elbows on the desk for support. His relief over finally hearing from Jo had pulled the plug on his emotional control, allowing him to acknowledge how deeply he'd feared that history had been repeating itself. "I'm sorry," he told her. "It's just that I've been half-crazy wondering where you were."

A sad smile formed on her lips. "I've only been gone three days. And besides, we wouldn't have seen each other anyway."

"We would have if you'd been home. I called you the day before yesterday to tell you I was on my way to Boulder, but you weren't at your apartment. I finally got in touch with Florence at the shop. She gave me some crazy story that you'd decided to take off for a few days to visit friends." Although he'd been almost obnoxiously insistent, Florence had refused to give him any more information. In the end, her attempts at reassurance had done little to ease his mind.

"That's what I told her to say."

"What's going on, Jo?"

"I'll tell you all about it as soon as I get home."

It took several seconds for what she'd said to register. He'd naturally assumed she was calling from her apartment. "Where are you now?"

"In St. George, Utah."

"What—"

"It's a long story. I think it would be better if I save it for when I get home."

"And how long is that going to take?"

She wearily ran her hand through her hair, stopping to rub the back of her neck. "That depends on you." It was barely seven o'clock in the morning and already the heat had settled over the desert like a thick wool blanket. A sticky layer of moisture coated her skin. Her glance landed on the small pile of coins on the triangular ledge beneath the phone. "I can't talk too much longer, Brad. I only have a couple of dollars in change."

"Damn it, Jo, you're not going to hang up on me until you've told me what's going on."

Despite the frantic concern she heard in his voice, she'd never felt such isolation. It was as if she'd been set adrift from everything that was good and loving in her life. Only one person's arms could shelter her from the pain ahead—and he would be the source of that pain. A trickle of moisture slithered down her cheek. She reached up to wipe it away. It was then that she realized she was crying. Her fatigue must have put her on edge. Why else would just the sound of Brad's voice bring tears? The time for crying would come later, when she actually told him about Karen and saw the joy that was sure to light up his eyes. "I think it would be better if I just told you why I'm calling and we took care of the other when I got home."

Brad responded to the note of desolation in her voice, and concern replaced anger. "What is it, Jo?"

"Nothing major," she said, putting all her effort into sounding confident and lighthearted. "Just a small favor." She swallowed. "Do you suppose you could send me some money? About fifty dollars?"

He didn't buy her forced cheerfulness. "Why fifty dollars?"

"I need gas to get home." She held her breath while she waited for his answer.

Brad couldn't believe he'd heard her correctly. "Are you trying to tell me that you drove your car all the way to St. George, Utah?"

"What's wrong with my car?" she asked defensively, hoping to throw him off and avoid more probing questions. But he was two steps ahead of her.

Although they'd been together less than a month, it was long enough for Brad to know that Jo would never leave home short of funds. "What happened to your money?"

"I lost it in Las Vegas." She mentally crossed her fingers that he would assume she'd been gambling. She should have known better.

"How did you lose your purse?"

"What makes you think—"

"Stop playing games with me, Jo."

She turned and pressed her back into the rough stucco. It was useless to evade his questions any longer. "A couple of men followed me—"

"*Damn it*—I knew it was something like that. Did they hurt you?" He was consumed with an instant impotent rage.

"No...I got away before they could do anything. What happened isn't important. All that matters is that I left my wallet in Las Vegas and now I need gas money to get home. I'm sorry I had to involve you in this, Brad, but everyone else—"

"What do you mean, you're sorry? Why would you even think of calling anyone else?"

The pain she heard in his voice created a tiny flare of hope; she ruthlessly extinguished it by reminding herself that he would be seeing Karen soon. "Brad, I have to hang up now. If you send the fifty dollars overnight mail in care of general delivery, I'll get it in the morning. Then, as soon as I get home, I'll call you so that we can make arrangements to get together...to talk."

"You don't have to wait until morning, Jo," he said with a sigh of resignation. I have a friend who owes me a favor. I'll get him to fly the money down to you this afternoon."

"You don't have to do that. Tomorrow—"

"For crying out loud, Jo. Would you please let me do things my way once in a while?"

Why was she fighting him over something so simple?

"All right," she said calmly. "I'll meet your friend at the airport."

There was a long pause. "Jo?"

"Yes."

"I love you."

The pain radiated through her chest. "I love you, too," she said, biting back fresh tears.

IT TOOK BRAD forty-five minutes to arrange for his friend to fly him to St. George, give instructions to the new foreman who'd taken Jack's place and then get to the airport himself. Three and a half hours later, he was climbing out of his friend's twin-engine plane and into the blast-furnace heat of the Utah desert town.

After retrieving his small suitcase and thanking his friend for the ride, Brad made his way toward the small terminal. As he neared the building, he spotted Jo's green Toyota out of the corner of his eye. It sat at the far edge of the parking lot, but even at that distance he could see someone inside the car.

A strange mixture of relief and anger stirred in him. He realized he was being unreasonable, but he couldn't control the fury that came over him whenever he thought about the risks Jo had taken on her trip. What had she been doing wandering around alone in Las Vegas, where two men could accost her? Not to mention the insanity of driving that ancient car of hers over the Rockies and into the desert.

Didn't she realize she had more than just herself to think of now?

The longer he thought about the risks she had so heedlessly run, the angrier he grew. In accepting his love, she had made a commitment to him to take care of herself. Hadn't it occurred to her what it would do to him if he lost her?

After eight long years he had finally opened up to someone again, and because of that he'd spent the last three days in his own private hell, convinced something had happened to her. She had put the sweetness back into his life, had restored his ability to dream...and had made him vulnerable.

Brad experienced yet another instant of fear when Jo didn't stir at his noisy approach over the gravel parking lot. As he drew closer, he saw that she was simply asleep, curled up in the front seat, her head resting on a pillow that she'd propped against the half-open window. He stopped beside the car and stared down at her, torn between giving free rein to his anger and crushing her to him in a fierce, relief-filled embrace. "Wake up, Jo," he finally demanded, choosing a middle ground between his warring emotions.

She softly moaned and turned away from the sound of his voice, bumping her arm into the steering wheel. Even that failed to awaken her fully. Brad reached through the window and unlocked the front and back doors. After tossing his suitcase in the rear seat, he reached for her and lightly shook her shoulder. "If you don't want to wake up, at least move over so I can get in."

Jo fought the voice that was trying to drag her out of the cool dark tunnel of her dream into a blinding light, but the struggle was useless. Yielding the battle, she opened her eyes, saw Brad and frowned in confusion. "Brad?" she questioned, sitting up straight and peering out the window at him. She clasped a hand to the side of her neck to ease the pain of a complaining muscle.

"What are you doing here?"

"Oh, I just happened to be in the area so I thought I'd drop by," he drawled, the words edged with barely controlled sarcasm.

"But—"

"Come on, Jo. You didn't really think I'd leave you out here all alone, did you?"

Perversely, his declaration of chivalry made her feel more like a helpless child than a rescued damsel. Her back straightened and her chin rose defiantly. "I've managed to get along all right on my own up until now. I didn't call you so that you'd fly down here to be my bodyguard. All I needed was your money."

His gaze swept slowly over her, taking in her disheveled appearance and sleep-swollen eyes. "You don't look like you're doing all right to me." He gave her a gentle but firm nudge. "Now move over so I can drive us somewhere out of this heat."

It was senseless not to do as he asked when she was as anxious to find someplace cool as he was. She swung her legs over the gearshift and clambered into the passenger seat. Although he wasn't a particularly large man, Brad's presence filled the small car. Jo moved as far away from him as she could, pressing into the door. To cover her actions, she busied herself rolling down the window, fighting a growing sense of panic at his nearness.

Couldn't he see that she didn't want him there? She wasn't prepared for the final confrontation. She knew the words she would use, but they weren't forming into sentences yet. *She needed more time.*

Brad's frustration mounted at her peculiar behavior. She was acting as if they'd had a terrible fight. What in the hell had happened while she was gone to make her turn from him like this? In spite of his pronouncement about finding shade, he couldn't wait any longer to ask her what was going on.

"Jo," he said, taking her arm and turning her to face him, "I want you to tell me what's wrong."

She removed her arm from his grasp, afraid to let him touch her in even the most casual way when every part of her cried out to be held by him...to be loved by him. "Nothing's wrong. I'm just tired."

"And I would imagine you're hungry, too," he said as reasonably as he could, trying to control his urge to demand answers from her. "But that's—"

"No—not hungry. I ate what was left in the cooler for breakfast."

Brad twisted around to glance at the back seat and saw the sleeping bag and picnic cooler sitting beside his suitcase. He turned so that he was facing forward again. He sat perfectly still for several minutes, blindly staring out the front window, his hands wrapped tightly around the steering wheel. "I can put up with a lot, Jo," he said with deceptive calmness, "but not being lied to. You haven't been visiting friends, have you?"

The pain she heard in his voice made her impulsively reach for him, but before she made contact with his leanly muscled forearm, she withdrew her hand. "I never meant to lie to you...." She shrugged helplessly, at a loss for words. It was impossible to explain without telling him everything.

"And I suppose that makes it all right." Still without looking at her, he started the car and backed slowly out of the parking space.

They were heading north on the main road when she asked, "Where are we going?"

"To a service station. I believe you said something about needing gas."

The terse exchange was the last that passed between them until Brad pulled into the parking lot of the Hilton hotel. "Why are we stopping here?" Jo asked.

"You look like you could use some sleep."

Denying the obvious would have been pointless. "Not to mention a bath," she said, trying to inject a note of normalcy into their conversation.

When Brad returned from the registration desk, he handed Jo the room key. "What time is your flight home?" she asked, still trying to put them on an even keel.

He started the car before glancing in her direction. "I don't have one."

"What do you mean, you don't have one?" she demanded too quickly. She forced herself to wait several seconds before adding, "How are you getting back to Casper?"

Instead of immediately answering, he drove around to the other side of the building. With pointed deliberateness, he took the key from the ignition and slipped it into his pocket. "I'm not. I'm going to Boulder with you."

"But you can't," she breathed.

"Wanna bet?"

In her panic she struck out. "Just what right do you think you have to come down here and—"

He grabbed her by the shoulders, hanging on tightly when she tried to twist away from him. "Jo—would you stop a minute and listen to yourself? Not five hours ago you told me you loved me. Now you're acting like you can hardly stand to have me around."

His words shattered her protective anger, leaving her defenseless. She saw the hurt and confusion in his eyes and hated knowing she was the cause. She bit her lip to keep from crying out at the injustice of what would happen to them in the next few hours. "I'm sorry," she whispered.

"Why can't you trust me?"

There was nowhere left for her to run, no place to hide. She had to tell him. "Let's go inside, Brad," she said, her voice lifeless, full of resigned finality.

He stared at her for a long time. "Whatever it is—we can handle it." Taking her hand in his, he brought it to his lips and pressed a kiss to her palm.

His naive confidence made her flinch. She turned her hand to caress the side of his face. "Maybe you'd better wait to hear what I have to tell you . . ."

Brad ignored her warning, convinced that together they could face anything. "I'll unload the car—you unlock the room."

As soon as he had carried in the suitcases, he walked back to the door and announced, "I'll be back later."

Jo frowned in confusion. "Where are you going?"

Brad gave her a gentle teasing smile. "First you do everything you can to get rid of me, and now that I'm voluntarily leaving, you act like you want me to stay."

Too emotionally drained to respond to his bantering, she simply shrugged noncommittally.

Brad came across the room and took her in his arms. "If you recall, you said something about wanting to take a bath," he reminded her. "I just thought you might like some privacy."

Jo felt tears burning the back of her throat. She threw her arms around his neck and buried her face in his shoulder to keep him from seeing the moisture forming in her eyes. "Don't be gone long," she said. Now that she had decided not to put off telling him about Karen, every moment they would have together became precious to her.

''I won't,'' he said, giving her a deep and lingering kiss filled with heartbreaking promise.

JO TURNED HER BACK to the shower to let the spray wash the shampoo from her hair. On her face, droplets of fresh water mingled with the salty tears. Soon Brad would return, and when he did, the time that remained to them would be measured in minutes.

It wasn't fair.

But then, life itself wasn't always fair. In the end, it didn't matter that Karen wasn't deserving of Brad's love. The choice of whether or not to give that love was his.

She turned off the shower and, after drying herself, wrapped the towel around her and returned to the bedroom to get her blow-dryer. Her hand was on the suitcase zipper when she heard a key slide into the lock. Rather than let Brad see her making an undignified dash back to the bathroom, she stayed where she was.

He came in carrying a bag from a fast-food restaurant. If he was nonplussed by the sight of her wearing only a towel, he didn't show it.

''I wasn't expecting you back so soon,'' she said, adjusting the ends of the light-blue terry cloth, which had started to separate.

''I thought you might be hungry after all.'' He put the sack on the table by the front window.

Slowly, purposefully, he walked toward her, stopping inches from where she stood. He brushed a damp curl back from her forehead. ''Do you have any idea what it did to me when you left the way you did?'' he asked, his voice gruff with the memory of what he had endured these past three days.

At last, she fully understood his anger at the airport. She flinched at her own stupidity and thoughtlessness. Not once had she stopped to consider how he would naturally react to her abrupt disappearance. "I never—"

But Brad was beyond listening to her explanation.

She caught her breath as his finger lightly traced a line along her skin where the towel crossed over her breasts. "I never—" The breath that had been caught became a shuddering sigh when his lips retraced the route.

"You never what, Jo?" he whispered, inhaling the clean smell of her, drawing it deeply into his lungs, willing it to become a part of him.

She automatically placed her hand against his chest to push him away. It was wrong to let him make love to her now, knowing what she did about Karen.

But she wanted him so desperately. *Just for today,* an inner voice pleaded, *just for these few hours.*

She was weary of fighting a battle she wanted to lose. She felt her resolve weaken and then disappear altogether. For once in her life she would do something out of pure selfishness. Despite what was sure to follow, she would allow herself this time with him...and then at least she would have her dreams. The hand that had been poised to push him away slipped around his neck to bring him closer.

With a deep throaty groan he took her into his arms. The fear and anger he had brought with him to St. George were channeled into an explosive desire that swept away everything but his need to be with Jo, to make love to her, to have her love him in return.

"Jo...this isn't the time or the place I had envisioned for us," he told her, his voice ragged.

"Shh," she whispered. "Don't talk...not now." She didn't want to think; she only wanted to feel.

He held her face cradled between his hands and pulled her close. His lips met hers, touching and then clinging; his tongue dipped into her mouth to taste the sweetness. He felt her body mold itself to his with a strength and suppleness that left him weak with wanting her.

Jo willed the towel to be gone so that she could know the feel of Brad's touch along the length of her bare skin. As if attuned to her thoughts, his hand went to the place where she had tucked one end of the material over the other. Gently he tugged until the cloth parted, leaving her naked.

For long seconds he stared at her, his gaze caressing the fullness of her breasts, the curve of her waist, the swell of her hips. "Such beauty wasn't meant to be covered," he said hoarsely, his hand trailing from her chin to her neck and then her shoulder.

Jo's breasts ached to be touched. She caught her breath in anticipation as his fingertips dipped below her collarbone. Unconsciously she swayed toward him, willing his hand to move lower. Finally he cupped the lush flesh against his palm, applying a gentle pressure with a circular motion that drew a throaty gasp of pleasure from Jo.

But it was the stroking of his thumbs that brought her nipples to hard peaks and sent fire racing through her body. "Brad...I want...I want..."

"What is it you want, Jo?" He looked into her dazed eyes. "What can I do that will please you?"

"I want to feel you...against me."

He smiled as he reached up to unbutton his shirt.

"No...let me," she said. With trembling fingers she worked the buttons through their holes and then let the shirt slip from his shoulders to fall to the floor. As if she had never experienced anything as wondrous, she explored the nuances of his tightly muscled chest, tracing parallel patterns through the light matting of hair with her fingernails, eliciting sounds of pleasure from him that heightened and fueled her own excitement.

She found the nub of his nipples and stroked them as he had hers. They hardened and grew taut in response to her touch. When she gently nipped at the flesh with her teeth, Brad sighed in deep satisfaction.

He touched her chin and raised her mouth to his. The kiss was unlike any Jo had ever experienced. With his lips, with his tongue, he took and then he gave, relentlessly demanding while gently coaxing. He silently poured out the years of loneliness in the way he took the sweetness of her offering. She arched against him, insisting he hold nothing back.

His hands coursed her body, stroking her waist, cupping her buttocks. He drew her closer to him, imprinting the feel of her on his bare chest.

"Brad—your jeans," she breathed.

He released her and started to move away. "Are they hurting you?"

A meaningful smile filled her eyes. "No," she said softly, "that's not the problem."

Her smile destroyed the little control he still had. With a fluid movement, he undid the fastenings and stepped from the rest of his clothing. She came forward and he folded her in his arms. Her warmth scorched him, building fires that raged in his mind. He'd forgotten how incredible it felt to make love to someone he also loved. The actual sensation of having Jo in his arms was beyond all his imagining.

Jo caught her breath when Brad bent and took a throbbing nipple into his mouth. He stroked and teased the taut flesh until her caught breath became a harsh de-manding sigh. "Brad—"

This time there was no need for him to ask what she wanted. Her body strained against him like a drawn bow. He lifted her in his arms and carried her the short dis-tance to the bed. Her legs parted and she reached for him, but he gently eased himself down beside her, not yet ready to take the final step of their lovemaking.

He took her cry of disappointment into him as he cov-ered her mouth in a devouring kiss. She softly moaned and moved against him. With long sensuous strokes, he ran his hand from her waist to her thigh. Slowly the path deviated until his fingers were pressed against the flat-ness of her belly and then skimmed past the apex of her long legs.

He parted the soft moist flesh he found there, dipped into the hidden recesses and gently caressed the places that made her gasp in pleasure. Unconsciously she be-gan to move against the pressure of his hand, establish-ing an ancient rhythm Brad innately recognized.

"Yes," she said in response to his increased pressure. And then a whispered, "Harder."

Brad continued to stroke the yielding folds until he felt her grow tense in anticipation, and then he joined her. His thrust was deep and possessing. She responded with a wild abandon that reached into the depths of his mind to bring him an exquisite joy. Even in their lovemaking they were a perfect match. Their life together would be everything he had known it could be.

Jo felt herself being swept up in a sensuous maelstrom where even the soft sound of her name on Brad's lips brought her the keenest of pleasure. Slowly at first, and then with breathless speed, the ecstasy that filled her body focused on a single demanding location. The waiting became a bewitching torture as she teetered on the edge in anticipation. And then she heard Brad call her name one last time and her world exploded in thundering waves of exquisite release.

Afterward, as she lay fitted into his side, she thought about what had to happen next. A fierce possessiveness overcame her, and for a moment, she convinced herself that she could live with never telling Brad she'd found Karen. But the fantasy lasted only a moment.

By letting Karen know that Brad was still in love with her, Jo had destroyed any possibility of keeping the woman's whereabouts a secret. If Jo didn't tell Brad, eventually Karen would seek him out herself.

From the heights of ecstasy, Jo was plunged into the depths of despair. A shuddering sob escaped her as she threw her arm around Brad's waist and clung to him.

Jo's sudden change sent a cold shaft of fear down Brad's spine. For long agonizing minutes he held her, listening to her tortured sobs, feeling his confidence ebb with every tear until he was left with the dread certainty that the dream they had shared so briefly had somehow been shattered.

"I think it's time we talked," he said.

Jo took her arm from around Brad's waist. She waited until she was sure the last of her tears had been shed, then sat up, pulling the sheet around her. It was too late to search for the right way, the perfect way, to tell him. "I found Karen for you," she announced bluntly.

At first the words were incomprehensible to him. Individually, they made sense. Collectively, they formed a statement that he just couldn't seem to grasp. What could she conceivably be trying to tell him? "I don't think I heard you right," he said, sitting up beside her and running a hand through his hair.

"Yes, you did, Brad."

"How—"

"The details really aren't important," she said quickly. When finally his mind allowed him to accept what she'd told him, the news hit with the force of a blow to his midsection. His thoughts were in a turmoil; his body refused to remain still. He swung his legs over the side of the bed, reached for his jeans and slipped them on. Jo. "What makes you so sure it's really her?" he demanded.

She brought her knees up and hugged them tightly against her chest. "I talked to her."

A frustration, a rage tore through him. "Why?"

She recoiled at the raw pain she saw in his face. She had expected many things from him when he found out about Karen, but not this. "Because I had to know—"

"What is it about you that wouldn't let you believe me when I told you that I loved you?" he nearly shouted. He walked over to the window, parted the curtain and stared outside.

After a while, his hand slid down the curtain to rest against his thigh. When he spoke again, the anger was gone, replaced by an aching hollowness. "I thought you loved me, Jo."

"I do . . ." The words caught in her throat.

He turned to look at her. "Just not enough to fight for me, is that it?"

Jo felt the blood drain from her face. She knew then that there was no way she could ever make him understand what she'd done.

CHAPTER TWENTY

BRAD PARKED the rental car in front of the house Jo had told him was Karen's. For long minutes he sat and stared at the elegant home. Finally a wry smile found its way to his lips. Obviously Karen had done all right for herself since leaving him. But then, that shouldn't have come as any great surprise. She'd always been resourceful.

It was a strange feeling to know that after all the years of searching, he was within a few steps of seeing her again.

A few steps? They seemed like miles.

With a determined effort to overcome his nervousness, Brad got out of the car and walked toward the house. His knock was answered by a leggy young girl with braces on her teeth.

"Yes?" she said impatiently, shifting her weight from one foot to the other, clearly letting him know she had little time to spare for strangers.

Brad was at first too stunned to speak at the impact of seeing the small child he had once thought of as his own now a nearly grown young woman. Only the large eyes and blue-black hair of the little girl he remembered so well were still unchanged. He started to call her by name, then hesitated, afraid the familiarity might frighten her. "Is your mother home?" he asked.

"Is she expecting—"

"It's all right, Tracy," a woman called out. "I've been waiting for Mr. Tyler."

Brad looked past the girl and saw that the achingly familiar voice had come from the end of the hallway. His and Karen's eyes met. Everything surrounding them ceased to exist. It was as if the eight years they'd been apart had never happened.

JO ARRIVED IN BOULDER in the middle of the night. She had left Brad at the hotel in St. George, making arrangements to get to Los Angeles. After a short but heated argument, she'd finally convinced him she was capable of driving home alone.

In the end, it was less her rationale that had swayed him than the certain knowledge that the trip would be torture for both of them if they made it together.

She had planned her homecoming carefully. She'd even spent three hours lingering over dinner in Glenwood Springs with the intention of killing enough time so that no one would be up to see her drive into town. She had chided herself that sneaking home was a coward's way of doing things, but it didn't matter. She felt empty, drained of the strength that she'd need in order to face the questions her friends were sure to ask the moment they saw her.

One more day. That was all she needed. By then Brad would have called, and she would have an answer for everyone.

As she climbed the steps to her apartment she told herself that no matter what the outcome was, she could live with it. It was the not knowing that was tearing her apart. She tried to swallow past the lump in her throat. No . . . it was more than not knowing, it was the look she had seen on Brad's face when she'd told him about Karen.

She'd been right—Brad's reaction to the news would haunt her forever. But the scenario she'd imagined had been all wrong. Not once had it occurred to her that Brad would feel betrayed by what she'd done, that he would take her actions to mean her love was so shallow that she felt no need to fight for him.

How could she have been so stupid?

She opened the door to her apartment and sought a sense of rightness in being there. But since she had opened herself up to Brad, the old feelings about hearth and home and the cocoon they created around her had disappeared. He had made her reach out into the world, beyond all that was safe and secure, and as a result, she'd lost the ability to return to her shelter.

Nothing was the same. It would never be the same again.

Desperate for something to do to keep herself busy, she unpacked her suitcase, then wandered into the kitchen to fix a cup of tea. She was reaching for the teabags when she heard a familiar rhythmic knock on the apartment door.

Amy.

She was torn between running to answer the summons and ignoring it. While Amy would be sympathetic about what had happened, she would be dumbfounded by the way Jo had handled everything.

As Jo stood there trying to decide whether or not to go to the door, the choice was taken from her. Amy came in on her own.

"I saw your light from the street, so I decided to stop by and officially welcome you home," she said, striding into the kitchen. "How were your friends?"

Jo frowned. "Friends?"

"You know," she prompted, "the ones you went to visit."

"Oh . . . those friends. You must have been talking to Florence." Jo nervously picked up a cup and turned it around and around in her hand. "What are you doing up this late?" she asked, hoping to throw Amy off and avoid any further questions about the trip. Tomorrow would be soon enough to face the inevitable.

Amy snorted. "I was on another of my famous dates."

"I thought the bad ones always ended early."

Amy nudged past Jo to get to the cupboard. She gave her several cursory but perceptive glances as she went about the process of making a cup of tea. "Something tells me there's a story here," she said, handing the steaming cup to Jo. As soon as she'd prepared another cup, she gently guided Jo over to the kitchen table. "Now, why don't you let me in on why you look like the poster girl for a pessimists' convention?"

Jo propped her elbows up on the table. When Amy was curious about something, she was like a bloodhound on a scent; once started, there was no way to distract her. Jo no longer even felt like trying. "I found Karen."

Amy's eyes narrowed speculatively. She brought her tea up to her mouth and softly blew on it while she studied Jo. "And I suppose you told Brad that you found her."

Jo nodded.

Amy put her cup of tea on the table and shoved it aside without taking a sip. "For crying out loud, Jo. Why would you do something like that?" She threw her hands up in the air. "Never mind. You don't have to answer that question. We've been friends too long for me to even ask." She let out a commiserating sigh. "Now what?"

"Now I wait to hear from him."

"He's with Karen now?"

Unable to trust her voice, Jo nodded.

"What if he decides . . ."

Jo held her cup balanced between her upraised hands and peered over the rim at Amy. It was the first time since she'd known her articulate friend that she'd ever seen Amy too upset to complete a sentence. "That Karen is the one he wants?" she softly finished for her.

"Yeah—or something like that."

Jo squared her shoulders. It was time she showed some backbone. "I've decided I'm not going to let myself dwell on that possibility," she said.

BUT BY THE TIME three days had passed and Jo still hadn't heard from Brad, the possibility that he'd decided to stay with Karen was all she could think about. To her dismay, she also discovered that what she'd thought of as her selfishness in not telling Brad about Karen until after they'd made love had turned out to be a particularly insidious form of torture. Instead of bringing the anticipated peace, the memory of his passion and tenderness now haunted her. She realized with a heartbreaking poignancy that she would have been far better off not knowing the depth and completeness of the love he had wanted to give her.

The pain of her loss peaked on the morning of the fourth day. By afternoon, a grim acceptance had begun to force its way into her consciousness. That evening, as she was preparing for bed, she reflected on the transition she was making from pain to acceptance. She realized that her gradually shifting outlook was creating a profound need for her to rethink the terms on which she'd been living her life.

Although she didn't sleep at all that night, there was a newfound determination in her step when she left for work the next morning. As soon as she reached the shop, she called Florence and Howard and asked them to come over. They arrived together ten minutes later.

"What is it, Jo?" Florence asked, concern in her voice.

"Have you heard from Brad?"

Jo gave herself a mental pat on the back for managing a smile. "No—and I don't expect to anymore." She was grateful Florence didn't try to argue with her. "But since, in a way, Brad's responsible for what I'm about to do, I suppose it's only fitting that his name be included in this conversation." She had given them an overview of her meeting with Brad but none of the painful details. "I want you to know that I appreciate your not pushing me to talk about what happened while I was away. I needed time to work things out. And now I have." She looked from Florence to Howard and acknowledged the unlikelihood of what she was saying with a shrug. "There may still be a few loose ends, but once you've heard me out, I'm sure you'll agree I've made one heck of a start."

Jo stopped to take a breath before going on. "But first things first. I think you'd better sit down for this one," she told them, a mysterious gleam in her eye.

"Sounds ominous," Howard said, pulling out a chair for Florence.

Jo sat across from them, perched on the edge of her seat. She was anxiously leaning forward, her body language giving away her nervousness. "First of all, I know I've told you a dozen times how much I appreciated your taking over the shop while I was away, but I'm not sure I ever thought to tell you what a terrific job you did and what extraordinary business managers I think you are."

"Jo, this isn't necessary," Florence said. "We—"

"Wait," Jo interrupted her. "There's more. I'm sure you've figured out by now that I could simply have closed the shop while I was gone, but I was hoping that leaving the two of you here together would make you realize life is too short to live it alone."

"Jo—" Howard started to protest.

"Just give me a few more minutes, Howard. I promise I'll get to the point." She reached over to the center of the table and tucked a loose napkin back into its metal holder. "I'm not as insensitive to your problem as I seem to be. I know that the two of you are caught in a situation where there doesn't seem to be any way out. However—" she paused for dramatic effect "—I think I may have come up with a solution."

This time the looks they gave her were openly skeptical.

"All that's keeping you from getting married is money, right?"

Howard looked at Florence and snorted. "*All*, she says."

"What if I could come up with a way for you to make the money you need?"

Florence answered. "Remember, Jo—we've been running this place for you. We know the shop doesn't bring in enough business for you to hire two full-time employees."

"But it does make sufficient profit for two people to supplement their incomes enough to let them live together comfortably."

Howard eyed her, suddenly keenly interested in what she was saying. "Just what is it you're leading up to, Jo?"

"It's time I moved on," she said, surprised at the catch in her voice over a decision she felt was absolutely right.

''I want to go back to school to get my degree. I've decided the University of Colorado could use one more dedicated student.'' While she would have liked to return to UCLA for the healing effect of a change of scene, she couldn't afford the out-of-state tuition. ''I'm even going to change my major from business to social science.'' The corner of her mouth turned up in a lopsided grin. ''And then, after I graduate, I'm going to set the world on fire with my ideas on social reform for senior citizens.''

''And you want—'' Florence started.

''I want you to buy the shop from me,'' Jo finished for her. ''No money down, with payments to be determined by a percentage of the month's gross sales. If things continue the way they've been going these last two years, there will be more than enough money for the two of you to live on and to put me through school, as well.''

Howard didn't even look at Florence; he simply reached for her hand. ''It's a deal,'' he said. He stood, bringing Florence up with him. ''I agree with you, Jo. As much as we love you and as much as we're going to miss you, it's time you moved on. You're just starting out in life. It's important that you stretch your wings; otherwise you might look around one day and discover that you've become earthbound.'' He looked at Florence. ''Now, let's you and me get out of here,'' he said.

''Where are you going?'' Jo asked, taken aback by his rush to leave when there were still so many details to work out.

''To city hall—for a marriage license.''

Florence's delighted laughter filled the air. She gazed into Howard's eyes, then threw her arms around him and gave him a kiss. ''I love you,'' she said.

Jo fought to hide the pain that radiated through her chest and made it difficult for her to breathe. She didn't want any of her own unhappiness to tarnish the specialness of Florence's and Howard's moment. "Am I invited to the wedding?" she asked, feigning a cheerfulness she didn't feel.

"Of course you are," Howard said.

"You shall be one of two guests," Florence added, looking at Howard meaningfully.

Jo caught on immediately. "Brad isn't coming back," she said with certainty. "If you make your plans with him in mind, you'll never get married."

"How can you be so sure?" Florence asked.

"It's been five days since I left him in Utah," Jo answered, fighting the tears that burned her eyes. "Time enough for a person to make up his mind about who he loved, don't you think?"

THE NEXT TWO DAYS passed in a blessed flurry of activity. With late registration for school and trips to the lawyer's office to arrange the sale of Yogurt, Etc., along with the day-to-day work of running the shop, there were times when Jo was almost too busy to think about Brad.

Almost—but not quite.

In unguarded moments, the sadness came close to overwhelming her. Consequently, she did whatever she could to protect herself. She filled the days with the business of getting on with her life. The evenings she spent with Amy, the two of them eating dinner together and then going to a movie.

In order to keep up her frantic pace and safeguard her peace of mind, she'd asked Howard and Florence to let her stay on in the shop until school started. They'd worked out a schedule that managed to keep her busy but allowed her a couple of hours off each afternoon for trips to the university and the lawyer's office to set up the sale.

It was a particularly busy day at the shop thanks to a large lunchtime crowd, when at ten minutes to one, Jo's calm efficiency was totally shattered. People were standing at the counter five deep when she heard the bell over the door announce yet another customer. She glanced up just in time to see Brad walk into the shop.

The blood drained from her face as her heart slammed against her ribs. Her mouth formed a silent cry of surprise. The chocolate topping she'd been about to sprinkle over a vanilla yogurt tumbled into the coconut bin.

Brad's gaze cut through the crowd, his penetrating blue eyes singling her out. For what seemed like an eternity he stared at her, the look an unabashed claim of his right to do so. Finally he strode across the room, pushing his way through the lines of customers. He stepped briskly around the counter and took her by the arm. ''I want to talk to you,'' he said. When she hesitated, he added a firm, ''Now!''

''I can't—'' Jo sputtered. ''I have customers.''

Brad turned to the assembled crowd. ''Ms Williams is going to be busy for a while. Help yourself to whatever you came in to get.'' His gaze swept the area around him. As soon as he spotted what he'd been looking for, he added, ''You can leave the money in the glass jar by the register.'' He took the cup of yogurt Jo was holding and set it down on the counter, then firmly steered her into the back room.

As soon as they were alone, Brad took her other arm and held her so that she was facing him. ''I want you to take a good long look at me, Josephine Williams, and then I want you to listen very carefully to what I have to tell you.''

Jo was too stunned to do anything but comply.

"I'm here, not in California," he said. "And I love you."

"But—"

"There are no buts. I've spent the last week thinking about us and I've decided I can put up with you trying to palm me off on someone else once, but I don't want you ever to try it again—*no matter how much you feel it's for my own good*."

"I thought . . ." *Don't you dare cry,* she sternly threatened herself. But the warning was useless. Tears formed, filled her eyes and spilled over her eyelashes.

He pulled her into his arms and held her tightly. "I know what you thought," he said gently. "But I couldn't come any sooner." He pressed a chaste, comforting kiss to her lips. "After I left Karen, I needed time to think about everything that had happened, so I drove up the coast. It's taken me most of this last week to sort things out. Except for the stop I made in Casper to pick something up, I came here as soon as I could. I felt it was more important that I come to you a whole person than to show up a few days earlier."

A memory of the predatory look that had been in Karen's eyes flashed through Jo's mind. "I can't believe Karen just wanted to see you so the two of you could reminisce about old times."

A roguish smile tugged at the corner of his mouth. "No," he admitted. "She had a little more in mind than that."

"And now, after your week driving up the coast, you know for sure that you're not in love with her anymore?" How was it possible for her to speak while at the same time she felt as though she were holding her breath?

"There was never any real doubt in my mind about who I loved, Jo. But I knew you wouldn't believe me unless I went to see Karen. The meeting turned out to be harder than I'd imagined and yet, in a strange way, easier, too. I understand so much now about so many things. I only wish I'd found out sooner—in time to come back to Boulder and . . ." He shrugged helplessly. "But that's behind me now. Perhaps my mother and I will be able to work things out in another lifetime."

He reached into his pocket. "She was right about one thing," he said, taking Jo's hand. "She was right about who should be wearing this ring." He slipped the pear-shaped diamond back onto the finger it had left less than three months earlier.

Speechless with happiness, Jo looked at the sparkling stone and then at Brad.

"Don't worry," Brad said quickly, misinterpreting her reaction, "this doesn't mean I expect you to leave Boulder. The plans for moving Tyler Construction to Denver are almost complete and I don't mind commuting to work.

"There's one more thing," he said, pulling a cassette tape out of his other pocket and showing it to her before dropping it onto the table. "It's a Neil Diamond tape—all love songs. From now on, every one of them is 'our' song—along with every other love song ever recorded. If I should ever again get a funny look on my face when I hear a love song, it's because I'm thinking about you. *Is that understood?*"

Her eyes sparkled. "Absolutely. And the same goes for me," she added.

At last, Jo allowed herself to believe what was happening. Brad had come back. He loved her. She had so much to tell him—but nothing that couldn't wait. "I accept your proposal," she whispered, wrapping her arms around his neck.

He eyed her. "Am I to take that to mean you also love me?"

"Oh, yes—" she breathed.

"Enough to fight for me from now on?"

She smiled. "Bring on the dragons."

"God, I've missed you," he said hoarsely. This time when he lowered his mouth to hers, the kiss he gave her was anything but chaste.

Behind them the door opened wide enough for Florence and Howard to see inside. As soon as they were sure Jo was all right, they closed the door again. Florence looked at Howard, happiness radiating from her eyes. "It looks like we can get on with our wedding plans," she said. "The best man has arrived."

Harlequin Temptation ™.

DID YOU ENJOY THIS STORY?
THEN WATCH OUT FOR AMY!

Now that Amy no longer has to protect Jo from all the Brad Tylers of the world, she has her own troubles brewing....

In Temptation #157, *Tomorrow's Love Song*, Amy assumes a false identity and sets out on her own to right a few wrongs. She has everything to gain— dollars in the multimillions. And everything to lose—the love of the one man who belongs in her future....

Look for #157, *Tomorrow's Love Song*, the second book in Georgia Bockoven's dynamic duo. Coming to you from Harlequin in June 1987.

S 246-A-1

Harlequin Superromance

COMING NEXT MONTH

What the press says about Harlequin romance fiction...

"When it comes to romantic novels...
Harlequin is the indisputable king."
—*New York Times*

"...always with an upbeat, happy ending."
—*San Francisco Chronicle*

"Women have come to trust these
stories about contemporary people,
set in exciting foreign places."
—*Best Sellers, New York*

"The most popular reading matter of
American women today."
—*Detroit News*

"...a work of art."
—*Globe & Mail, Toronto*

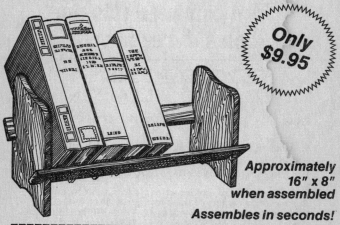